"We're partyin' today! Eat, drink, and be merry!"

To the players, who'd been discouraged by the

Catastrophe, Marielle's cheery proclamation was

the best possible encouragement.

Adventurer, you whose weight is borne by your winged soul! The mystical world of Theldesia is home to dragons and giants, magical beasts, and demihumans. Fragrant green winds blow across this new yet ancient land that opens before you like a blank page. Fill it with your life.

L☉G HORIZON

8

AKIBA CHRONICLE AFTER CATASTROPHE **0**

1 — Bridge of All Ages

Located on the southern edge of Akiba, this grand stone bridge is the departure point for Adventurers. There's also a stable at the foot of the bridge that rents horses to newbies (five gold coins per day).

2 — Great Silver-Leafed Tree

Some of the leaves on this enormous tree are silver. Since the surrounding area is open, it's a good place to meet up for an adventure or a date.

3 — Old Akiba Station

A huge building said to have been a public transportation center in the old era. Flowering plants used in elementary potions grow here, but be careful—the station interior is a maze.

4 — Street Stall Village Alley

If a player wants expendables or commodities, they need only head over to Street Stall Village Alley, where everything from food to potions can be found. Haggling at the small stalls is one of the best parts.

5 — Akiba Guild Center

At the Hall Office, Adventurers can apply to join a guild or withdraw or deposit funds at the bank. A fledgling Adventurer's staunch ally! Use it well!

6 — Production Guild District

The place to be for Adventurers who aspire to the production classes. All sorts of production equipment is available free of charge. A wide variety of major guilds provide solid support for material procurement as well.

7 — Town Gate

A transport device that lets players teleport between towns...when functional. Currently, it isn't. Stalls are sometimes set up on certain days, and it's a great place to hunt for bargains!

8 — Akiba Temple

Unless someone chants a resurrection spell for them, players unlucky enough to lose their lives on an adventure will wake up here in the temple. It's a magnificent, beautiful place, but don't visit too often!

Fragrant green winds blow across this new, yet somehow old land. The imaginary world of Theldesia is home to dragons and giants, monsters and demihumans. With a burden weighing upon your soul, go forth, O winged one <Adventurer>! This land spreads out before you like a blank page; make your mark in it!

LOG HORIZON

2 THE KNIGHTS OF CAMELOT

MAMARE TOUNO   ILLUSTRATION BY **KAZUHIRO HARA**

YEN ON

NEW YORK

CONTENTS

SHIROE
▶ MACHIAVELLI-WITH-GLASSES

NAOTSUGU
▶ PANTIES WARRIOR

AKATSUKI
▶ LOVELY ASSASSIN

AN INTELLECTUAL ENCHANTER WHO ONCE ACTED AS COUNSELOR FOR THE LEGENDARY BAND OF PLAYERS KNOWN AS THE DEBAUCHERY TEA PARTY. HE MAY BE A VETERAN PLAYER, BUT INSIDE, HE'S A UNIVERSITY STUDENT AND HARD-CORE GAMER WITH HERMIT TENDENCIES.

A TRUSTY GUARDIAN AND SHIROE'S GOOD FRIEND, NAOTSUGU IS A CHEERFUL, TOUGH YOUNG GUY AND FORMER DEBAUCHERY TEA PARTY MEMBER. HE TOOK A TEMPORARY HIATUS FROM *ELDER TALES*, ONLY TO GET TRAPPED IN THE GAME WORLD ON THE DAY HE RETURNED.

ALTHOUGH SHE FORMERLY HID THE FACT THAT SHE WAS FEMALE AND PLAYED AS A SILENT MAN, AFTER BEING SWALLOWED UP BY THE GAME, SHE CHANGED HER BODY TO MATCH HER REAL-WORLD SELF AND BEGAN PLAYING AS A SLENDER, BRILLIANT ASSASSIN.

THIRTY THOUSAND JAPANESE GAMERS HAVE BEEN TRAPPED IN THE WORLD OF *ELDER TALES*, A VENERABLE, OLD ONLINE GAME.

A MAN WHO CARRIES THE NICKNAME "MACHIAVELLI-WITH-GLASSES" IS ONE OF THEM—OUR PROTAGONIST SHIROE. IN THE JUMBLED RUINS OF THE TOWN OF AKIBA, HE WAS REUNITED WITH HIS OLD FRIEND NAOTSUGU, THE ASSASSIN AKATSUKI, AND MARI, GUILD MASTER OF THE CRESCENT MOON LEAGUE.

ONE DAY, MARI TOLD SHIROE'S GROUP THAT SERARA, ONE OF THE CRESCENT MOON LEAGUE'S NEWBIE MEMBERS, WAS BEING MENACED BY THE BRUTAL BRIGANTEERS GUILD IN THE NORTHERN EZZO EMPIRE. SHIROE AND HIS FRIENDS RESOLVED TO RESCUE HER.

WHEN THEY CROSSED THE SEA AND MET UP WITH SERARA, THEY DISCOVERED NYANTA, A PLAYER WHO HAD BEEN A SORT OF MENTOR TO SHIROE. INCREDIBLY, HE HAD HELPED SERARA BY KEEPING HER HIDDEN.

HAVING WON A DESPERATE BATTLE AGAINST THE BRIGANTEERS, THE FIVE ADVENTURERS MOUNTED THEIR GRIFFINS AND FLEW AWAY, BOUND FOR AKIBA.

[THE CATASTROPHE]
A TERM FOR THE INCIDENT IN WHICH USERS WERE TRAPPED INSIDE THE *ELDER TALES* GAME WORLD. IT AFFECTED THE THIRTY THOUSAND JAPANESE USERS WHO WERE ONLINE WHEN *HOMESTEADING THE NOOSPHERE*, THE GAME'S TWELFTH EXPANSION PACK, WAS INTRODUCED.

[ELDER TALES]
A "SWORD AND SORCERY"-THEMED ONLINE GAME AND ONE OF THE LARGEST IN THE WORLD. AN MMORPG FAVORED BY SERIOUS GAMERS, IT BOASTS A TWENTY-YEAR HISTORY.

[ADVENTURER]
THE GENERAL TERM FOR A GAMER WHO IS PLAYING *ELDER TALES*. WHEN BEGINNING THE GAME, PLAYERS SELECT HEIGHT, CLASS, AND RACE FOR THESE IN-GAME DOUBLES. THE TERM IS MAINLY USED BY NON-PLAYER CHARACTERS TO REFER TO PLAYERS.

[PEOPLE OF THE EARTH]
THE NAME NON-PLAYER CHARACTERS USE FOR THEMSELVES. THE CATASTROPHE DRASTICALLY INCREASED THEIR NUMBERS FROM WHAT THEY WERE IN THE GAME. THEY NEED TO SLEEP AND EAT REGULARLY, SO IT'S HARD TO TELL THEM APART FROM PLAYERS WITHOUT CHECKING THE STATUS SCREEN.

[THE HALF-GAIA PROJECT]
A PROJECT TO CREATE A HALF-SIZED EARTH INSIDE *ELDER TALES*. ALTHOUGH IT'S NEARLY THE SAME SHAPE AS EARTH, THE DISTANCES ARE HALVED AND IT ONLY HAS ONE-FOURTH THE AREA.

CHAPTER.

1

RETURN TO AKIBA

-190

-180

-170

-160

-150

▶ LEVEL: **90**

▶ RACE: **FELINOID**

▶ CLASS: **SWASHBUCKLER**

▶ HP: **10872**

▶ MP: **9477**

▶ ITEM 1:

[FAIRY KING'S BELT]

A SWORD BELT SAID TO HAVE BEEN ORDERED BY THE FAIRY KING AS PART OF HIS BATTLE KIT. MORE THAN JUST BEAUTIFUL, IT IS DESIGNED TO STREAMLINE ALL GESTURES, FROM DRAWING TO ATTACKING. IT HAS AN EFFECT THAT INCREASES THE CRITICAL HIT RATE DURING PREEMPTIVE STRIKES.

▶ ITEM 2:

[LAPIS FLY-WINGED SWORDS]

THRUSTING SWORDS THAT REQUIRE A LARGE AMOUNT OF HIGH-LEVEL INSECT MATERIAL. THEY FLEX FREELY, AND DEFENDING AGAINST THEM IS DIFFICULT. ALTHOUGH VERY HARD TO OBTAIN, THE SPARKLE OF THE BEAUTIFUL JADE-COLORED SHELLS AND TRANSPARENT WINGS GIVE THEM A UNIQUE PRESENCE. THEY'RE POPULAR WITH ADVENTURERS WHO WANT WEAPONS THAT ARE BOTH IMPRESSIVE AND HIGH PERFORMANCE.

▶ ITEM 3:

[CAIT SITH'S BOOTS]

LONG, STURDY, FLEXIBLE BOOTS THAT ARE FAVORITES OF CAIT SITH, THE CAT FAIRY. A TREASURE-CLASS ITEM OBTAINED AT THE END OF A LONG QUEST. IF YOU CLICK YOUR HEELS TOGETHER WHILE WEARING THEM, A TINY CAT FAIRY WILL APPEAR AND CARRY YOUR PACK FOR YOU.

<Mustard>
A condiment.
Do not rub into wounds.

▶ 1

Rose. Red. Yellow. Orange.

Three griffins flew above a sunset ocean that seemed littered with broken shards of light.

Driven by night gathering in the east, the sky was gradually fading to purple, the darkness deepening. However, this only heightened the beauty of the rose-madder evening sun as it receded into the west, trailing long tails of light over the ocean at its feet.

The young man in silver-gray armor who rode the lead griffin looked back and waved hugely, a cheerful grin on his face. The wave seemed to be a signal.

At Naotsugu's gesture, Shiroe told the slender girl who clung to his back to hold on tight.

At a small tap from Shiroe's boots, the huge griffin he rode tilted just the tips of its wings—each of which measured three meters—ever so slightly. As the monster sliced through the wind, it sketched a wide arc, setting a course toward land.

After taking to the skies, the five who'd escaped Susukino—Shiroe, Akatsuki, and Naotsugu, plus Serara, the young Crescent Moon League Druid they'd rescued, and her guardian, the Felinoid Nyanta—had flown straight across the Laiport Strait without stopping and were now approaching the Ou region.

As indicated by the slowly sinking evening sun, the world would soon be covered in darkness. And even though they were traveling on griffins—flying mounts that ordinary Adventurers didn't have—Shiroe and the others had wanted to put as much distance between them and Susukino as possible that day, and so they'd continued their journey quite late for a group traveling through the wilderness.

Setting up camp is considerable work. It takes a fair amount of time to pitch a tent and prepare a meal. Those who have not done so may not realize it, but simply gathering dry branches to build a campfire can take over an hour.

Since the Catastrophe, Shiroe and the others had learned how to live in the wastelands and forests that spread across this world, and during their journey to Susukino, they had been careful not to push themselves. However, today, the day in which they rescued Serara, they had wanted to cross the strait as quickly as possible and reach an area where there would be no possibility of pursuit.

The three griffins predicted one another's courses and descended in gentle arcs, finally alighting together upon a hill.

"I'm not scared or anything."

Akatsuki sounded a bit defensive as Shiroe held out a hand to her, helping her down from the griffin.

From the way her gaze swam, she actually was feeling timid. That said, she seemed to have grown used to the new experience of flying during the journey.

What she was just a little afraid of was the griffin itself.

Griffins were enormous monsters with the upper bodies of eagles and the lower bodies of lions. Fully extended, the span of their powerful wings measured five or six meters. Like their taloned forelegs, their sharp beaks were those of eagles, and since they were so big, to the fine-boned Akatsuki, they probably seemed apt to take off her head with one bite.

As soon as she touched the ground, Akatsuki quickly backed away. Shiroe smiled—a little smile, so she wouldn't notice—and took a large chunk of meat from the magic bag he'd shifted to rest at his lower back. He held the meat out to the griffin.

To all appearances, it really was a terrifying monster. But, like other animals that appeared when summoned by magic whistles, it was the picture of loyalty. As he patted its neck, the griffin happily swallowed the meat in one gulp.

"So hey, that went well," Shiroe's friend Naotsugu said on approach. He had dismounted from the back of his own griffin and was climbing up the hill.

"It certainly did. Mew handled that quite skillfully."

Nyanta and Serara came toward them from the opposite direction.

"—Um! Thank you very much! I was really impressed."

"Yes, well, don't worry about it. We didn't do anything special," Shiroe answered, as Serara bowed her head.

Even though he thought his words were brusque, he couldn't think of anything else to say. He felt shy and awkward, and all he could do was avert his eyes.

Up on the hill, where he could look out over the whole area, Shiroe opened his menu, preparing to report in via telechat to Marielle. She had probably been waiting to hear from them for a long time; as Marielle received Shiroe's report, her voice was clearly relieved.

Come to think of it, Shiroe and the others had practically stolen this journey north from Marielle's group.

The chaos that had followed the Catastrophe. The gloomy atmosphere in town. Friends divided. Everyone haunted by a feeling of helplessness and uncomprehending irritation.

Shiroe hadn't been able to stand that atmosphere. That was why he had undertaken the journey to save Serara.

Of course it was true that he had wanted to help Marielle and Henrietta of the Crescent Moon League. However, it was equally true that there had been more to it than that: Inside, he had felt an indescribable disgust.

"Really, don't worry about it. Just don't."

Shiroe had done this for himself. That was all. It made his words get tangled up, and he ended up making a clumsy report.

"Mew've always been a bashful one, Shiroechi."

Nyanta spoke with a serenity that set his listeners at ease.

"Captain Nyanta."

"Shiroe and Nyanta—have you two known each other for a long time?" Serara asked.

"Yep, they sure have. Me, too." Naotsugu fielded the question, interrupting from the sidelines.

"We have, indeed. Long ago, when *Elder Tales* was still just a game, Shiroechi, Naotsugucchi, and meowrs truly often rampaged around together."

...*When* Elder Tales *was still a game.*

Those words sank into their hearts with a keen sadness.

He was right. This wasn't *Elder Tales* any longer. Ever since the day of the Catastrophe, although it looked like *Elder Tales*, it had degenerated into a reality dozens of times harsher.

Possibly because her thoughts had taken her that far, Serara's face also fell slightly. It troubled Shiroe, but there was nothing he could say to her.

"My liege, we need to set up camp."

Shiroe felt as if Akatsuki had rescued him. He called to the others. Nyanta and Serara must have realized that pessimism wouldn't do them any good; they actually seemed relieved, and they began looking for a place to pitch the tent.

The sun was down, but there was no sign of any powerful enemy creatures in the nearby zones.

Naotsugu and Serara began to pitch a small tent. At this time of year, as long as one had a sleeping bag, spending a night under the stars was no problem at all. If it happened to rain all night, though, things would get annoying.

Coming to a silent agreement, Akatsuki and Nyanta headed for the forest together. They probably intended to gather dry branches.

It was inefficient to start setting up camp at this late hour.

Even though they had magic light, both setting up the tent and gathering kindling took time in the darkness. By the time they dug through the hill country undergrowth, set up several stones as a windbreak, and started a fire, nearly two hours had passed since the griffins' landing.

At this rate, they weren't likely to get enough rest by morning, but even so, the group's faces were cheerful. After all, they had come through the hardest part of their journey to rescue Serara.

Since they had crossed so many zones via the griffins, there was very little chance that they would be pursued. They still needed to return to Akiba safely, but since they had already met up with Serara, speed was not nearly as important as it had been when they were on their way to her.

They could even spend a second night in these hills if they felt they needed to.

That breathing room showed on everyone's faces.

While Nyanta and Akatsuki headed to the forest—which was really more of a series of scrubby thickets—in search of kindling, and Naotsugu went to the river to draw water, Shiroe and Serara skillfully pitched the tent. Although not a magic item, sailcloth tents were essential equipment for adventures. They were quite bulky and heavy, but in a world with magic bags that canceled out the weight of items, it wasn't hard to carry them around.

Before pitching the tent, Serara had apparently had a telechat with Marielle, who was waiting for them in Akiba. Shiroe, of course, had completed his own report a little while earlier.

Marielle always smiled cheerfully, but that didn't mean she was not worried. Possibly because of the sudden relief, she had actually sounded tearful during his own report.

But as he sat in front of the tent unpacking their things, Shiroe was able to imagine how happy Serara's report had made Marielle, just by listening to Serara's side of the exchange.

"Hey up there! I got the water!"

The one making his way up the hill was Naotsugu.

He had brought up water from the spring in portable waterskins. The sun had set completely, and the jet-black forest was sharply silhouetted against an evening sky clearer than highly polished turquoise. In a short while, Nyanta and Akatsuki would return from the woods.

At any rate, their mission to rescue Serara from Susukino had been a success.

2

"Whoa. What the heck?! This's awesome!!"

Naotsugu's muttered words seemed overcome with emotion.

A campfire crackled in front of the five, sending up sparks.

"My liege, my *liege*. This is, what's the word…? *Paradise*."

Even Akatsuki—who was normally almost too serious and rarely showed much emotion—raised her voice happily, her flushed cheeks tinted by the orange flames.

Shiroe nodded in response, but he wasn't exactly calm, either. He was worked up. It was only that Shiroe, hopelessly clumsy, couldn't make the excitement show through in his attitude.

"Mya-ha-ha, there's lots more where that came from."

As if he couldn't even hear Nyanta's reassurance, Naotsugu chowed down single-mindedly.

Fragrant venison roasted, the fat crackling and popping.

That in itself was a major event.

It had begun when Nyanta and Akatsuki had brought back a deer they had bagged while gathering firewood.

Wild animals weren't rare in this other world. On the contrary: Here, where the population of Japan was only one one-hundredth of what it was in the real world, wild animals had an environment so suited to breeding that it must have seemed like heaven.

This meant that in forests, hill country, and other lush areas, it was common to see deer and wild birds, as well as boars, mountain goats, and other livestock turned feral. Of course, there were dangerous animals like wild dogs, wolves, and bears as well. Boars and bears in particular had formidable fighting abilities, comparable to goblins, so caution was necessary.

However, if they avoided those few dangerous animals, deer and wild birds were relatively easy to deal with, and they were useful both as food resources and as perfect practice opponents for low-level Adventurers.

Thus, it had come as no great surprise when Akatsuki and Nyanta returned from the forest where they had been gathering kindling with a deer in tow.

Under the perplexed eyes of Shiroe's group, Nyanta had dressed the deer and, wonder of wonders, produced venison shish kebabs that were shockingly tasty. Even the way they sizzled and crackled over the fire was completely unlike everything that had come before.

The sweet scent of roasting fat.

The realization that real food had such a complex, rich aroma was astounding. Shiroe and the others were suddenly so hungry it felt as if they hadn't eaten for days, and they couldn't take it anymore.

With one bite of the slices that Nyanta held out for them, their senses were flooded with the melting sweetness of meat juices flavored with salt and rosemary. This wasn't a "food item." It was *food*. When the difference stared them in the face like this, it was overwhelming.

They were as different as lightning bugs and lightning.

"It's delicious…but…why?"

Even Shiroe couldn't help but sound startled.

Naotsugu and Akatsuki were dumbfounded, too. Only Serara and Nyanta beamed proudly.

It was the most delicious meal they'd had in a month.

Part of the sad reality of this other world was—or should have been—the rule that none of the food items tasted like anything. That rule had plagued Shiroe and his friends, and each of the more than thirty thousand Japanese players who'd been trapped here, with the taste of despair.

Whether they ate omelets or curry, pottage or grilled fish, the food tasted like nothing more than soggy rice crackers. …Worse, actually, since they didn't even taste very salty. It was so bad that Naotsugu had labeled it "edible cardboard."

Over the past few weeks, they had despaired utterly and resigned themselves to the logic of this other world… And now, right before their eyes, that logic was disintegrating.

As far as cooking went, what Nyanta had made for them wasn't very complicated, and there was nothing pretentious about it. He'd dressed the deer; flavored it with spices, herbs, and rock salt; sautéed it in a frying pan; and roasted it right over the fire.

It might not have been first-rate fare, but compared to the soggy, unsalted rice crackers that had darkened their days, the taste was heavenly.

"Yum! This is fantastic. Captain Nyanta, you're amazing! I love you second-best, right after panties!!"

"Oh, mew're making too much of this."

As Nyanta spoke, he threaded the venison onto metal skewers he had taken out of his bag and began to roast them one after another. Serara, who was sitting next to him demurely, knees together, busily set out dishes and used a small knife to peel an onion for garnish.

"Captain. Hey! Maestro Nyanta. Why does it taste like this? I mean, why doesn't it taste like rice crackers?! Requesting-testimony-from-the-defendant city!"

As he asked his question, Naotsugu had a skewer in each hand.

"Mew can have as much as mew like. There's no need to wolf it down like that," Nyanta told him, but Naotsugu didn't seem to believe him. It was as if he couldn't quite relax without gripping what he was planning to eat.

Ordinarily, it would have been Akatsuki's job to hit him with a "Greedy, stupid Naotsugu," but even she was muttering, "Delicious, wow, amazing," as she munched busily on roast venison.

As Nyanta dexterously carved the organs, he continued.

"When mew cook, mew collect all the ingredients, select the dish mew want to make from the menu, and then mew have a finished food item. Correct?"

What he was describing was the ordinary item creation method in *Elder Tales*.

"When mew cook like that, no matter what mew do, the finished food item has that particular flavor. All mew have to do is collect the ingredients and cut, roast, or boil them directly, without opening the menu. Just like in the real world."

Nyanta's explanation was quite casual.

"But we—"

Akatsuki gulped down meat. Shiroe handed her a canteen, finishing the sentence for her.

"We tried that, but even by that method, the end result is just a mystery item. Isn't it? When we tried to grill fish, it turned into a slimy paste or into weird charcoal that had nothing to do with fish. …It isn't possible to cook normally in this world, is it?"

From what he and the others knew, that was simply how things worked here.

Since this was a game, if one lacked game skills, what they did would fail. It was basic logic.

"That's what happens when mew aren't a Chef, or if mew are a Chef but your cooking skills are poor. As in reality, to cook, mew need cooking skills. In other words, if Chefs cook in the mewsual way, without mewsing the menu, the flavors of the ingredients will shine through in the resulting dish."

Although Shiroe was dumbfounded by Nyanta's words, he was soon convinced.

When he thought about it, their salting of food items before consuming them had been odd already. If it had only been possible to create food from the food menu, wouldn't they have had to select SALT FOOD from the menu to be able to add salt at all?

Players had a minimum of five experience points in the production classes, including Chef, even if they hadn't acquired those classes. Even though it was one of the most rudimentary cooking operations, the act of salting food appeared to be the most advanced "realistic cooking" technique possible for any player with a non-Chef subclass.

"Then, uh, Captain, does that mean—"

"That's right, Naotsugucchi. I'm a Chef. …Now, how about another skewer?"

With Nyanta's encouragement, Shiroe and the others dug into the meat.

A midsized deer was enough to feed five with plenty left over. It would probably prove to be all the food they needed the next day as well. Nyanta passed around an apple brandy he said he'd made up in Susukino, and the lively nocturnal banquet continued.

Once again, Nyanta formally introduced Serara to the other three.

Serara stood politely from where she'd been sitting by the campfire with the others and bobbed her head.

"It's nice to meet you. I apologize for not greeting you sooner. I'm

Serara; thank you very much for rescuing me. I'm a level-nineteen Druid, my subclass is Housekeeper, and I'm still really new at everything."

She sure is an energetic girl...

Many things about her combined to give Shiroe that impression: her tranquil, girlish face; her small, round, gently sloping shoulders; the hair tied into a ponytail that hung down her back...

"It's like, in terms of the three cutest girls in class, you'd be number three, but you'd get the most love letters."

"Uh—huh?!"

At this discombobulating assessment from Naotsugu, whom she'd only just met, Serara found herself at a loss for words. Akatsuki landed a resounding knee kick on Naotsugu's face.

"No *knees*! Quit with the *knees*!"

"My liege, I've kneed a rude individual."

"And now you're reporting it after the fact?!"

What had Naotsugu been thinking? He hadn't even tried to protect his face. Closer inspection revealed that he was holding a venison skewer in each hand and that he'd desperately toughed it out so that he wouldn't drop them. Seeing that, even Serara laughed a little.

"Fu-fu-fu!"

"...Uhm. This is Naotsugu. He's a Guardian. A very dependable fighter."

"He's also vulgar and an idiot."

At Shiroe and Akatsuki's explanations, Serara nodded, still smiling.

"I saw you fight on the front line. I'm sorry my clumsy healing spell couldn't recover you completely."

"Don't worry about it," Naotsugu replied. "You still saved my butt."

Serara apologized repeatedly for her low level, but on that point, Shiroe agreed with Naotsugu. He felt that Serara's focus after she had steeled herself and her resolute use of all her strength were more than worthy of recognition. In any case, with time, anyone could raise their level. She had nothing to apologize for.

"Naotsugucchi's always been like this. Please think of him as a ribald person and pardon him. Besides, Serara, he was complimenting mew just then."

"Huh?"

Serara looked up at Nyanta, who was sitting beside her, his already narrow eyes narrowed further in a shrewd smile.

"He's saying mew're the most popular girl in class. Naotsugucchi's bashful."

"Hey, Captain, hold up. That's not how it is. And anyway, I'm less of a pretty-girl guy than a panti*eerg*!!"

Another of Akatsuki's knee kicks hit home, cutting off Naotsugu's words.

"Owwww… You're getting more and more ruthless there, short stuff."

"My liege, I've caved in the pervert's face. I've also confiscated his meat."

"Huh?—Uh? Aaaaaah!!"

Akatsuki was gnawing away at the venison skewers she'd taken from Naotsugu during her lightning-fast knee kick.

"That was a total foul…"

As Nyanta handed the dejected Naotsugu some fresh-grilled venison, he shifted the topic to Akatsuki. "And who is this young lady?"

Picking up on the shift, Shiroe began introducing Akatsuki to Nyanta.

The girl who'd traveled with him and Naotsugu. An Assassin and Tracker. A skilled professional, someone who could be relied upon.

Akatsuki, who had watched Nyanta fixedly with deadly serious eyes, finally bowed her head and greeted him. "I am Akatsuki, the inexperienced, venerable sage."

When Naotsugu started kicking up a fuss about how much differently she treated *him*, Akatsuki shoved some half-done meat into his mouth. *Short stuff! Stupid Naotsugu!* The other three just laughed at their endless squabbling.

"And this is Shiroechi. He's a very intelligent youngster who acted as a counselor for a group I mewsed to be part of."

As Shiroe gave a slight nod acknowledging Nyanta's introduction, Serara seemed overawed and thanked the sorcerer, over and over.

She's a nice, cheerful girl, Shiroe thought.

Absently, he wondered how old she was.

From what they could gather, their appearance in this other world was influenced by their bodies in the real world. However, their figures and rough modeling were based on the character data from the *Elder Tales* MMORPG. Anyone who arbitrarily guessed someone's age based on their height or figure ran the risk of insulting them. Shiroe had learned this through experience from Akatsuki.

However, from the way Serara spoke, he didn't think she could be all that old.

A high school kid or maybe even a middle schooler…

Elder Tales had been the sort of game that charged monthly play fees and therefore tended to have a higher average user age than many free network games. However, that was just on average, and middle school players weren't rare enough to cause astonishment.

Come to think of it, the twins had been about that age.

The whole noisy escape from Susukino must have put him on edge. Maybe it was the relief of having reached a safe place or the feeling of freedom that surrounded the lively meal, but Shiroe found himself thinking back to when he'd met them, just before the Catastrophe.

▶ 3

Of course, when Shiroe had first met the twins, this other world wasn't an other world yet, and *Elder Tales* was still a game.

Shiroe had been spending his days playing the game as a slightly eccentric solo player (as a high-level Enchanter, he could hardly have been anything *but* eccentric), operating out of the town of Akiba.

After the Debauchery Tea Party had dissolved, Shiroe had been a rootless wanderer in the truest sense of the word. There hadn't been any negative connotations to it, though, and Shiroe had rather enjoyed gaming that way.

In Akiba's plaza, one could hear voices recruiting party members wherever they went, and at the time, since *Elder Tales* was still only a game, it had a recruiting channel system that let a player send messages to all areas of the server. He'd used that system to join and battle with stray parties from time to time, and he'd occasionally accepted invitations from Marielle and other acquaintances and gone to dungeons with them. Of course, he'd traveled around on his own as well, exploring zones that interested him while collecting items.

Shiroe's Scribe subclass was one of the production subclasses. Scribes' main talent was the ability to copy books, diagrams, and magical textbooks. In *Elder Tales*, producing items was nearly synonymous with compounding materials: To produce items, one needed other items to use as material.

For a Scribe, those materials were paper and ink. That said, not just any paper and ink would do. For ordinary manuscripts, it was all right to use the inexpensive ink sold by NPCs, but it took magic-infused ink to create rare tomes and high-level spell books filled with power. Creating this magic-infused ink was another Scribe task, and in order to do so, the Scribe needed materials such as dragon's blood and precious ores found deep in dungeons.

In order to get these diverse materials, it was necessary to go to all sorts of zones, explore them, and get through their battles. With such tasks, even after the Debauchery Tea Party disbanded, and even after *she* wasn't there to run Shiroe ragged anymore, Shiroe had kept himself busy.

It was the twins who spoke to Shiroe first, while he was living this way.

"Mister, mister. Yo, hold up!"

"Um… Excuse me. I'm very sorry to bother you. Would it be all right if we asked you something? We had a question…"

The pair who'd addressed him didn't even come up to Shiroe's shoulder.

The boy was wearing cheap armor and had a katana slung across his back.

The girl wore a white robe and carried a long staff with bells on it.

"Sure. What is it?"

From what Shiroe remembered, they'd been in the crowded streets of Akiba.

One look at their gear was enough to tell him that the two were unmistakably newbies. Not only that, but since it was gear that was distributed free of charge at the very beginning of the game, they were probably *complete* newbies. The voices he heard over the voice chat function seemed to belong to middle schoolers or elementary schoolers. Either way, they were young.

"My spells are weak, and Touya's wounds won't heal. I was told to go buy a better spell, but I'm not sure where they're sold… Do you know, sir?"

Filtered through voice chat, the girl sounded very well-mannered.

"I want some techniques, too. If you know, mister, tell us. Pleeease!"

Their names floated above their heads in green letters. The girl was Minori, and the boy was Touya. They were both level 6.

The first quest in *Elder Tales* was a tutorial. Players who chose the town of Akiba as their starting point were forcibly sent to a dedicated zone known as Major Colonel's Tutorial Ground, where they were made to practice the game's basic operations.

Parenthetically, Major Colonel was a non-player character with rather problematic specs: While he looked like a mild-mannered, white-whiskered gentleman, once he was riled, there was no telling what he would do. From his name, it was hard to tell whether he was a major or a colonel, and it made him quite popular with a certain set of players.

Major Colonel's training lasted about an hour, and once they'd completed the training, even players who'd just started the game were level 4. Taking that into account, these two were probably perfect newbies who'd just started the game that day or the day before.

"Is this your first day here, guys?"

"Yes, sir." "You betcha."

The pair spoke at the same time.

Shiroe might not have been very good with people, but it wasn't as if he hated them. He just had a habit of keeping a wary eye out for strangers who might approach him with profit and loss on their minds.

In that sense, Shiroe didn't dislike newbie players. They wouldn't know that Shiroe was comparatively wealthy, and since they hadn't yet developed the desire to play the game efficiently, the idea of using him would never enter their heads.

Even with pessimistic reasoning like that, as a player who loved

Elder Tales, Shiroe wanted to make beginners feel welcome. This was particularly true when he thought of his own responsibilities as a veteran player.

"I see… Yes, I'll show you. It's this way."

Showing them around town didn't even take enough effort to count as "trouble."

With that thought in mind, Shiroe took the lead and started walking.

After that first meeting with the twins, Shiroe ended up playing alongside them frequently. This was because Touya, who was the polar opposite of shy, would shout to get his attention whenever he saw Shiroe around town and because Minori was very polite and would always call on him to thank him.

The two really were twins; they'd been born very close together, and Minori appeared to be the elder. A mature older sister with the temperament of a committee chairwoman, she kept an eye on her little brother, who, although bright, was a daredevil that didn't know how to hold back. That was the pair's fundamental play style.

Both twins were in their second year of middle school, and they were so young they seemed like little kids to Shiroe. Since Shiroe had been playing for so long, he'd met all kinds of players, but not many of them had been middle schoolers. Because such an age difference left little in common to talk about, even when he'd gotten to know similar players in the past, he hadn't taken the opportunity to go adventuring with them. However, these twins looked up to Shiroe and so sometimes traveled around with him.

Elder Tales was the twins' first online game, and the brand-new experience had them both excited. They both told him about it in the first field zone they visited together.

That initial adventure was a considerably noisy affair.

The second he spotted a monster, Touya would charge at it like a guided missile. Minori would follow him in a panic, and they'd fight hard and desperately until they were almost in tears.

That heartwarming scene was repeated many, many times.

Elder Tales had something called a Coach System. In simple terms, it was a system that allowed high-level players to play alongside low-level players. When Shiroe used this system with the twins, although he was technically level 90, his level temporarily dropped to match theirs. In addition to his level, his HP, ability values, attack power, and general status were all considerably reduced.

The purpose of the system was to lower players' strength to match that of their low-level friends so that they could adventure together.

Of course, Shiroe kept his veteran knowledge of the game, and even though he was stat-weak, he still had fairly expensive equipment. All of this meant he was far tougher than the average beginner; however, if that difference had been converted into levels, it would only have equaled one or two. It was a handy, useful system to use when coaching other players.

Making use of that system, Shiroe raced after the twins.

He fired attack spells at the enemy to decrease their numbers, but Enchanters' attack spells weren't all that powerful to begin with, and his lowered level made them pitifully weak. However, even so, the support seemed to encourage the two newbs.

"Thanks, mister! Okay, next we're charging that enemy over *there*!!"

"Honestly, Touya, would you wait just a minute?! *Listen* to me: You're low on HP!!"

Sometimes, he'd let them pull him around the hunting grounds all day long.

Touya was a Samurai, one of the three Warrior classes.

In *Elder Tales*, spells and sword techniques were known as "special skills." In addition to proper names and effects, each special skill came with set values for required MP, cast time, and recast time. Cast time was the amount of time between the point when a player selected a special skill and the point when the skill activated—the equivalent of "charge" time. Recast time was the amount of time that had to pass after a special skill was used before it could be used again.

One of the distinguishing features of the Samurai class was that many of their techniques had long recast times.

Although the techniques were powerful, most of them couldn't be used several times in a row, and many of them were major techniques that could only be used once or twice per battle. This made Samurai the complete opposite of Monks, who built combos from multiple small techniques.

Since Samurai had many powerful special skills, when they managed to settle a battle quickly, they had the highest attack power of the Warrior classes. In turn, this made Samurai a popular and exhilarating class.

On the other hand, if an Adventurer didn't make the best use of the class's features, they'd run through all their special techniques too quickly and be unable to react during the recast time, no matter what happened. The class's weak point was that players could run out of on-the-spot coping methods and insurance, making it a difficult class to master.

"Goooooooooo! Helm Splitter!!"

Touya, who'd charged ahead, brought his sword down on a goblin from the front. The attack went right through the goblin's shoddy armor and inflicted huge damage, but the subsequent recovery rigidity left Touya wide open.

"Gugaaaah! Gafu! Gafu!"

The horde of goblins didn't let that chance escape them: They rushed him. Touya panicked, but while he was frozen up, he couldn't even evade.

"Aah! Touya! Get back, that's dangerous! Uu... Purification Barrier!!"

As Minori swung her belled staff, an effect like a shining pale blue mirror appeared, blocking the goblins' attack.

Minori was a Kannagi, one of the three Recovery classes.

The Recovery classes recovered HP, healed their companions' abnormal statuses, and had a variety of spells to boost friends' abilities.

All of the Recovery classes had similar spells by which to recover their companions' HP. However, each class had its own unique special recovery skills as well, and those skills provided the three classes' defining characteristics.

Kannagi were apostles of the ancient gods, and their unique recovery ability was Damage Block. This type of spell put up a certain type of barrier for either one specific companion or for the whole party and would negate all damage until the total reached a set amount.

In terms of general recovery ability, Kannagi were the weakest of the three classes, but in some situations, the ability to completely negate damage before it happened gave them an extremely powerful advantage.

On the other hand, because the ability meant the player had to predict the type and range of enemy attacks beforehand, it was tough to master it.

All the main classes in *Elder Tales* were designed to make it hard to get better. Since this was part of the game's complexity, there was really no help for it, but in any case, Touya and Minori didn't seem to mind. They were just enjoying the game.

Since they pestered him to, Shiroe showed the twins around a variety of zones near Akiba, and went shopping with them, and answered all sorts of questions.

"Would you like me to give you some slightly better equipment?" he'd asked once. Even good equipment would only be level 10 or so. At level 90, Shiroe could easily purchase that at the market, in the hundreds if he so wished.

However, Touya turned down his offer. "Huh? I don't need that. I mean, we're out here playing the game, right? Collecting stuff's the best part. If I just *take* it, it's like I'm playing for nothing."

Minori, bowing again and again, said, "I'm sorry. I'm sorry. Please excuse Touya's impertinence. It's just that you're doing so much for us already, Shiroe! Having you play with us makes us much happier than any present could!"

Precisely because they were like this, Shiroe was able to relax and coach them. The twins didn't treat him as a veteran player who was worth using, and playing with them was a fun experience.

Things had gone on that way right up until the day of the Catastrophe.

▶ **4**

"Twins, huh? How 'bout that. And then?"

"'And then' what?"

"Do you not know what happened to them after that, my liege?"

After Shiroe told them about his meeting with the twins just to make conversation, they hit him with *that* question.

The orange light from the fire threw their wavering shadows onto the hilltop tent, and the mood in the camp was peaceful.

"They're on my friend list... I've seen them several times since the Catastrophe, actually."

"So they did get pulled in, huh?"

"We were together right up until it happened, so yes. We were all sent back to Akiba, but then we got separated."

"I was teleported from a ruin as well."

In the instant the Catastrophe occurred, all players seemed to have been forcibly relocated to the nearest town. As if they'd remembered that, both Serara and Nyanta looked thoughtful.

"You shoulda said something to 'em," Naotsugu said. "I bet they've got it pretty rough. Amateurs getting caught up in something like this..."

All the members of the Debauchery Tea Party had been good at looking out for people. Some had been better than others, but among them, Shiroe remembered, Naotsugu had been particularly good at making sure the newer players were taken care of.

I guess you can't really be a Guardian—the guy who protects everybody—if you're not good at looking after people. ...Although, in Naotsugu's case, I think the way he talks puts him at a disadvantage.

Even if he treated Akatsuki like a kid, then got knee kicked for it, every time a battle broke out Naotsugu was the sort of guy who'd do his absolute best to make sure his companions went unharmed.

"Well, mew had a lot going on, too, didn't mew, Shiroechi?"

As he spoke, Nyanta poured hot tea into his tin mug. It wasn't real tea, he'd said; just a mixture of herbs and dried apple peel. Even that makeshift blend felt like a blessing to Shiroe and the others, who'd drunk only plain water for so long. Akatsuki was holding her cup in both hands to warm them, as if it was something very precious.

"True. For the first few days, we were pushed to the limit, and I didn't have the leeway to think about much else. Besides, the next time I saw them, they'd both joined a guild."

To be accurate, Shiroe hadn't been the only one who hadn't had any leeway. None of the players had. No one had the energy to think about anyone besides themselves.

"Oh yeah?"

"The recruiting was aggressive back then."

At Akatsuki's words, Naotsugu nodded, saying, "Now that you mention it…"

"What were they, level twenty? That or close."

"I think they've probably leveled up a bit more by now."

"Then joining a guild was probably their best move. I mean, they barely knew right from left."

As Naotsugu spoke, he stretched hugely and, in the same motion, turned completely around to face Shiroe.

"So, was that Minori girl cute?"

"……Buh?"

Now that he thought about it, Shiroe had only looked at the twins closely when *Elder Tales* was still a game. At the time, they'd been nothing more than polygon models on a screen, so there'd been no way to tell whether Minori was cute or not. Since he hadn't spoken to them face-to-face since the Catastrophe, it wasn't the sort of question he could answer.

"Yeah, that. Forget about that. You used voice chat, right? Couldn't you tell from her voice whether she was cute or not?"

Even after Shiroe told him he didn't know, Naotsugu persisted.

Akatsuki seemed a bit disgusted by their conversation. She just looked at them coldly, as if to say, "Good grief, there they go again."

When Shiroe glanced at Nyanta as a last resort hoping for help from her reprisal, Nyanta was busy being chivalrous. "Serara-chi, aren't mew getting a bit chilled?" But even as Shiroe thought it wouldn't hurt Nyanta to spare a few scraps of that chivalry for his old friend, Naotsugu pressed him further.

"Hmm. If I had to say, 'Yes, she was cute' or 'No, she wasn't,' I'd say… Look, I really don't know. When she talked, she sounded feminine and polite—as if she'd been well brought up, you know? Maybe. I thought she might have been from a family with good breeding, although not quite like Henrietta's family."

As Shiroe explained, remembering as he spoke, Naotsugu nodded along at almost every word. He seemed incredibly happy.

"Well, sure. That's just how middle school girls should be!"

"Heck, why specify an age range?!"

"Stupid Naotsugu…"

He nodded, agreeing with Akatsuki—*absolutely!*—but immediately afterward, she told him, "You're being ridiculous, too, my liege."

"When we get back, let's check up on 'em. Date city! I'll be the vanguard! You're the wingman, Shiroe! Girls are so great."

"Well, we agree on that, I guess."

"So you *do* like panties, huh, Shiro!"

"No, I don't!! I'm no more interested in panties than the average guy."

Even as he thought this was turning into a hassle, Shiroe agreed to Naotsugu's proposal. The hassle came not from having to contact the twins, but from having to take verbal jabs from Naotsugu, and there was no help for that.

Naotsugu had been getting bullied by Akatsuki lately, and so even Shiroe was sympathetic.

After that, their fireside party continued late into the night.

They spoke tirelessly about guilds and each other, about delicious food and this world's starry sky, and the night grew later and later.

The five Adventurers' laughter echoed over the orange flames and the first flavorful meal they'd eaten in ages. It was so pleasant that no one was willing to speak up to end the experience. It was gentle and comfortable, and they didn't want it to be over.

Akatsuki and Serara had begun to nod off, leaning against each other. It was adorable, and even Naotsugu, who was always getting mauled by one of the pair, smiled wryly and draped a blanket over them.

By the time Nyanta finally declared it time for bed, the eastern sky had already begun to gray.

"Ahh. Man, did I *eat*! I haven't had food that awesome in ages. It would've been worth the trip to Ezzo just to get that meal. Yeah, all trips should be like this."

Naotsugu's steps were a bit unsteady from his fatigue and full belly, but the words he murmured were exactly what everyone was feeling.

The five of them curled up in their sleeping bags and drifted off to sleep in the warmth of the fire.

▶ 5

From the next day on, their journey went smoothly.

After all, Shiroe, Naotsugu, and Akatsuki had made it safely to Susukino all by themselves. Now their group had acquired Nyanta, a brilliant attacker, and Serara, who, although her level was low, could use recovery spells.

If Serara could heal superficial wounds of the sort they'd pick up in a fairly aggressive attack, their range of potential tactics expanded. There was no danger of losing to the monsters or wild animals in the field zones.

That said, it wasn't a forced march, either.

Shiroe and the others took care to travel at a more leisurely pace than they had during the first half of their journey. After drastically oversleeping at their first camp, they chose a good time to leave during the morning and traveled by griffin. Since there were restrictions on how long they could use the griffins, they landed at a little past noon and traveled slowly, by horse or on foot, beginning to look for a place to camp early in the afternoon.

They pitched their tent before dusk, then took their time preparing dinner. Naturally, what they made was camp cooking, but compared to the meager fare they'd had up to the present, everything was a fantastic feast.

Of course, Nyanta also did his best to bring variety to their meals. The stew he simmered slowly over the small fire was very well received, and it brought a splendid warmth to their camp under the stars.

The five of them talked about all sorts of things.

Serara didn't discuss the details of the harassment she'd experienced in Susukino, but although still frightened, she seemed to be getting over it now, which was a great relief to Shiroe and the others.

However, unexpectedly, Serara seemed to have fallen for Nyanta, and the only one who hadn't noticed was Nyanta himself. The fact that Serara seemed to think she was successfully hiding her feelings from Shiroe and the others—including Nyanta—was both adorable and heartwarming.

When she was apart from Nyanta, Serara's eyes would inadvertently begin to search for him. At dinnertime, when they gathered around the flames, she always sat unobtrusively beside him, looking happy.

The fact that Nyanta planned to come back to Akiba with them and make the town his new base of operations seemed to be the best news Serara had heard yet. She had hugged the catman in spite of herself, coming very near to upsetting the pot, and had been terribly embarrassed.

As he watched her, Naotsugu smirked like an unruly little kid who had just come up with a prank. Shiroe thought it was a bit mean of him, but he did understand what he was feeling. As might be expected from the fact that he'd called himself an old man, Nyanta hadn't had a single romantic rumor attached to him at the Debauchery Tea Party. To the two of them, who knew Nyanta's past, this was huge news and a noteworthy event.

"Still. I wonder what she sees in middle-aged guys…"

"That's not nice, Naotsugu. This is Captain Nyanta, remember? It's the Captain's magnetism."

"Serara has good taste." Akatsuki spoke nonchalantly while the two of them snickered together.

"You'd go for Nyanta, too, Akatsuki?"

"The sage is a first-class swordsman."

Akatsuki nodded politely in response to Shiroe's startled question. Shiroe thought that was a weird basis for evaluation, but he satisfied himself with the thought that her respect for his battle tactics worked precisely because they were both close-range attack classes.

It was true that Nyanta's laid-back maturity made him very reliable.

Although he kept advertising himself as an old man, viewed objectively, Nyanta was probably in his early forties or late thirties. He had a slender build, and although his eyes were a little squinty, he was quite good-looking.

Hm… Could Captain Nyanta…? I bet he could…

As Shiroe thought—with his fingers near the tip of his chin, a pose he tended to fall into when doing so—something seemed to occur to Akatsuki. She came closer and tugged at his sleeve.

"My liege. My liege."

"What?"

"You aren't a swordsman, my liege, but I think you're very skilled."

Realizing she'd meant to cheer him up, Shiroe gently touched Akatsuki's smooth bangs and thanked her. Looking slightly troubled, Akatsuki announced, "I haven't said anything important," and deliberately turned away, which tickled him a bit.

As they were flying over the Aabu Highlands, ominous dark clouds that seemed mixed with India ink began rapidly bearing down on them from the distant southwest.

Naotsugu spotted the lowering clouds up ahead and strained to get a better look. They were far away, but every once in a while he thought he saw cracks of white light running through their interiors.

"Heeeey! Shiro~. Captain Nyanta~."

Without taking the time to launch the telechat function, Naotsugu yelled down to Shiroe and the others, who were flying about ten meters below him.

"Looooks like we've got some incoming rain clouds~."

When Shiroe heard him and strained his own eyes, he saw that the sun really did seem to be blotted out in the west. Possibly because the air was growing heavier, the griffins were having trouble gaining altitude.

"Shiroechi. It's a bit early, but I think we'd do well to find a place to shelter from the rain."

That proposal came from Nyanta, who'd calmly set up a telechat. Shiroe checked the rain clouds again, then raised his right hand. Together they veered away from the path of the wind and began their descent.

The village where Shiroe's group took refuge was one of the small hamlets that dotted the vast Aabu Highlands. In the old era, the location had probably held a farming village. At the intersection of several unpaved roads, about twenty wooden buildings huddled close together.

They almost hadn't made it in time.

Right after the griffins landed just outside the village, with a roar they felt deep in their chests, lightning began to race across the sky. It was one of those abrupt early-summer weather changes.

Shiroe and the others hastily made for the center of the village.

The place seemed to be a typical farming village, the sort that could be seen all over each of the five territories on the Japanese server.

In the world of *Elder Tales*, where it was said that scientific civilization had been mostly destroyed and the environment had reverted to what it had been a thousand years ago, rich soil had returned along with the thriving wild animals, and in areas where there were few monsters, farming had made a comeback.

Of course, the residents of this sort of farming village weren't players.

They were non-player characters, and they called themselves People of the Earth.

When *Elder Tales* was still a game, a large percentage of the quests had involved traveling to villages like this one, which were nearly ubiquitous, and solving all sorts of problems and incidents. This type of village was often the setting for an adventure or the stage for some sort of event.

The village streets were filled with housewives in white blouses and skirts of thick, soft material and young cowherds with dogs at their heels, all rushing around; no doubt they'd noticed the change in the weather. Farming people of all ages and types appeared, hastily putting away farming tools or struggling to herd sheep into sheds.

As Shiroe and the others had predicted, the large house in the center of the village was both a shared storehouse and a public hall. This sort of thing was common in frontier settlements.

"Hellooooo!"

Naotsugu called into the interior. He'd taken the lead and was the first one inside the big wooden building, where the refreshing smell of dried grass hung in the air.

"Yes, yes. You're travelers, I take it?"

The old man who appeared was an NPC, and he introduced himself as the village's organizer. He looked to be about sixty, with white, close-cropped hair and thick glasses. As might be expected from a pioneer organizer who lived in the wilderness, in spite of his age, his spine was still straight, and he seemed fit as a fiddle.

After he listened to their story, his manner brisk and professional, he offered to lend them a roof for a night at a low rate.

Shiroe's group thanked him and entered the storehouse.

It seemed to be a place where hay was put up for the winter, and it still held a mountain of leftover straw. By that time, the rain clouds had completely blanketed the area. The early-summer rain pelted the village with drops that, while not cold, struck like large lead shot.

As Shiroe turned back to the village street from the door, glancing up at the dark sky, he heard a cheerful voice behind him.

"This's great. I love haystacks!"

Naotsugu sounded delighted.

In this other world, which had inherited the convenience of the game world, sleeping bags and tents performed fairly well. However, although they were passably comfortable, in the end sleeping bags were sleeping bags. Sleeping on the ground all night left them chilled, and their muscles were often stiff and sore.

Compared to that, sleeping on a haystack would be just as comfortable as sleeping in a bed at an inn.

"Mew're right. This looks quite cozy."

Akatsuki, who'd been exploring the large storehouse confirming the locations of windows and the back door, nodded too. Although the building was wooden, the walls had been daubed with clay that acted like plaster, and there were no drafts. The interior was cool and dry, and it smelled clean.

Now, with the rain pounding down as if it were trying to put holes in the roof, they felt they'd been quite fortunate to reach this frontier village.

"Do mew suppose there's a place to start a fire?"

"Nyanta, I found a hearth over there."

Nyanta had already begun to worry about dinner, and Serara pulled him away. As if to say they left all that to the others, Naotsugu and Akatsuki had begun to break down the haystack. They seemed to be preparing to make beds for the five of them.

"Hey, what's with that itty-bitty bed? Is that for a hamster or something?"

"Shut up, stupid Naotsugu. Make your bed over on *that* end."

As Shiroe was listening to the two of them squabbling, smiling wryly, the old man they'd met earlier spoke to him.

"Have you come from the town of Tsukuba, traveler? Are you all Adventurers?"

"Hm? Yes. We're Adventurers. We're actually on our way to Akiba," Shiroe responded. The old man seemed pleasant. *Adventurers* was the word non-player characters used to refer to players. "Would you like some?"

"Why, thank you kindly… Is this…tea?"

Shiroe had taken some of Nyanta's special sweet tea from his bag; he poured it into a tin cup and handed it to the old man. He poured his own into the lid of his flask and sat down on a nearby sawhorse.

The old man pulled up a chair hewn from a log and sat down near Shiroe.

"What do you think? It's pretty good, isn't it?"

Shiroe smiled at the old man. The man was drinking the tea; he seemed surprised at its slightly bittersweet taste, as if he'd never had anything like it before. Grinning from ear to ear, the man told him it was wonderful.

"Huh. You're making *that* one right."

"Of course. This one is for my liege."

"Oh yeah? I see… It must be pretty tough to make a human-sized bed, huh?"

"Don't make fun of me, pervert."

Still quarreling, Akatsuki and Naotsugu were getting the beds set up. With their voices as background music, Shiroe and the old man slowly drank their tea. Outside the eaves, the streets were beginning to turn muddy, but given that the old man didn't seem concerned, this sort of rainfall probably wasn't all that unusual.

"Your friends are nice and lively."

"They are that. They're a bit embarrassing."

"No, no. You need that much energy when you live on the road. It's only natural for Adventurers such as yourselves."

Among the players, it was said that the NPCs had been one of the things most changed by the Catastrophe.

In the *Elder Tales* game, as in all other games, non-player characters hadn't had personalities. As characters, they were much more sophisticated than those in a badly designed home RPG, as they would answer simple questions; however, this was due to the sort of artificial intelligence that could respond to set keywords, and so in reality they'd been no more than automatons.

After the Catastrophe, though, in this other world, non-player characters seemed to be almost perfectly human. The members of the Briganteers might not have thought so, but at the very least, Shiroe did.

They thought, breathed, ate, and lived.

It was possible to drink tea with them this way and to talk with them about all sorts of things. Each of them had a name, and they all had memories.

They weren't human, but they weren't monsters, either. They were probably one of the elements that made up this world.

Since the Catastrophe, because they'd placed great importance on training together on the outskirts of town, Shiroe, Naotsugu, and Akatsuki hadn't stayed in Akiba for any length of time. In addition, since Akiba was a starting point for Adventurers, it had fewer NPCs than PCs compared to other towns of the same size.

As a result, up to this point, Shiroe hadn't had much opportunity to really get to know any non-player characters. However, as he and the man conversed, it was difficult for him to remember that this was a game character, and the more they talked, the more impossible it was to think of him as anything except human.

"People of the Earth don't travel much, you see."

The old man was watching Akatsuki as he spoke, and he smiled broadly, like a good-natured old grandfather.

The term *People of the Earth* didn't signify a race, the way *human*, *elf*, and *dwarf* did. It was what non-player characters called themselves in contrast to the players, or *Adventurers*.

These names had existed when *Elder Tales* was operated as a game, but no players had called them People of the Earth back then. They were players. The mechanical characters were NPCs. That was all.

Now, however, things were different.

" 'People of the Earth,' you said...?"

"That's right. This village is a good place, and there isn't much that troubles us."

When People of the Earth called players Adventurers, the name held great awe and dread. From their perspective, players were beings with fundamentally different abilities and a culture completely unlike their own.

By battling repeatedly, Adventurers grew and grew, and they could develop fighting ability that was tens or hundreds of times greater than what they'd had at first. On top of that, even when lethally wounded, they weren't completely destroyed: They had eternal souls that returned to the temple and were resurrected. They even went to the ruins that remained all over the world and fought—and defeated—giants, undead, dragons, and other terrible, menacing monsters.

These transcendent beings were what they called Adventurers.

People of the Earth didn't have that sort of fighting ability. If they were wounded, they collapsed, and if they died, they couldn't be revived. The term referred to the normal people of this world.

Of course, as the game specs dictated, some non-player characters were given abilities that were equivalent to, and sometimes surpassed, player abilities. The People of the Earth considered these beings to be different from both themselves and the Adventurers, and they referred to them as the Ancients.

In this system of classification, the People of the Earth were the weakest beings. If an Adventurer felt like it, they could easily take their lives or property.

The People of the Earth seemed to have undergone a population explosion since the Catastrophe, and their numbers were five to ten times greater than before, but the difference in fighting ability was a lethal one.

However, as far as Shiroe could see, the fact didn't seem to cause them resentment or grief. Possibly this was because, to them, that was the natural way of things: This world, where they'd been born and raised, had always been that way.

Even the name is like that: People of the Earth... They live with the land. I don't think I could match that...

As he and the old man spoke about it reticently, Shiroe felt this very keenly. How many People of the Earth did the world hold? Even in the Aabu Highlands alone, there had to be more than a hundred villages like this one.

Come to think of it, I don't know much about the People of the Earth, do I? I don't know what they normally eat or what they do… That's really, really…

Spurred on by a sense of wrongness he couldn't put into words, Shiroe was about to ask the old man about it when a cheerful voice hailed him from behind.

"Shiroechi. Great mews!"

Nyanta approached them, and there was a spring in his step. Serara skipped playfully at his side; from the smile on her face, she already knew what the news was.

"What is it?"

"We called at a few of the houses in the neighborhood. When we spoke with them, they sold us provisions."

"It's amazing! We have milk. And cheese. There's sausage and bacon—oh, and eggs! Eggs, too! We bought sugar in Susukino, so we can make cookies!"

"Mm, yes, and we now have cabbage and potatoes as well."

Triumphantly, the two of them displayed their loot. This much food would easily tide them over until they reached Akiba, even if they didn't hunt.

"Is that all right?"

Shiroe asked the old man just to be safe, but he nodded and said, "Of course.

"The weather was good this spring, and our livestock multiplied. I'd wager the villagers are glad of the chance to make a bit of money. …Ah, that's right. I have some barrel-pickled berries," the old man added, as if he'd just thought of it. "If you'd like, would you buy those as well?"

No doubt he was also eager to make "a bit of money."

"We'd love to."

The old man counted among the People of the Earth set off, leading the way, and Shiroe followed.

Touya swiped roughly with his left hand at the mud on his cheek.

His battle gauntlet was made of beast hide and steel wire, so his cheek stung where he'd rubbed it, but that was just what he needed.

If it was hard enough to hurt, he could keep the tears in his eyes from spilling over.

"Step it up. Get the lead out!"

His party leader was yelling, his voice harsh.

Their battle lines had collapsed again today, and he seemed thoroughly annoyed by it.

Touya could sympathize. Touya's class was Samurai. Samurai were one of the three Warrior classes, and it was his job to be the tank.

A tank's role was to support the battle array on the front line. All parties had one or more tanks to draw monster attacks and provide support. If they did that, the attackers could put their abilities to work and attack from wherever they liked in relative safety, without worrying about the monsters' attacks.

In order for that to happen, there were two requirements. The first was not to die. If the tank died, there would be no one to draw the monsters' attacks, and the damage would spread to the players with weak defense: the magic users and healers. If that happened, the battle lines would collapse. The second was to draw enemy attacks to himself, ensuring the safety of the rest of the party members. Even if he survived, if he didn't draw the monsters' attacks, his companions would end up taking damage and, again, the battle lines would collapse.

Mr. Shiroe showed me the ropes, so I understand the basics, but...

Even if he understood the basics, understanding them and putting them into practice were two different things.

True, supporting the battle lines was a tank's duty. It was practically the reason tanks existed. Touya didn't want to just stand by and expose his party to danger. However, without the support of his companions, it couldn't happen.

In order for the tank to survive and continue supporting the front line, he needed recovery support from the rear. Even the Warrior classes, with their excellent defense, would collapse if they had to keep taking monster attacks. To avoid that, sporadic recovery support from the rear guard was necessary. At the same time, the Warrior classes had to draw monster attacks so that the healer could concentrate on recovering, without worrying about enemies in the surrounding area.

These were two sides of the same coin. If either one was missing, Touya, the Warrior on the front line, would fall—and the battle lines would collapse.

In addition, in order to draw the enemy, he had to fan their hate more than anyone else in the party and keep their attention on him. The Warrior classes had lots of special skills to pull the enemy's attention to them and concentrate attacks on themselves. Many of these were provocative skills known as taunts. These special skills were a type of mental manipulation that wiped everyone but the Warrior off the enemy's radar.

"After you've drawn them, it's a matter of having courage, a cool head, and the strength of will to believe in your companion's recovery. Touya, you trust Minori, so that's easy, right?"

That's what Mr. Shiroe told me, but…it's not enough…

Ordinarily, if enemies and allies had roughly equal strength, taunts would function without any problem. However, if another party member's level was much higher than the tank's or if the attacks were too fierce, this wasn't necessarily the case.

In other words, even though the tank's job was to draw the enemy on the front line, the enemy would decide that an attacker or healer posed more of a threat.

That was the issue with Touya's current party.

The man who'd been put in charge was a level 46 Summoner. That put him right in the middle as far as *Elder Tales* rankings were concerned, and his level was twice as high as Touya's.

In comparison to the Summoner's attack power, Touya's ability to control the front line was lethally inadequate. Enemies decided that the Summoner was more of a threat than Touya, who was supporting the front line. Naturally, the man's excessive attacks provoked the enemy monsters' anger, and their attacks targeted him instead of Touya. However, although the Summoner had twice Touya's level, his defense was far lower.

In a situation where the enemy's attacks were split between Touya and the leader, the healer's attention would be divided as well. If two party members were taking damage from attacks, the amount of recovery was spread out, and in the worst-case scenario, there wouldn't be enough to recover either of them.

On top of that, if their teamwork broke down, the formation they'd put together in advance would fall apart, and the members in charge of attacking wouldn't be able to tell which enemy they needed to take out in order to salvage the situation. Should they act according to plan and take out the enemies Touya was fighting at the front, one at a time, or should they save the Summoner, their leader, by switching their target to the enemies swarming him? If the players in charge of attacking lost their focus, their attacks wouldn't be focused either, and the individual kills wouldn't go as planned.

As a result, the battle would drag out, and the wound in the already disintegrating battle lines would widen. It was a perfect vicious cycle.

I guess that's why Mr. Shiroe used the Coach System. If he'd just played as himself, the monsters would have gone for him…

Touya had finally made that connection the other day.

Shiroe certainly hadn't matched his level to theirs for show on a whim or out of sympathy, he realized. He'd done it to train them in the basics of group combat.

On that point, the Summoner, his current leader, was different.

The target monsters at that day's hunting ground were level 25. They were lizardmen, with higher levels than Touya and the other beginners, and fighting the monsters stretched them to their limit.

However, to the leader, they were puny monsters more than ten levels below him. He couldn't stand to chip away slowly at low-level monsters like that. *"I'm not matching your pace. You match mine. That's how it should be."* He'd said that to Touya and the others very clearly.

To the Summoner, this was just a babysitting job that his guild master had foisted on him. If they didn't collect or earn their quota, he'd probably get some sort of warning from the guild's top brass.

As far as he was concerned, Touya and the others were holding him back.

The leader, who was wearing a dark crimson robe, made no attempt to hide his irritation.

All his companions were exhausted, and their eyes were dull and vacant. Four of them had died today. The fact that they'd had to go back to the temple and make a fresh start every single time had only added to their leader's annoyance.

However, even then, the man hadn't changed his methods. If he'd used the Coach System and matched his level to Touya and the others, it would have balanced their combat teamwork, but he didn't seem able to stomach the idea of bringing his level down. "Our battles are *already* slow!" he'd railed. "If I do that, they'll get even slower, and we won't make our quota."

In one of Akiba's back alleys, one of his companions, a Bard, staggered and nearly fell even though the path was perfectly clear.

"…I'm sorry. …I feel kind of dizzy…"

The girl apologized to Touya, who'd helped her stay on her feet. All he could see in her eyes was a stagnant, murky fatigue.

"It's not much longer now. C'mon, you can do it."

Touya lent the girl his shoulder, trying to encourage her. The Bard was a level or two below Touya; she was light, and the sour smell of her sweaty, grimy mantle clung to his nostrils. Touya knew he was about the same. They weren't given the time or breathing room to bathe.

I guess that's pretty rough on the girls, but…

He glanced at the girl out of the corner of his eye. She didn't seem to have the energy to care about her shabby appearance anymore. She was moving her lips, silently counting her steps, as if she'd collapse from exhaustion if she didn't distract herself.

Touya bit his lip.

Why had things turned out like this? The idea, which he should have been sick of thinking by then, dragged itself around his fatigue- and anger-muddled mind, unable to find a way out.

When, trailing behind their leader, the party reached the central plaza, they were made to form ranks. The leader, his lip curled in a sneer, glared at Touya and the others. Then he began going from member to member, collecting the material items they'd won that day.

Just having a guildhall didn't give the guild limitless storage space for items. Hamelin sold off any middling items it couldn't use at the market immediately after a hunt.

"You've been sitting on a lot there, Touya."

The leader taunted him in a sticky voice. Although Touya's level was low, he was a Warrior. Naturally, it made him physically stronger than the other classes, and he was able to carry a lot. His load was the result of his attempt to reduce his companions' fatigue as best he could.

"I worked hard to carry it."

Even the leader had to be aware of that. Touya spoke without meeting the man's eyes. The urge to hit him welled up inside him, but they were already in the noncombat zone. Besides, his companions' strength was nearly gone. He didn't want to start trouble in a place like this and shorten their already brief break.

"Huhn!"

The leader snorted contemptuously at Touya, then put all the items he'd collected on the market.

"So, all the power you lot have is just barely enough to collect bargain-bin items like those. Well, even then, your room and board is covered for you. Be grateful for that. …Even though it's because of your Pots."

In spite of himself, Touya ground his molars together.

…*Minori.*

If they hadn't had his sister shut up in the guildhall, a virtual prisoner, he wouldn't have let this smug-faced thug shoot his mouth off. Even he could feel the animosity creeping into his gaze, and anger was welling up inside him like heavy oil. To keep it from showing, Touya looked away, turning his gaze to the dusty street.

In any case, the leader was only middle management.

That scumbag. If I cut him, I'd just get my sword dirty. …How long is this going to go on? How did this happen? …We don't need the Pots. I don't even want 'em. If they do, they can have 'em all. But even Minori's at the end of her rope. If only we hadn't joined this guild…

*   *   *

"—We just got back. Yes, thanks. Yeah… We're fine."

Suddenly, a pure white light lanced through Touya's gray-hazed field of vision.

It hadn't even been a month yet, but the voice was already nostalgic. It was a voice he'd nearly forgotten: Shiroe's pensive, slightly troubled speech.

His head came up as abruptly as if he'd been stung; he scanned the plaza.

The market? No.

The stalls? No.

The smithy? No.

The weapons shop, the guard shop, the tavern, the inn… He looked and looked for the face he knew must be there… He was very close to despair. Touya didn't know the face that belonged to that voice.

He'd only ever heard the voice over voice chat. Touya didn't know what Shiroe would look like now, after the Catastrophe. When that thought occurred to him, he felt as if his chest was being crushed.

Still, when a group of a dozen or so noisy travelers entered through the arched gate that linked the plaza with the main street, Touya's eyes were drawn to them. Several town-dwelling guild members had surrounded a small group that had obviously just returned from a long journey. A young man stood at the center of the group, but he didn't seem at all excited and in fact looked a little troubled.

It was Shiroe.

"Don't you worry! Once our Chefs heard what you told us, you'd never believe it. We've been taste testin' like it was goin' out of style every day. What would that be in English, 'a taste-testin' storm'? When we heard you were comin' back, they started skippin' around and gettin' ready for a party."

"Whoa, a feast?! Can't-wait-for-that city!"

"That's wonderful mews."

"Mari, you really didn't have to do all that. Not over this."

Feeling frantic, as though he couldn't move quickly enough, Touya opened his mental menu. He aligned his cursor with the player in front of him and called up the name and guild display. Guild: Unaffiliated. Name: Shiroe. Class: Enchanter.

It was the expert player who'd spent a little while with Touya and Minori before the Catastrophe struck, teaching them the basics of the game. Even now, Touya and his sister talked about the young man as if he were their big brother.

"Mist—"
Touya began to raise his voice, but then he froze, as if he'd been cut off. He'd thought Shiroe had looked his way.

It might have been an illusion, but when Shiroe looked at him, Touya had sensed something inside him, something that had grown far stronger than before.

Shiroe was also living here, in the world after the Catastrophe.

The moment he sensed that, the shock had frozen Touya's tongue.

The world had changed.

The Catastrophe had done something final and irreversible to it. They'd been pulled into another world, something all young dreamers fantasized about at least once or twice. Not only that, but the game world had turned real. It was like something out of a heroic legend.

However, a good look at the situation revealed a gray prison.

"A guild to aid beginners." Touya and Minori might have been wrong to fall for words like that. *Still*, Touya thought. Even without that, this was a world where the "haves" were powerful people.

Money, items, experience points: All resources benefited the people who collected them. Those who had money gained more of it; those who had items got more of them. Those who had lots of experience points—in other words, the high-level players—fought stronger monsters and leveled up. In this world, where the law of the jungle prevailed, that was the Truth.

The "haves" got even more power, and the "have-nots," eternal latecomers, could only stare at the backs of the "haves." That was part of the true shape of the *Elder Tales* world, the world of the online game. Now that the game had become real, that harsh truth showed even more clearly, and on top of that, since it was no longer a game, they weren't allowed to quit.

Touya's thought patterns were still young, and he couldn't put that truth into words and explain it clearly. Even so, because he *was* young, he was sensitive to its real shape.

The fact that they were the same.

It was a fundamental natural law, in every place, in every world. If "survival of the fittest" was allowed, then it was only proper that some people were strong and others were weak. The world wasn't rough on the weak because this was a game. The real world had been the same way. True, open exploitation and discrimination had been forbidden, but that hadn't meant those things hadn't existed.

Touya knew.

He'd had legs that wouldn't move. They'd taught him the truth well enough.

Both Touya and Minori were novice players. Novices had low battle strength and didn't know much about the world, and on top of that, they didn't have property. That meant they were powerless.

Touya thought there probably wasn't anyone as well versed in being powerless, or in being a child, as he was. He bit his lip as he thought and tasted iron.

The weak didn't have the power to protect themselves, and there was no miracle in any world that would save them for free.

What were the words Touya had swallowed? *Help me? Save me?* Now that he'd cut them off, even he didn't know.

In Touya's mind, Shiroe was an expert at the game. He'd seemed to know more about *Elder Tales* than anyone. Maybe Touya had thought Shiroe would rescue them from any hardship.

…But how could he say that?

Did he have any right to ask a mere acquaintance—someone who'd played with them for a week or so before the Catastrophe, when *Elder Tales* had been just a game—for help?

Take someone bankrupt, for example, or someone deep in debt. A person like that could never just ask a stranger, someone who wasn't even family, for help. This was reality, and that was what that meant. Even Touya knew that much.

In order to survive in this world, even Shiroe had to be paying some sort of price.

There was no way he could impose on him like that.

As Touya thought this, he lowered the fist he'd clenched.

At some point, a fine rain had begun to fall in the plaza.

CHAPTER.
2
DETERMINATION

► NAME: TOUYA

► LEVEL: **6**

► RACE: **HUMAN**

► CLASS: **SAMURAI**

► HP: **668**

► MP: **331**

► ITEM 1:

[CERTAIN-KILL UNSIGNED SWORD]

A TWO-HANDED SWORD SPECIFICALLY FOR SAMURAI. CAN BE EQUIPPED AFTER REACHING LEVEL 10. IT'S A MAGIC ITEM CREATED FROM UNSIGNED SWORD, A CHEAP WEAPON SOLD IN SHOPS. THE "CERTAIN-KILL" MODIFIER MEANS ITS CRITICAL HIT RATE HAS BEEN RAISED SLIGHTLY.

► ITEM 2:

[PERSIMMON TANNIN LEGGINGS]

JAPANESE-STYLE PROTECTIVE GEAR FOR YOUR LOWER BODY. THE ASTRINGENT JUICE OF PERSIMMONS IS SAID TO HAVE PRESERVATIVE AND WATER-RESISTANT EFFECTS, AND THESE GAITERS ARE SOMEWHAT WATER-RESISTANT, AS WELL AS STRONG AGAINST COLD AIR ATTACKS. SINCE THEY'RE LOW-LEVEL EQUIPMENT, THEIR EFFECT IS MODEST.

► ITEM 3:

[WOLF FANG *NETSUKE*]

AN ACCESSORY GIVEN AS A REWARD FOR CLEARING THE BEGINNER QUEST "ATTACKING WOLF PACK." WHEN EQUIPPED, IT RAISES A PLAYER'S PHYSICAL STRENGTH SLIGHTLY. AS AN ITEM, IT HAS ABSOLUTELY ZERO RARITY, BUT TOUYA WON HIS WHILE TRAINING WITH SHIROE, SO HE IS FOND OF IT.

<COMPASS>
WHEN A LIGHTNING SPELL HAS
BEEN USED NEARBY, IT WILL
TELL YOU THE DIRECTION IN
WHICH IT WAS CAST. YOU CAN
ALSO USE IT TO FIND NORTH.

Guilds—communities of any size created by Adventurers—were a system that played a central role in player interaction within *Elder Tales*. They were a continuous relationship contract created when two or more unaffiliated players joined up, establishing the guild. Adventurers affiliated with the same guild received various privileges, such as common safe-deposit boxes and the use of a dedicated communication function.

Guildhalls, one such privilege, were zones that guilds could own or rent.

For example, the guildhalls in Akiba's guild center were roughly divided into four ranks: halls with three, seven, fifteen, or thirty-one rooms. Having a guildhall of a size that corresponded to that of one's guild was plain common sense. The halls could be used to store various items that wouldn't fit in members' individual bank safe-deposit boxes, as well as to house equipment used in item production.

The biggest guilds sometimes used an entire external building to do this, instead of the guild center.

There was a theory that the world of *Elder Tales* was the future shape of the real world and the town of Akiba (the Half-Gaia Project reproduction of Akihabara) held many ruined buildings. Many of these ruins were uninhabited, and although they cost quite a sum, it was possible for guilds and individuals to buy or rent them.

By making changes on the Settings screen, anyone who purchased one of these zones could customize it by leaving items there, permitting combat, or setting entry and exit permissions for individual users. Enormous guilds, in turn, would purchase one of these buildings and transform it into their headquarters.

In guild center terms, the guildhall of the Crescent Moon League was a B-rank hall, one with seven rooms.

While it certainly wasn't vast, it held sufficient facilities for a guild of their size: With four rooms, one workroom, one storeroom, and a midsized conference room, it was, in Marielle's words, "handy."

However, the conference room would be crowded with even fifteen occupants, and it certainly wasn't large enough to hold a banquet for a group of more than thirty, including Shiroe and his companions.

For that reason, Marielle and the other guild members had decorated all the rooms in the guildhall, with the exception of the storeroom, for the party to celebrate Serara's return.

The rooms were decorated here and there with modest fresh flowers, and a clean cloth had been laid over a table that was normally used as a manufacturing surface for small articles. The guildhall had been swept sparkling clean from corner to corner, and some rooms had been equipped with low wisteria-cane tables and lots of cushions so that guests would be able to sit in circles and chat. A temporary row of wisteria-cane chairs had even been set up in the corridor.

These weren't expensive items: The Crescent Moon League's craftsmen had manufactured the very best things they could make and brought them to the guildhall.

Marielle and the others had gone to the outskirts of town to meet Shiroe's group, and as soon as they returned to Akiba after rescuing Serara, the travelers were jubilantly invited back to the guildhall. Since they'd been in touch via telechat nearly every day, the Crescent Moon League members had known full well for several days that Shiroe and the others were returning.

Having heard the secret of "real cooking" from Nyanta—also via telechat—the Crescent Moon League Chefs had spent those few days combining lots of ingredients and making food for the party.

According to Marielle, in order to get used to the new way of cooking they'd learned—in which Chefs cooked directly, without using the item creation menu—the Crescent Moon League Chefs had made scores of dishes over and over, barely even taking time to sleep.

Even the samples had been wildly popular with the Crescent Moon League members, who had been given only depressingly monotonous food up till now, and it had become another cause for celebration alongside Serara's return.

Of course, it wasn't as if there were no problems with this new cooking technique.

First, with the new method, one had to take the time to actually prepare the food. In the previous method, when cooking was performed from the item creation menu, even stews and pickles were done in ten seconds, but with the new method, one had to give stews time to stew and fermented foods time to ferment.

In addition, when making dishes from the item creation menu, the required ingredients were limited to five at most. Subtle seasonings, oil, and secondary ingredients had probably been left out of the game for convenience's sake. However, with the new method, naturally, ingredients one didn't have on hand wouldn't be included in the finished dish: Curry made with only meat, potatoes, onions, and spices wouldn't have carrots in it.

They'd also discovered that their cooking skills seemed to be reviewed when they attempted to prepare dishes that were over a certain difficulty level. If a Chef's cooking skills weren't at the required level, no matter what ingredients were used, the attempt would fail and the dish would turn into a weird blackened object or a slimy, sticky glob. The general trend seemed to be that using special cooking techniques such as frying, roasting, and steaming required more advanced cooking skills, but they didn't completely understand the particulars yet.

There was an even more basic issue as well.

Up until now, if players used the same ingredients and selected the same target item from the item creation menu, a food item would come out exactly the same no matter who made it. It would look the same, of course, and the flavor would be the same as well (although it would be the characteristic soggy rice crackers flavor).

However, with the new method, since the item creation menu wasn't used, the quality of the finished dishes varied widely, even if the Chefs who made them had the same levels and skill values. Even if a player's cooking skills were advanced, it was the actual player who was doing the cooking. Cooking skills became a number that showed the difficulty of the dishes a player was *allowed* to make and no longer showed what sort of dishes the player *could* make.

The new method did have many limitations, but that didn't mean it was worthless. On the contrary, the discovery had tremendous value. Viewed from the perspective of common cooking sense at home on Earth, the fact that it took time, the fact that it required a variety of ingredients, and the fact that flavors changed depending on who was cooking were only natural.

More than anything, the Crescent Moon League guild members were as sick and tired of the flavorless, factory-made, energy bar–like food items as Shiroe and the others had been.

"I tell ya, we let the food items break us, and we completely lost sight of the fact that livestock feed isn't *food*! This stuff we're eating right now? *This* is food!"

As the young Crescent Moon League magic user said during the banquet, until they'd chanced upon genuinely delicious food, they had failed to realize how terrible the food they'd been living on actually was.

The flurried dinner preparations and decorating had ended, and the guildhall to which Shiroe and the others were invited as the guests of honor was steeped in a festive atmosphere.

Shiroe and his group were shown to the great table that had been set up in the conference room and given aperitifs, along with the reassurance that "All the food will be completely ready in another hour!" Having changed out of their traveling clothes, Shiroe and his friends were each welcomed warmly.

Although Shiroe and the others enjoyed being entertained, the Crescent Moon League members who were entertaining them also enjoyed the banquet. It was the first boisterous gathering filled with food this splendid, luxurious, and—best of all—delicious to be held since the Catastrophe.

"We're partyin' today! Eat, drink, and be merry!"

To the players, who'd been discouraged by their life since the Catastrophe, Marielle's cheery proclamation was the best possible encouragement.

*   *   *

For a while, the conference room was filled with words of gratitude. But then, suddenly saying, "I'll just go take a look," Nyanta
stood. Serara hastily followed him. From the sounds that came after,
the heartwarming pair had gone to the temporary kitchen that was
currently taking up the entire workroom, where they had joined the
Chefs of the Crescent Moon League and threw themselves into the
party preparations like battle-scarred veterans.

When using the new cooking method, the list of food items registered on the item creation menu was useless. Each Chef could only use
the dishes and cooking methods they personally knew, and this was
greatly affected by the sort of cooking experience they'd had in the
real world.

To that end, Nyanta and the Crescent Moon League Chefs compared
their culinary knowledge, shared the recipes they knew, and created a
festive banquet with even more flair.

The Crescent Moon League members who hadn't been able to fit
into the conference room found places in the other rooms, drinking
and carousing wherever they liked.

Dish after dish was brought out.

Fried chicken, omelets bursting with tomatoes, a salad of corn and
lettuce, seafood paella with saffron, an unleavened bread a little like
naan, and spicy mutton soup. Roast venison flavored with rock salt
and herbs. Fruits of all colors piled high on a platter, and delicate
biscuits topped with lots of custardy cream.

Serara walked from room to room with platters of food, waiting on
the guests. In every room, players told Serara, "This is a banquet to
celebrate *your* safe return. Sit down and enjoy it!" However, Serara
only laughed and told them, "You were the ones who saved me. Let me
thank you," and continued diligently serving.

This behavior was so touching that Serara's fan base at the Crescent
Moon League grew remarkably, and in every room, she was pressed into
taking part in a toast—"Have this, at least"—until she grew quite drunk.

Shiroe and his friends were also in great demand.

Naotsugu was surrounded by younger players and was discussing
battles with them.

The Crescent Moon League was still a young guild. Only a few members, Marielle included, were level 90. Even Marielle and the others were *only* level 90 and hadn't seen what lay beyond.

"What I'm saying is, as long as you and your companions' levels are similar, that's enough. It's what's *beyond* the level that's important, not the level itself."

"Beyond the level… You mean the mysteries?!"

Shouryuu, a Swashbuckler whose red face might have been the product of intoxication, quizzed Naotsugu, who was wolfing down a skewer of sweet and spicy chicken. Shouryuu was a young player who was in charge of organizing battles and hunts at the Crescent Moon League, and he'd gone on several excursions with Naotsugu. To him, Naotsugu probably seemed like a hero.

"Mm. I mean—panties!!"

At Naotsugu's forceful declaration, everyone in the room was taken aback for a moment and the atmosphere seemed to curdle. Even Shouryuu's expression said, "What is this guy talking about?"

Possibly the atmosphere struck Naotsugu as dicey, too. He cleared his throat several times, then continued, as if trying to smooth things over.

"…Uh… Kidding. That was a trendy little joke. Now that I've got your attention… Let's see… So, as long as you depend on level when you fight, whenever an enemy beats you, it'll be because your level wasn't high enough, right? So what happens if you play like that until you hit the highest level? If you've maxed out your level and there's an enemy you can't beat, you'll never beat it, because you can't boost your level higher. See? If that happens, you're through. There's no way you'll ever win. Despair city.

"To keep that from happening, you need to work with your friends and get a bit tricky. If you don't do those two things, you'll always lose somewhere in the end. It's too late to figure that out once your level's as high as it'll go. A guy who's never worked with his friends won't be able to turn into a team player right off the bat just because he's come up against an enemy he can't beat. On the other hand, you can cooperate and use your head no matter how low your level is. Do that, and you'll go straight to the top. It's important to keep asking yourself, 'Is there anything else I can do?' Our man Shiroe's an expert at that.

I mean, he's Machiavelli-with-glasses, y'know? The guy'll use any cheap trick to win!"

That speech seemed to make a pretty good impression.

Of course, if Shiroe had been listening, he probably would have said, "Don't use me as the punch line."

After that, the conversation turned into a lively discussion of what sort of tricks to use when fighting a particular enemy and what should be done in this or that situation. For better or worse, the players in this world were gamers. Even if they'd been tossed into another world, once their souls had regained some of their energy, they wanted to learn.

Meanwhile, Akatsuki was being held captive in one of the rooms.

It was a room used by the women of the Crescent Moon League.

The room was decorated with potpourri and a vanity, and although simple, it felt neat, tidy, and somehow elegant. In its center, Akatsuki was surrounded by five women.

"All right, Akatsuki. It's about time you resigned yourself, my dear."

"I refuse."

Akatsuki's expression was, as always, so serious it made her look cross, but her eyes were flicking right and left, searching for some way to escape. However, she was completely surrounded, and she couldn't find an opening.

"Don't be afraid. We'll be gentle."

"Would you get it through your head that that's a villain's line?"

The leader of the women, Henrietta—a Bard with bright, elegant, honey-colored curls—was bearing down on her, flexing both hands menacingly. Frightened, Akatsuki took a step back...straight into the arms of the tall woman standing behind her, who caught and hugged her.

"You're so little and cute!"

"Don't say 'little.' I'm older than you are. Probably."

The Crescent Moon League's guild master was Marielle.

It was quite rare for a woman to serve as the head of a guild, and it meant that the Crescent Moon League attracted rather more women than most other guilds. Not a few of these players were, like

Henrietta—the Bard who managed the guild's accounts, absolutely crazy for cute things.

Akatsuki's slight stature and sweet, doll-like face had won her many fans in the Crescent Moon League. There were, of course, guys with secret crushes on her, but the ones who were really enthusiastic and hard to deal with were her female fan club.

"Ta-daaa! We've got three summer dress styles for you today."

"Wait. What sort of fight would anyone wear those to?!"

Henrietta had begun to present the showy girls' dresses, her cheeks flushed a bit in embarrassment—as though she had the wrong idea about something—but Akatsuki interrupted her almost immediately.

Since she was dealing with women, Akatsuki couldn't respond with a physical attack of the sort she visited on Naotsugu. All she could do was kick and squirm. Not only that, but since the women thought even *this* was cute, Akatsuki was left without any way to fight or the energy to do it.

On top of that, the dresses they brought out—a violet cotton frock, an organdy dress frothy with lace and frills—were so young and feminine they made her dizzy.

"I am my liege's ninja! I can't wear frivolous clothes like that!"

"We have Master Shiroe's permission. Come now. Give up."

"I've been tricked! My liege! You set me up, didn't you?!"

Going to her fate almost in tears, Akatsuki was mobbed by the crazed women.

▶ 2

The banquet reached its zenith, and the enjoyable time passed in a whirl of repeated thanks and congratulations, toasts and compliments on the feast.

They ate enormously, drank fantastically, and made merry.

It must have been about the time when the moon had set completely.

The Crescent Moon League guildhall, which still held a faint echo of the banquet's heat, was wrapped in the unique atmosphere that follows festivals: a satisfied, slightly wistful, happy tranquillity.

The tables that had been set up here and there were littered with bottles of alcohol, plates of half-eaten food, and buckets of ice that had been used to chill drinks, like beaches after a typhoon.

The guild members lay all around the room, under tables, on sofas, or curled up hugging cushions.

Naotsugu was sprawled out on his back in the conference room, snoring, his arms and legs spread-eagled. Akatsuki, who'd been dolled up by Henrietta, the Crescent Moon League's expert in all things feminine, had fallen asleep (possibly from exhaustion) on a large cushion that enfolded and nearly buried her.

"—Whoops."

Shiroe caught a bottle that had been teetering on the edge of the table, then picked up a few more and tossed them into his rucksack together. The bag, a magic item that canceled out the weight of anything put into it, was also a powerful ally when cleaning up rooms.

Shiroe and Marielle were the only two awake in the conference room full of sleepers.

The table that had been pulled into the corner of the room still held a stack of several large plates and some leftovers, but everything that could have been bumped into and scattered across the room by a tipsy partygoer had been cleared away. Marielle, who'd been moving around the conference room laying wool blankets over her sleeping companions, put her hands on her hips and stretched. Then she spoke to Shiroe.

"Think this'll do it?"

"Sure."

Somewhere, he heard a small murmur, as though someone was talking in their sleep.

As Shiroe responded to Marielle, he smiled a little at the voice. Of course he kept his own voice low, so as not to wake anyone.

"What now? Are you gonna sleep, too, kiddo?"

"I'm not all that tired."

"I see…"

Marielle came over to Shiroe, looking into his face as if she were seeing him for the first time in a very long while.

"…In that case, why don't I fix us some tea? Let's go to the guild master's office. No sense in hangin' out here."

Beckoning to Shiroe, Marielle left the conference room. "Wait just a sec," she whispered. As they went, she checked each of the rooms. In every one, sated from their feast, guild members slept on sofas, cushions, or right on the floor.

"Tomorrow's gonna be a big ol' cleanup day."

"I'll help."

"Now how could we let our guests help us clean?"

When Marielle looked at the guild members, her expression was warm and gentle. Just being able to see her like this was enough to make Shiroe glad they'd accepted the mission.

Tidying up only the bottles and platters that looked hazardous, the two of them made for the guild master's office. It was the ultrafeminine room where, before their journey, they'd heard Marielle's story and resolved to make the trip to Susukino.

Only the large work desk seemed suited to the term *office*. The rest of the space was coordinated in pastel colors to the point where it might as well have been Marielle's private room.

"What'll you have?"

"Anything's fine."

"All righty. Let's see what we've got. …Hm…"

Marielle brought some black-leaf tea from the beverages that were left in the kitchen. Made with black tea leaves, the tea could be drunk hot or cold, and varieties blended with fruit had a particularly clean, brisk flavor.

The two of them sat on the sofa, finally relaxing for a bit.

Shiroe was always the last one to fall asleep after a commotion like this one. It wasn't that he disliked parties; on the contrary, he loved them. It was just that the more fun he had, the more he felt that he wanted to watch over it to the very end, and it kept him from falling asleep. It was a very old habit of his, and Nyanta and the others had always teased him about it.

Marielle seemed to share that feeling; the way she'd looked lovingly at each of her companions as she'd covered them with blankets had made an impression on him.

From the guildhall, they could feel the sleepers' presence and, quite faintly, hear the sounds of people turning in their sleep. It was far more reassuring than complete silence.

"You really saved us this time, and I mean that. Thanks so much."

"Enough. We didn't do anything that special."

Still slightly giddy from the festive heat of the banquet, Shiroe's mood was light as he answered. He hadn't expected to be thanked this heartily. Well, to be completely honest, he'd assumed they'd be thanked, but he'd never dreamed that *everyone* would thank them this way.

He remembered the huge smiles of the good-natured Crescent Moon League guild members.

If anything, Shiroe tended to be shy with strangers. He thought he was probably hard to approach, unlike Naotsugu and Nyanta, but the Crescent Moon League members had even come to him, offering him food and expressing their gratitude.

I never thought we'd make them so happy…

In actuality, he'd been prepared to be told that they had been out of line: Outsiders poking their noses where they didn't belong; who did they think they were?

He hadn't been able to forgive the world for becoming what it had become, and he'd gone out of his way to undertake the long trip up to Susukino in an attempt to burn through that irritation… In other words, he'd done nothing more than push his own incredibly personal standards onto everyone else.

Shiroe was fully aware of how arrogant that had been.

I don't regret it, but… I do know it's nothing they should be thanking me for.

For that reason, being thanked so freely left him at a loss as to how to respond. He felt rather humbled and ashamed.

"If that wasn't anythin' special, I don't know what is. We'll have to think of a way to thank you."

"No, really, don't worry about it… How were things here while we were away?"

"Here, huh…?"

At Shiroe's question, Marielle's expression clouded slightly.

Shiroe didn't ask her why. He only waited, swirling the tea in his glass.

"Akiba's…settled down a bit, I think. It's more settled than it was anyhow."

" 'Settled down'…?"

"Yep. PKs are way down. And public order… It doesn't seem bad to me. I guess it depends on what you're comparin' it to, but still. At the very least, it feels better than when it was real awful. All of that's better."

Marielle continued, searching for the words as she spoke.

"…Listen, though. This atmosphere's no good. I can't really say what bugs me about it, but… What I mean is… Hmm. I can't tell you, 'This or that is bad, and that's what's wrong,' but even so, somethin's broken somewhere. I'd like to do somethin' about it, but there's nothin' to be done. I'm pretty sure it's 'cos the rankings have been hashed out."

Rankings.

There was something disturbing and sinister about the sound of that word.

"We're a pretty small guild, y'know? Just under thirty of us. Plus, four of us are level ninety, and about half of us are level fifty or under. I'm not complainin', mind, but as a practical problem, it's a fact. It's somethin' objective, and we can't change it. For instance, right now, D.D.D. is Akiba's biggest combat guild. From what I hear, they've got over 1,500 members. I bet they've got more level nineties than we can shake a stick at. That's another objective fact we can't change."

Marielle set her glass on the table and continued, kneading her fingertips together.

"Now I'm not sayin' that's bad. The big guys have their own big-guy problems; believe me, I know. But how should I put it…? Things like that are buildin' up, and it's gettin' to the point where we can't fix it… As you'd expect, the big guilds with all the equipment are doin' well; that's only natural. In some areas, places like that are settin' the mood and the rules for the town. Like preferential use of the market, say."

"They're doing things like that?"

"These aren't clear-cut 'rules,' mind. It's just, with numbers like that… The big guilds are the ones who are actin' all important. One way or another, see, they've got the power. If players that belong to those guilds act important to match, they get away with it, and they think that's how it should be."

Ridiculous.

Of course the big guilds had more members, and naturally they'd be more efficient at some things. For instance, the main source of income for fighting guilds was loot won from monster battles. In battles fought specifically to win loot, known as "hunting," larger numbers were linked to efficiency. When it came to making efficient use of the materials won as loot, having lots of production classes and companions in-house let the guild develop many situations to its advantage. Still, that didn't make each individual player who was affiliated with the guild any stronger, and it certainly didn't make them more important.

She would probably have laughed it off.

She would have looked at the players who could do nothing but live huddled together in narrow-minded groups and laughed loud and long as she declared:

"You people aren't even the teensiest bit cool."

"Remember I said PKs were down? It's the same reason. This guild here is tougher than that guild there. ...Or weaker. With that hashed out already, there's no point in fightin' anymore just to make it clearer. Nobody who knows they're gonna lose will go near somebody that could bite 'em. They just find another huntin' ground. But most of those other huntin' grounds are either far away or the huntin's no good. Sure, PKs are down, but all it means is that the guilds have managed to segregate the zones they go to. The tough guilds have claimed the best huntin' grounds as their turf. We can't fight in town, so nobody's lockin' horns that way. Still, even so, these invisible territories are takin' shape. That sounds like 'rankings' to me."

He hadn't been drunk to begin with, but Shiroe felt the center of his head growing cool and clear. This was even worse than the deterioration of public order he'd been imagining. True, it wasn't the worst it could have been. PKs were down, apparently, and there were probably fewer quarrels as well.

But still, somehow... I don't like this. It makes me sick...
It wasn't the least bit cool, Shiroe thought.
A sense of revulsion churned inside him.

"I can't tell you, 'This or that is bad and that's what's wrong,'" Marielle had said. For example, occupying hunting grounds might not be an admirable move, but was it wrong? Not necessarily. At the very least, there were no laws in this world, which meant no one could declare it was illegal.

Patrolling a set area in order to gather items efficiently was a common method, and the more experience a player gained in an area, the more efficient they'd get. In other words, becoming an expert on an area wasn't a bad strategy at all.

Not only that, but the big guilds were expending significant resources to implement that strategy: They were using their members to police their areas.

Shiroe had no intention of criticizing that strategy without hearing their side of the story.

If those without power were allowed to criticize that sort of thing, the result would be something like "reverse discrimination" by the weak, and so he understood just what Marielle meant when she said that no one in particular was wrong. No doubt this was just "the way things went."

However, even then, he couldn't quite reconcile himself to the idea.

In this lawless other world, was it all right for those with power to dominate those without? If asked whether it was okay for the answer to that question to be this uncool, the answer was no. However, Shiroe knew that if the argument were taken to the extreme, his only grounds for saying no were his own preferences.

"Didn't the smaller guilds try to do anything about it?"

"Well... Yes. Over the past two weeks, for example, there was talk of the smaller guilds formin' a liaison committee, holdin' down some huntin' grounds and handlin' it that way. ...It didn't work out, though. Even with smaller guilds, there are slight differences in numbers, y'know? There were little differences of opinion that got people upset, and some couldn't keep from bein' selfish, and they fought, and things fell apart. Then several small guilds thought, *If that's the way it's gonna be...*, and they merged with the big guilds or with each other."

They did, hm? Shiroe thought.

There was probably no help for that, either. It was easy to say "hold on to hunting grounds," but whether a hunting ground was "good" or not changed depending on its level. No doubt there had been a nearly infinite number of ambitions regarding the hunting grounds each guild wanted to frequent, depending on the guild's personality, its number of members, and their levels.

Working together and occupying a hunting ground would take a large number of people who were able to curb their egos and cooperate. The larger guilds might be able to exercise control, but in a gathering of smaller, weaker guilds, debates were bound to break out, and the group would fragment.

Come to think of it, the influence of the frozen transport gates and the Fairy Ring trouble showed through in this issue as well. There were tens of thousands of zones on the Japanese server. With only about a thousand guilds, it was hard to imagine having a shortage of hunting grounds under ordinary circumstances.

However, now that the intercity transport gates were out of order and the Fairy Ring timetables were a complete mystery, the Adventurers' movements were drastically restricted. Players with griffins, like Shiroe's group, were extremely rare. Now that players had to rely on horses or their own two feet, the number of hunting grounds that were within a day's journey of the town was more limited than it had been in the game.

There were about fifty zones that fit that description near Akiba. As far as hunting grounds were concerned, there might be three hundred or so. If those were ranked by quality of experience points, proximity to the town, and apparent safety, there would naturally be a scramble for the popular spots.

Since the Catastrophe, all zones had been made available for purchase. The zone prices were determined by factors beyond the Adventurers' comprehension, but at the very least, one of those conditions seemed to be area. This meant that zones with enough area to be hunting grounds would be too expensive to purchase, but there was no need to buy them: Any guild with enough members could use their human resources to "occupy" them.

*   *   *

"...Plus. The Knights of the Black Sword are aimin' for ninety-one."

"Huh?"

Ninety-one. She probably meant the level. Since *Homesteading the Noosphere* had been introduced, the level maximum had probably been released, so that in itself was no surprise. If the level maximum had been let go, it should be possible to grow past level 90, the previous maximum level.

However, in order to do that, wouldn't it be necessary to hunt monsters that were at or above level 85? Shiroe had his doubts about whether anyone could skate on ice that thin in the real battles of this other world.

"The big guilds are tough as things stand, but you know they can't expect any new players to join up. So, it sounds like they think the issue of level height is gonna have a big effect on their power. That's behind the player acquisition wars, too. And y'know the Knights of the Black Sword have always aimed for the top..."

Shiroe nodded, acknowledging what Marielle had pointed out.

Even in Akiba, the Knights of the Black Sword were a proud fighting guild, elitist to the point of seeming somewhat exclusionist. Not one of their members was under level 85. They didn't even *accept* members under level 85. A pureblood combat organization: That was the Knights of the Black Sword.

"The Knights of the Black Sword still have that level restriction on joinin' up. Of course they're still a prestigious major guild, too. The Crescent Moon League can't compare. But D.D.D. and its 1,500 members are keepin' the Knights on the ropes. After the Catastrophe, D.D.D. snapped up several smaller guilds. Well, with that level restriction on entry, the Knights of the Black Sword can't assimilate any smaller guilds. That's why they're workin' to get past level ninety, tryin' to beat out quantity with quality."

"But how—"

That was the heart of Shiroe's question. He understood the motive. He also understood the feeling and the strategy... But was there any way to achieve it?

"By usin' EXP Pots."

"—EXP Pots…"

EXP Pots were a famous support item in *Elder Tales*. They were potions that, when drunk, slightly raised a player's attack power and self-recovery abilities and nearly doubled the amount of experience points won in battle.

Ordinarily, players couldn't get any experience points from monsters more than five levels weaker than they were. A secondary effect of the EXP Pots was that, although it wasn't much, players were able to gain a few experience points from monsters as much as seven levels below them.

The effects of the potions only lasted two hours, but as a result, during the time they were effective, it was far easier to earn experience points.

Although these support items were powerful, it wasn't necessary to go through a large-scale battle or jump any other hurdles to get them. In fact, almost all players had used them at one point or another.

As a popular, long-running game, *Elder Tales* had continued to raise its level maximum over the course of its run. That made it difficult for newbie players who'd just begun the game to catch up to those who'd been playing longer. As a result, the administrators had given various assists to new players, and the potions were one of them.

In specific terms, players under level 30 automatically received one potion per day, free of charge. They were a present from the administrators, given in the spirit of helping players reach midrange levels quickly and enjoy the game.

"But those potions are—"

"…There's this guild called Hamelin. They advertised themselves as bein' out to rescue newbies, and after the Catastrophe, they attracted a lot of 'em. Everythin' was a mess then, and it's true that most weren't in a place where they could've helped newbs. We couldn't do anythin', either. But Hamelin… They're sellin' off the EXP Pots they collect. Hamelin's gettin' rich, and the big guilds are workin' to boost their levels with those potions. I dunno who's in the wrong here; maybe nobody is. But that's the way things are goin', and there's nobody who can stop it…"

► 3

The heat of the banquet was gone completely.

Even though it was early summer, the night wind was cool, and it blew strongly enough to set the tail of his tunic flapping.

Cloud shadows skimmed across the ground. The moon was so bright it cast shadows, even now in the dead of night. It was past midnight, and Shiroe walked through the streets of Akiba as if he was chasing the contrast between moonlight and shadow.

He didn't have a particular destination in mind.

It was as if he were running from this mysterious, black emotion. Running from it or possibly trying to see it clearly. Even Shiroe didn't quite understand what he was feeling.

He felt as if there was a huge, heavy mass in his chest. It was like the ocean at night, but nowhere near as refreshing; the mass was unidentifiable, so black and thick it could have been made of coal tar, and he failed to grasp it completely. He felt as if he had a huge amount of energy, but it wasn't focused on anything. It was simply *there*.

…*Although it's* only *there*.

Shiroe knew it, too.

There was nothing for him to unleash this emotion on.

There probably was a villain somewhere, of course. The Hamelin guild certainly wasn't good. If he got the opportunity, Shiroe wouldn't mind fighting them the way he'd fought the Briganteers.

Still, even if Hamelin was bad, they were just a small-time villain. Hamelin wasn't behind Akiba's current situation. All sorts of things that "couldn't be helped" had piled up, one on another, to make the atmosphere in Akiba what it was. That atmosphere was what he couldn't stand.

Besides, Shiroe was well aware that, if he turned that feeling on Hamelin exclusively, he'd be punishing them for something that wasn't their doing.

Shiroe walked, holding his breath.

There was nothing cool about taking things out on other people.

He didn't want to lash out at someone just to make himself feel better.

That left Shiroe unable to vent the pitch-black emotion inside him. To Shiroe, taking it out on Hamelin would make him even worse than they were.

But in that case...

In that case, he had nowhere to vent the feeling.

So Hamelin was a small-time villain. Fine.

Who was the main villain?

Who was in the wrong?

Was it the big fighting guilds, who must have had an inkling of how their EXP Pots were supplied, but were turning a blind eye to it in order to increase their power?

Was it the newbies, who were fully aware they were being exploited, but had relaxed into the fact that they were weak and let the idea of being "protected" hold them captive?

Was it the small and midsized guilds, who knew there was inequality between the guilds and had come together in order to do away with it, but had gotten distracted by their own interests, failed to cooperate, and could do nothing but squabble with one another?

Was it all the players who knew that the atmosphere in the town was deteriorating but just stood by and watched, irresponsibly acting as if it had nothing to do with them?

Yes. That was wrong.

They were all wrong.

Still, those "wrongs" were small ones; for the most part, the people in question were nothing more than foolish or self-centered. None of them was the mastermind that lurked on the far side of all that was wrong. There was no fairy-tale "evil" whose defeat would solve everything. This was nothing so simple or convenient.

Everything was warping, little by little, and it was frustrating. That was all.

Shiroe was there, too, in the midst of that distortion. Things were getting more and more uncomfortable in Akiba; a warped order was becoming established, and here he was, with a higher level and more equipment than the majority of Akiba's citizens, and what was he doing? Nothing. He had a good grasp of the situation, and still he let the moments slip by, letting things pass without comment.

There was no difference between him and the "unconcerned citizens of Akiba" that he found so irritating. Add in the fact that friends of his were personally involved in the problem, and he might be even worse.

Although Marielle had said it had failed, they'd managed to start discussing an alliance of guilds. Shiroe himself hadn't made it even that far.

The fact that he—*he*—was thinking that the smaller guilds who could do nothing but squabble with one another were in the wrong was so pathetic and laughable that he bit his lip almost hard enough to bite through.

I'm uncool. …I may be the least cool one here.

At some point, he'd reached the crest of a bridge. An old, mossy stone bridge built in a European style spanned the Kanda River. When he leaned on the railing, the scent of water and the sound of ripples spread under the moonlight.

…Then what should he do?

Without consciously putting that feeling to work, Shiroe *thought*. He had the sort of personality that felt compelled to *think* when it encountered a problem, and it was also a "job" he'd grown used to, thanks to the Debauchery Tea Party.

Story after story was set up and destroyed.

Shiroe's right hand held the red card soldiers, and the black card soldiers were in his left. They crossed paths, sounding the notes of logic with spears of denial and swords of assent. Meaningless facts were weeded out, possibilities examined, and deductions flowed away down the dark river.

The answer wouldn't come. How could it? He'd known from the start that there were no easy answers. Shiroe had been saddled with a handicap from the very beginning, one that was much too large. Not only that, it was a handicap he'd picked up by choice.

Even thinking of it as a handicap is presumptuous. It's just a bill: what I get for having done nothing but run away. I'm a solo player because that's what I wanted to be.

What would *she* have said? Shiroe lifted his gaze from the surface of the river to the moon. The pure white moon illuminated the predawn streets of Akiba with a luster like that of a highly polished fossil.

She was a dynamic person... And she wasn't like me; she wasn't a coward, and she didn't drag regrets behind her.

He could picture her laughing with her big mouth wide open as she resolved everything with the force of a typhoon. He could also picture her tossing Akiba aside because it felt like too much work.

The most realistic was probably the scenario in which, after she'd rampaged around saying and doing everything she wanted, she dropped the situation into his lap as homework: "You figure out a way to clean up the mess, Shiro! That's fine, right?! Got a problem with it? Of course you don't! You're one of the best, Shiro, so get things squared away ASAP!"

He called up the telechat function.

Those two names on his friend list.

Touya. Minori.

The twin siblings who were probably in Hamelin.

Right. He'd known as soon as he heard the story. Shiroe and the twins had gotten separated, and right now, they were probably caught up in this problem. ...All because Shiroe had left them on their own. Because, in the instant the Catastrophe occurred, he had prioritized meeting up with his old friend Naotsugu.

He wanted to help them. He wanted to help, no matter what it took. However, this wasn't like when they'd gone to rescue Serara.

For one thing, in the Crescent Moon League's case, Marielle had been there. When Shiroe had rescued Serara, he'd done so as Marielle's proxy. In other words, he'd been working for a client.

Of course he'd wanted to save the girl, but he knew that somewhere he'd had an excuse available: "I've accepted a request. All I'm doing is carrying it out."

For another, although Shiroe wanted to rescue Touya and Minori now, even more than that, he wanted to do something about *everything*. He'd felt the same way during their escape from Susukino. Back then, although there hadn't been many players in the same situation as Serara, there must have been a few others. On some level, Shiroe had felt bad about abandoning the rest of those players and rescuing only her.

However, there, too, he'd used the fact that his current mission was to rescue Serara as an excuse, closed his eyes to the rest, and returned to Akiba.

If he used a similar excuse again this time, Shiroe was sure he'd lose all ability to fight.

Rescue the twins, then, and abolish the tyranny of the big guilds, improve the atmosphere in Akiba and establish a new order... Could Shiroe do something like that? He was a solo player, not affiliated with even a tiny guild, let alone one of the big guilds... And so the answer was no, he couldn't.

Not even affiliated with a guild, hm...?

The thought gave Shiroe a dull, penetrating pain.

Now that he thought about it, Shiroe had always considered guilds to be something people belonged to. He'd felt they were nothing to do with him. Guilds had always been "there," and whether that was good or bad, whether they suited him or not—he'd viewed them as an outsider.

That attitude had been irresponsible.

That was what he thought now.

Wasn't that just like the riffraff who talked about the current atmosphere in Akiba as though it was nothing to do with them, even though they lived there?

Up until now, Shiroe had never participated in a guild, and he'd never had responsibilities toward one. On top of that, he'd forced his own preferences and convenience on others... The arrogance of that attitude staggered him.

"Guilds. ...Guilds, huh...?"

"Mew still dislike guilds, Shiroechi?"

Nyanta appeared from the shadow of a building; a few fragments of asphalt scattered, clicking, as he moved. He narrowed his quiet eyes in a smile, asking a question of Shiroe's monologue.

"——!"

Shiroe was startled, but he shrugged his shoulders and moved over slightly, making room.

"No, I don't. ...Or at least, I don't think I do."

Shiroe thought his hatred of guilds had probably stemmed from several unfortunate encounters. His relationship with the Crescent Moon League, both before and after the Catastrophe, had softened his obstinate prejudice.

At this point, he could even understand that he'd been arrogant.

However, on the other hand, he also remembered the PKs he'd met near Akiba and the gang of would-be bandits he'd encountered in Susukino. It was true that the guild system was easily corrupted. In the big guilds, where turf wars were the normal way of things, it was easy to imagine that morals would deteriorate.

"…Yes, those aspects may exist."

Nyanta responded to Shiroe's thoughts.

"On the other hand, though, incorruptible things aren't to be trusted. Birth, illness, old age, and death are the underlying principles of the mewniverse. Anything born will rot. It will suffer from disease and pain and will grow old and weak. Someday it will die. That's a painful thing, but if mew deny it, mew're denying birth as well. I know mew know this, Shiroechi. Perhaps it was particularly comfortable 'there,' but that's simply because we all tried to make it comfortable, and we did. Any treasure gained without cost or trouble is no treasure at all in the end."

…Yes. He was right.

Everyone had put in effort as a matter of course, and the work had seemed so natural that they hadn't even realized it was work. Now, though, he knew how precious that had been and how much unseen effort the cat-eared friend beside him must have invested.

It was the same sort of work Marielle did.

How much support did the Crescent Moon League gain from her smile? Did it not give the guild a strength, one that not even a wealth of rare items nor gold coins could hope to match?

That meant that if the town of Akiba had been comfortable until now, it had been because somebody somewhere was silently putting in invisible effort.

"Captain… What should I do?"

At Shiroe's words, Nyanta looked up at the same moon.

In the wind, his black ears flicked, then went still.

"Mew should do the most incredible thing possible."

"Incredible…?"

Shiroe looked at Nyanta. His expression was as calm as ever, but in the moonlight, he looked even more mature than usual.

"Mew hold back too much, Shiroechi."

He'd heard those words before, at some point, from Naotsugu.

Shiroe chased their meaning, the meaning he had let slip past him back then.

He thought seriously about what the words would have meant if they hadn't just been said lightly, in the moment.

What they meant.

What he'd done for Naotsugu.

What he'd done for Akatsuki.

In other words, those two had already known…

"I've been keeping them waiting?"

"That's right."

"And they did wait?"

"That's right."

"They stayed here with me, without going elsewhere…"

"That's right."

They were waiting for me to invite them to my *guild?*

Shiroe looked down. The lump in his chest, that black, ocean-like mass, rumbled and roared. The feeling he hadn't been able to vent roiled under the lid he'd clamped down onto it, coming near to boiling over.

The sounds of the summer insects. The quiet noise of the water. The pale moonlight. Shiroe stood stock-still in the midst of it, clenching his fists, desperately suppressing everything.

They'd had expectations for him.

They'd bet on him.

They'd waited for him.

He had pondered and analyzed and worried, or he thought he had. Why hadn't he seen it? Had he really been that slow-witted? Even though his distrust of himself and his sense of inferiority were as high as a levee, the frozen restraints were being washed away by happiness, and familiarity, and trust.

"Will I be in time?"

"Of course."

"Captain Nyanta. You join, too. ...It would make me really happy if you came with me. I need you there."

As he delivered the invitation, Shiroe watched Nyanta steadily. Nyanta laughed a bit self-consciously and said, "I'd like a good veranda."

"Sure," Shiroe agreed. "We'll build you one. We'll get you a fine veranda."

He wanted the most incredible thing. If he was allowed to want it. It came with a responsibility so huge that Shiroe couldn't support it by himself, but he did have a plan.

If he had friends who would shoulder it with him, then...

▶4

The dark room was damp.

The uncarpeted floor was made of ancient concrete, and it absorbed heat like a sponge. This meant that even in early summer, at times like this, just before dawn, it was as cold as graveyard earth.

Wrapped up tightly in her drab, dirty mantle, Minori turned over. She'd done it so many times already she'd lost track of how often.

The night was long, and it felt endless.

Maybe it was because her "bed" was much too hard and cold, or maybe it was her anxiety for the future. Her weary body wanted rest, but her sleep was shallow, and she woke easily at the smallest thing.

Grinding pain was what she felt when her consciousness drifted up from the dark of night. All she could remember were indistinct dreams that grew vague and melted into the darkness, leaving only unease and regret.

She spent most of the day cooped up in a tiny room, being forced to work as a Tailor, and her hands hurt as if the muscles were dead wood. Today, no matter how often she stroked them with her chilled fingers, the pain refused to recede.

Her little brother Touya slept next to her, hugging his knees.

Nearly twenty of her companions were asleep in this room.

The guild Hamelin.

It was a midsized guild that had advertised mutual aid for beginners.

It was the guild Minori and Touya had joined.

After the Catastrophe, the town had been engulfed in confusion and a feeling of claustrophobia. The sudden disaster had left everyone dazed; no one had known what to do. Minori thought the reason the town hadn't erupted into large-scale riots in those first few days was that most of the players hadn't known how to take what had just happened and had been hoping it might be some sort of elaborate joke.

She and Touya had been the exact same way.

For the first few hours, they hadn't known what had happened.

For a few days after that, although they knew what had happened, they hadn't known why.

The "why" was still unclear. What they finally did understand now was that those first few days had been terribly valuable and that, while they'd been distracted by the question *Why did something like this happen?*—a question that had no answer—they'd lost that time forever.

Her memories of the days that followed were hazy.

She remembered being hungry. They hadn't really known how to eat. She'd bought several food items at the market and shared them with her brother Touya. When they tried to leave the town, they were attacked, and before they knew what was happening, they'd been stripped of everything they owned.

By the time they remembered that Shiroe had advised them to leave all unnecessary items in a safe-deposit box at the bank whenever they left town, they were already penniless.

She had heard that many players were contacting their acquaintances and working to gather information.

However, she and Touya were newbie players, and they didn't have anyone to turn to. There was just one person they could think of, and they hesitated to contact him.

They might have been able to contact him right after the Catastrophe. However, after spending several days in a stupor, they'd lost all their property, and in this world, they would have been far too much of a burden.

Minori felt that she and Touya got along well.

She'd heard it said that when they reached middle school, brothers and sisters often began to detest each other. The fastidiousness and sense of independence among their age group made siblings of a near age a target for strict exclusion. Her classmates said they couldn't even stand to look at their siblings.

Maybe the rest of the world was like that, but not Minori and Touya. They were close.

They never even wanted to fight, and the desire to help Touya was never far from Minori's mind.

There was a reason for this.

After an accident when they were small, Touya had lost the ability to walk. There was no problem with his legs themselves, but he had been left with nerve damage.

It wasn't that Minori felt sorry for him, and thus didn't fight with him. The accident had been a terrible thing, and she sometimes wished she could take his place, but there was nothing she could do.

Even to her, his older sister, Touya seemed to be cheerful and a hard worker. Even in his situation, he never got angry or irritated with the people around him. Life was challenging when a family member was disabled, and Touya was always trying to make things easier for their father and mother.

She remembered that when they took him to and from the hospital twice a month, she and Touya had only talked about silly, trivial things. He'd joke around about manga and the Internet like any other middle school boy. From what the doctor said, Touya's exams were sometimes quite painful, but he never let it show.

Sometimes Minori thought that Touya's childish ways of speaking and acting were really intentional, something he did out of consideration for others.

Minori thought Touya was a fine little brother. Of course, as his older sister, she also thought he was a dummy who acted like a little kid, got carried away easily, and didn't think before he did things.

Still, fundamentally, she could count on him. Even if his legs wouldn't work for him, and no matter what difficulties he ran into in the future, she was sure Touya would continue to be himself.

Since that was the case, even if she'd only been born a few hours ahead of him, she had to fulfill her duty as his big sister. She was Touya's guardian. When Touya had to do something, she wanted to provide him with the necessary power.

A kind of respect—the sort of feeling that doesn't grow easily between siblings, particularly when they are young—had made the two of them close.

They'd started playing *Elder Tales* for a similar reason.

After his exams, Touya was exhausted and unable to go out, and he'd shown an interest in an online RPG. The two of them were already tired of all the ordinary indoor games, and they'd wheedled their parents into letting them play the game (on the condition that they didn't neglect their schoolwork).

It was a world where Touya could run around as much as he wanted, without worrying about anyone else. Touya had been thrilled and enjoyed himself immensely, and the game had excited Minori as well; it was like nothing she'd ever experienced before.

Almost immediately, they'd fallen head over heels for *Elder Tales*.

However, because of their situation, Minori was well aware that some things just couldn't be helped.

Sometimes being a child was very hard.

It meant it wasn't possible to make your thoughts and dreams come true just by doing your best.

Minori was a child, and that made her just as much of a burden as Touya with his damaged legs. Sometimes being a child *was* a handicap, and it put just as much weight on someone else.

For example, even if she wanted to take Touya to the hospital herself, Minori couldn't drive. Since she was a middle schooler, this was only natural, but it meant that burden fell on her parents.

Her abilities weren't enough. She couldn't take care of herself. She couldn't save anybody. She couldn't make her wishes come true the way she wanted to. —All of these characteristics made the faces of people she loved cloud over. In other words, they made her a burden.

Here, in the world of the game, having a low level made you so much of a burden that it was almost considered a sin.

She'd seen Shiroe from a distance, just once, after the Catastrophe.

The moment she'd seen the tall shadow with glasses, she'd known it was him.

Yet she hadn't been able to call out to him.

After all, next to that figure, grimy with blood and dust, were a heavily armored warrior, who seemed to be as much of a veteran as Shiroe, and a beautiful girl, like a fairy of the night.

Shiroe had his own battles to fight.

That thought kept Minori from approaching him. In this chaotic world, everyone had their hands full trying to protect themselves. How could she beg an acquaintance, someone who'd only played with them a handful of times, for help?

When she closed her eyes, a menu opened behind her eyelids.

Minori's friend list was short: Her brother Touya. A few of the newbie players she'd met at Hamelin. …And Shiroe.

Shiroe's name shone brightly, and she stroked it gently with an imaginary fingertip.

To Minori, who'd lost nearly everything she could call her own, it was a treasure no one could take away.

I wish we could have learned a little bit more from Shiroe…

She pulled her mantle closer around her chilled body. Tonight's darkness seemed even deeper than usual. The dull pain in her chest kept her from sleep.

Suddenly, a soft bell-like tone sounded in Minori's ear.

She caught her breath sharply and then was startled at how loud it sounded there in the dark room.

In her mind's eye, Shiroe's name—the one she'd just touched—was pulsing.

She was afraid she might have triggered the telechat function by mistake, but when she checked, that didn't seem to be the case. Shiroe was calling *her*. At this hour, just before dawn.

The bell chimed again.

Minori knew from experience that only she could hear it. Still, if she spoke, the Hamelin members might notice, and she risked waking her companions who slept nearby.

Even so, it was hard for Minori to ignore the sound of the bell.

Using her mental menu, she answered in a tiny, nearly inaudible voice. "Hello?"

"Um… Good evening. This is Shiroe. Do you remember me?"

"……—"

It wasn't just that the familiar voice was nostalgic. It seemed like a bridge to pleasant, distant days, and it made Minori's heart spill over.

In her dark, damp bed, wrapped in a dirty woolen mantle, Minori sniffled quietly.

"…That is Minori, isn't it?"

The flood of feelings that washed over her had made her nose begin to run a bit, and she didn't register Shiroe's words the first time. She couldn't reply. If she spoke, the others in the room might be suspicious. Even more than that, though, she didn't want Shiroe to hear her voice this way, cracked and damp with tears.

In her heart, she nodded dozens of times, but aloud, Minori could only murmur yes in a small voice.

"_____"

"……"

The sound of breathing flowed between them. Minori struggled desperately to keep her unreasonable nose from snuffling; she was frightened that Shiroe would be disgusted with her, and she was so tense that the inside of her eyes seemed to flicker. Why had he called at this time of night? Why her? The questions raced around and around in her mind.

"…Minori. Listen carefully. Cough very quietly; once for yes, twice for no. If I get something wrong or you have something to tell me, cough three times. …Understand?"

At Shiroe's question, the realization hit Minori like a lightning bolt:

He knows. Shiroe knows all about this.

The situation she was in. The sort of place Hamelin was.

She felt her ability to think, which had been half-numbed by her days of monotonous forced labor, coming back to life.

I don't want to cause trouble for Shiroe. Not for him…

Now that she was a part of Hamelin, she understood full well.

Beginners didn't have any systematic knowledge of this *Elder Tales* world, even if they were ten levels higher than Minori and Touya.

In this world, "knowledge" was a powerful weapon, and the lack of it was what kept newbies chained to their status as beginners. The common sense Shiroe had taught them as they played had become the strength she and Touya used to survive in this other world. Even in Hamelin's terrible environment, she and Touya were able to maneuver a bit better than the other newbies, and this was due in large part to the few scraps of knowledge Shiroe had shared with them.

Shiroe was their benefactor. Minori had always thought so.

She'd wanted him to be even more than that.

"If you understand, cough once."

Minori scraped what little warmth she had together, moistening her throat ever so slightly.

She gave one tiny cough.

Her throat was drier and achier than she'd realized, and even *she* thought the sound she managed to produce was pathetic.

She was indebted to Shiroe. She had to repay that debt. As Minori thought this, she swallowed several times to wet her throat, listening carefully.

"You and Touya are in Hamelin, aren't you?"

One small cough.

"You're giving your EXP Potions to Hamelin."

Another small cough.

"...Are you all right?"

"......"

A nearly palpable silence filled the dark room.

Having heard that much, Minori knew what Shiroe was asking and what he was trying to do.

However, precisely because she understood, she felt a pain that nearly crushed her heart. Minori had no idea *how* Shiroe was planning to do it, but the method wasn't the problem. The problem was that Shiroe was very close to resolving to save Minori and Touya.

What sort of price was he on the verge of paying in order to do something about their situation? In this other world, where everyone had to fight to survive, what would it end up costing him to save the two of them, burdens that they were?

How much were they worth, really?

There was only one answer to that question.

We're all right. We're absolutely fine. ...They feed us every day, and my Tailoring level is going up, little by little. Touya and I can get by here. I'm sure Touya would say so, too. ...We're fine...

As she admonished herself, her heart's voice sounded as if it belonged to someone else. In order to shut the door she longed for, the one that was dangerously close to opening, Minori gave one small cough. Just one.

We're fine.

"Really?" Shiroe asked again.

His voice was gentle, and it reminded Minori of one of the times they'd played together.

That time, Touya had charged at the enemy, she'd run in to provide backup, and their careless actions had ended up drawing enemy reinforcements.

While Shiroe had used a sleeping spell to render the reinforcements powerless, Touya had fought desperately, and she'd recovered both of them. There were hordes of enemies, and their HP displays were always dyed red. She'd exhausted her MP in the excitement, and again and again she'd thought, *We're finished! It's all over!* but in the end, although they were limp and exhausted, all three of them had survived.

She'd heard that in *Elder Tales* level 90 was the highest level there was.

If he'd died, he would have lost experience points as a penalty, but they'd made him wander the border between life and death right along with them, when they were barely level 10. She'd felt wretched and ashamed; she'd apologized desperately, and she'd hit Touya on the head with her fist and made him apologize, too.

We can't let Shiroe damage his valuable experience points over the two of us, she had thought. ...But Shiroe had only laughed, looking almost like a little kid.

"I had fun. It's an adventure, you know? There are some skills you only learn when you're in trouble. ...I think you're a little too proper, Minori. You did have fun, didn't you? I liked it."

His voice had been kind, and that kindness had saved Minori. She could sense the same kindness now, across the telechat's invisible line.

…And so she coughed, just once more.

We're fine.

If she did that, then the next time she met Shiroe, she might be able to smile and talk with him. Of course, she'd need a bit more time. Right now, she was filthy, and she looked like a street urchin. She hadn't even bathed. It was so bad she felt she couldn't even call herself a girl at this point.

There was a small, smoldering pain deep in her chest, but it had to be better than causing trouble for Shiroe. Even Minori was having a hard time believing that logic anymore, but she forced herself to listen to it.

"…All right. You're fine; I understand. In that case, let's play together again. I'd really like to. It was fun. So just…hang on for a little while."

"……—!!"

But that meant he didn't understand at all!

Or, no, it might be because he *did* understand everything…but even so.

Conflicting thoughts clashed in Minori's chest, turning into hot tears deep in her nose and forcing their way up. Why was Shiroe so stubborn? And why did he say such kind things?

Frustration that her own attempt to be considerate hadn't been understood; shame, confusion, guilt at having pulled him in… Sadness. And in equal measure to those negative emotions: happiness, kindness, joy, hope…and trust in Shiroe.

Those two contrary sets of emotions mixed, churning Minori's heart like a washing machine. She had to say something. She just didn't know what to say.

If she was going to stop Shiroe, this was her last chance.

She had to cough. How many times? Once for "save us"? Twice for "don't"? In the midst of tears she'd been unable to hold back, Minori coughed once. Then she coughed two more times.

"What's wrong? Is there something you want to say?"

……I coughed three times. I… No, I don't want to say anything—Shiroe isn't… He isn't our mom or dad. He's nice, but that doesn't give us the

right to impose! We'd only drag him down. There's no reason for him to carry us!

But she couldn't say the words.

In a musty, silent room in Hamelin's guildhall, Minori tried desperately to keep her breathing, which sounded nearly asthmatic, from echoing.

"I said to cough three times if there was something you wanted to say, didn't I? Okay. I'll hurry, so I can hear what it is. I've already made up my mind, though. I'll do what I can. I told you when Touya was with us, remember? 'A vanguard that can't trust their rear guard will pay for that crime with their lives. The same goes for a rear guard that can't trust their vanguard.' So, when you say you're okay, I believe you. Believe in me, too. I'll come to help you, I promise."

With the small sound of a severed connection, the telechat cut off.

Minori curled inward, hugging herself.

Her nose wouldn't stop running, and it was all Shiroe's fault for being selfish and not understanding. Emotions she couldn't put into words overflowed, and it felt as if there was a storm inside her ears; she didn't understand herself.

Still, something warm and certain, something that hadn't been there an hour ago, had begun to grow inside her.

▶ **5**

When Henrietta opened the door, she saw that all the other participants were there already.

It had been two days since their raucous celebration, and after a day spent cleaning, the Crescent Moon League guildhall had regained its former calm.

"What's happened? Your call was so sudden..."

"C'mon, Henrietta. Have a seat."

Marielle, Henrietta's guild master, motioned for her to sit.

The Crescent Moon League conference room—which, until yesterday, had been littered with bottles and the leftovers from their feast—was now neat and tidy, and the air felt fresh.

Four men and women were seated at the enormous table.

The Crescent Moon League was represented by its guild master, Marielle; by Henrietta, who was in charge of the accounts; and by Shouryuu, who handled combat and hunting. For all practical purposes, these three led the Crescent Moon League.

Shiroe sat facing them.

Oh... Master Shiroe.

"Mr. Shiroe says he has something he wants to discuss with us." Shouryuu, who was younger, bowed to Shiroe as he spoke.

"We dunno what the 'somethin'' is yet, either."

Marielle and Shouryuu's words aside, Shiroe's expression was hard. His eyes had a tendency to seem sharp—or rather, he had a habit of staring—but even so, there was a quiet forcefulness about him today. His determination seemed so strong that those endearing round glasses failed to soften the effect.

Hm...

Henrietta filed that look away for later.

Even under ordinary circumstances, Shiroe was a reliable young man. However, this Shiroe seemed like another person entirely. Henrietta thought it might not do to lump them together.

"Thank you for your time. I'm the one who called this meeting today. ...First, I want to thank you for the banquet two days ago. Both you, Mari, and everyone at the Crescent Moon League. Thank you very much."

At Shiroe's words, Marielle waved her hands wildly.

"Don't you worry about that! It was nothin' to write home about, really!"

Shouryuu also waved his hands, denying any need for gratitude. The banquet had looked impressive, and the food had been superb, but there hadn't been much actual expense.

Above all else, the Crescent Moon League members had also enjoyed themselves immensely. The celebration had really been for them as well. The idea that they'd have to formally express their thanks someday was already being discussed within the guild.

"No, no, it's perfectly fine. After all, I got to play with darling Akatsuki to my heart's content."

Remembering Akatsuki's adorable reactions, Henrietta smiled dreamily. Never mind the fact that Akatsuki herself had had tears in her eyes.

"That aside, then, I'm here on different business today. It's the opposite of last time: I've come to ask for your help."

My, my. That's… Hm.

Henrietta watched Shiroe from behind her smart, rimless spectacles. She couldn't deny that his request was somewhat unexpected.

From what she had seen, Shiroe was a strong player with a compassionate personality. He wasn't the type who would hesitate to help an acquaintance in trouble… The way he had, as ashamed as she was to admit it, helped the Crescent Moon League with Serara.

On that expedition, Shiroe and his friends had been a fantastic proxy for the Crescent Moon League's rescue party. No doubt they'd done dozens of times better than Henrietta and the others could have. If he felt he'd be useful and could do something well, Shiroe wouldn't hesitate to lend a hand.

But if it was the other way around?

To Henrietta, in addition to being sensible and compassionate, Shiroe seemed like an introspective and very…clumsy young man. He was far worse at accepting help from others than he was at helping them.

And now Shiroe was asking for help.

What sort of request could it be?

Of course Henrietta had no intention of using Shiroe's reluctance to ask for help to her advantage and bargaining down their debt of gratitude. No doubt the thought was even further from Marielle's mind. However, she really did find it odd that the man himself would clearly state that he wanted their help.

"Ask for anything, Mr. Shiroe!"

"Yes, he's right. The Crescent Moon League is in your debt, Master Shiroe."

Matching her words to Shouryuu's, Henrietta gave a welcoming response of her own. Under the circumstances, she had to: The Crescent Moon League really did owe Shiroe a great debt.

However, at the same time, Henrietta was concerned about Marielle. Ever since Henrietta had entered the room, Marielle had looked rather tense.

Of course, she was acting friendly on the surface, and Henrietta didn't have the least suspicion that her consideration or kindness would falter. She'd been friends with Marielle for a long time. She knew full well that Marielle could never dislike Shiroe.

In that case, though, what was the gravity in Marielle's expression?

Does Mari know what Master Shiroe intends to ask?

Shiroe didn't smile at Henrietta and Shouryuu's words. He pushed his glasses up with a finger and went straight to the heart of the matter.

"Two young players of my acquaintance are…being detained by, or forced to be part of, a certain guild. I want to help them."

Shouryuu nodded, responding to Shiroe's words.

"It's that sort of thing, is it? You'd just have to cancel their guild contracts, wouldn't you? Do you want us to set up a diversion, so you can complete the procedures for removing them from the guild? That's easy. …Oh. Or did you mean the other thing? Did you want us to take care of them after you've gotten them out? To leave them with the Crescent Moon League? Of course, they're welcome here. The more the merrier; we'd love it."

Shouryuu's reply was cheerful.

However, at his words, Marielle's face grew even tenser.

—I shouldn't think that's it. No doubt Master Shiroe could save those two without any assistance from us. He wants our cooperation badly enough to ask for it formally. What sort of request could it be…?

"It looks as though this unsavory guild is collecting new players and extorting EXP Potions from them. They're most likely selling them off to bring in operating funds. I don't think that in itself is unforgivable.—Not at this point, at least. If asked whether I like it, though, I'd have to say that I don't."

As he continued, Shiroe's tone was mild, but Shouryuu had frozen.

Now, when it was too late, he'd finally registered what was being said.

"That guild… Is it Hamelin by any chance? You're right; they certainly aren't a...very good establishment. Not good at all. However, they have major guilds backing them..."

The doubt Henrietta expressed was only natural. If the guild in question was Hamelin, it numbered Silver Sword and the Knights of the Black Sword among its customers. Both guilds were powerful in Akiba. In terms of combat guilds, they were in the top five.

"Yes, that's right. I intend to have them leave."

Shiroe said it quite plainly.

A heavy silence filled the conference room.

Marielle gave a small sigh.

So Mari did know, or she guessed...

That would certainly explain the tension in her expression.

"H-have them leave? Erm... Do you mean you want to destroy them? That's— Really? In any case, is it even possible to force a whole guild out? Even if you player killed them right and left, well, you'd probably damage their pride, but I don't know if you could destroy the entire guild..."

Shouryuu's voice was timid.

Henrietta had that same doubt.

The only ways to disband a guild were for the guild leader to decide to disband it or for all its members to leave. That was how the system worked.

It was possible to kill player characters through PKs. However, this world took after *Elder Tales*: It was gamelike. Here, where resurrection from death happened automatically, killing couldn't do any serious damage. It might be possible to affect the guild members' morale or property, but it wouldn't influence the continued existence of the actual guild.

That meant that Shouryuu's doubt—*"Is it even possible to force a whole guild out?"*—was correct. Logically speaking, it wouldn't be possible to bring that about through external interference.

It might be possible for a huge guild to use its abundant resources as bait to lure in all the members of a smaller guild, crushing that guild as a result. She'd heard of similar strategies around Akiba.

However, even if one poured resources into bribes and fund provision, there was no guarantee that the target guild would collapse. If the Crescent Moon League were targeted by that sort of acquisition maneuver, even if most of the members were lured away, as long as Marielle stayed there and kept fighting by herself, the Crescent Moon League would still exist as far as the system was concerned.

Destroying a guild was that difficult and that hard to pull off. It wasn't a matter of picking a target and crushing them. If that had been possible, the current situation in Akiba would have been much different.

In any case, these words—"Destroy that guild, make them leave"— were the sort of things players yelled as insults or when picking a fight. They were a type of threat, not a genuine plan.

Shouryuu wondered if he should take Shiroe's words as an expression of enthusiasm, a sort of goal. A declaration along the lines of "I'm gonna take you down!"

"No, I mean it literally. I'm going to have them leave Akiba."

...But Shiroe denied Shouryuu's idea point-blank.

His voice, nearly devoid of emotion, was so calm it was almost cold. Henrietta sneaked a glance at Shiroe's expression. If she'd seen anger there, or irritation, or determination, Henrietta probably wouldn't have felt so convinced.

However, the only expression on Shiroe's face was a smile so faint it might not have been there at all. Although technically a smile, it only curled the corners of his mouth slightly, and it had nothing to do with amusement or delight. It was a hunter's expression.

Shiroe's mind was already made up to the point where determination was unnecessary.

Ah... Master Shiroe...

He was going to do it.

That was what Henrietta thought right then.

She also thought it would be pointless to try to stop him. They probably wouldn't be able to overturn Shiroe's resolution.

Henrietta's father was a professional stockbroker, and she remembered him wearing a similar expression. He wore it when he took on a big gamble or when he was selling desperately in the midst of a panic that rocked the market. He wouldn't come home for days on end, and when he did come home, it was only to take a quick nap and a shower before he bolted out the door again, and there, in the entry hall, before dawn, he'd smile this same smile. A tiger's smile.

At the same time, Henrietta could also understand Marielle's distress.

Hamelin was backed by several big guilds. Silver Sword and the Knights of the Black Sword, its customers, were trying to use the increase in experience points from the EXP Pots to transcend level 90. It was a reckless method of growth that only A-class guilds with abundant capital could pull off, but it certainly might be possible to reach the next level that way.

From an ethical perspective, extorting EXP Pots from beginners and selling them off was a crooked move. It repulsed Henrietta, and if someone were to suggest doing something similar at the Crescent Moon League, she'd oppose it with everything she had.

However, she couldn't categorically declare that it was an unforgivable crime.

Even if there had been heavy mental pressure or some variety of intimidation, the beginners had joined the guild of their own accord, and they were staying there. Since that was the case, the extortion and reselling didn't violate the rules of the game. And, in this other world, that meant it wasn't illegal.

Laws… Laws, hm…? They really are more ephemeral than a mirage on a summer morning. It's difficult to tell whether they're there or not. Besides—

There were feasibility issues as well.

Say that act—legal or illegal—was evil. Were there any people or organizations in Akiba who could take them to task over it? The answer was no.

The influence of the big guilds was vast, and no player was quixotic enough to go against them when there was no particular merit in doing so. The members of the big guilds were already using their guilds' names to win preferential use of all the town's facilities. Not only that, but their domineering, unkind treatment of players who belonged to smaller guilds was growing conspicuous.

Under the circumstances, sympathizing with Shiroe's views would mean making enemies of the big guilds. Marielle's Crescent Moon League might be small, but it was an organization, and she was its leader. Henrietta was beginning to understand what her severe expression meant.

Leaving aside the question of what was just, no one had the power, authority, or muscle to serve that justice. That made "justice" no more than pie in the sky. As a result, it didn't matter whether it existed or not: Nobody even cared. That was the unvarnished truth of the current Akiba.

Mari...

Henrietta bit her lip.

She was indebted to Shiroe. She also liked him as an individual.

He was, with the qualifier "among men without a shred of cuteness about them," a young man she wouldn't mind having as a close friend. However, even so, there were some requests she couldn't agree to.

She probably should have stopped Shiroe's dangerous rampage with a heartfelt warning.

Still, when she saw that fearless resolution, the words wouldn't come.

Shiroe was normally so introspective that it made him look reserved. This was the first time she'd seen him show fighting spirit. Was it all right for someone like her to interfere with it? When she asked herself that question, there was no way she could be confident in her answer.

Watching Henrietta falter this way out of the corner of her eye, Marielle hesitated several times, then opened her mouth.

"Kiddo... Look, I know how you feel. I really do, but... I... No, y'see, we're..."

Her reply was probably meant to be an apology. She wasn't going to make Henrietta and Shouryuu, the guild's executives, do it. As the guild's leader, she was going to turn Shiroe's request down herself.

Henrietta knew that Marielle had been prepared for Shiroe to be displeased, or even to hate her, when she began to speak.

However, Shiroe interrupted her firmly.

"Mari. I'm sorry, but let me finish. I'm halfway through now. This is still only half. Hamelin is just a bonus. On its own, it's nowhere near enough. It's far too minor. A little thing like that is just a reward on the way. At this point, let me be blunt: I don't like the town's current atmosphere. It's petty and uncool and ugly."

As the others sat dumbfounded, Shiroe kept speaking, as though he alone had been convinced of everything from the start.

"…And so I'm going to clean up Akiba. Hamelin is just a side benefit. I'm helping Minori and Touya because they're my friends, but even that—it's secondary. There are a lot of other things that we need to do. We can't waste time on this."

Shouryuu, Henrietta, and even Marielle were as still as statues. Shiroe continued talking regardless.

"When did being a small guild become something bad, something that meant you had to creep and hide? Yes, Susukino was rotten. With only two thousand people, it's no wonder the strong guilds swaggered around as if they owned it. But Akiba's our hometown. It's the main base for more than half the players on the Japanese server. The server's biggest town. Akiba, uncool, with a nasty, uncomfortable atmosphere, and everyone looking down as they walk… Why should it be like that? That makes it seem as though we were all born to become losers. Occupying hunting grounds, the big guilds' rapid advances, discord between rivals: I'd never say those things are bad, but I can't stand to watch myself being strangled like this. Is any of it worth making newbies cry? We've been tossed into another world, and we have to work together to survive; is it worth kicking that whole situation to the curb? Sure, there are thirty thousand of us, but there are *only* thirty thousand of us. Aren't we underestimating it?—We're not taking this other world seriously. We're not desperate enough."

They had no words.

It was an outrageous speech.

From the fact that Marielle—not to mention Henrietta and Shouryuu—was frozen, she certainly hadn't seen this coming.

Rescuing friends they could understand. However, crushing a whole guild to do it was already over the top. When, above and beyond that, the talk turned to changing the current trends and situation, it sailed past "over the top" and left the realm of sanity entirely.

However, when they heard what he had to say, what shook them more than the substance of his words was Shiroe's voice. It was a calm voice, with no tension or excitement about it, but it held hidden steel. There was a sharpness to it that would cut on contact.

Cautiously, Henrietta let out the breath she hadn't realized she was holding.

She'd misjudged him, this young man called Shiroe. She'd thought he was strong and kind, but introspective and shy. ...She'd been wrong. The essential part of this youth was terribly pure. He was single-minded regarding goals, and both his thoughts and methods were straightforward. He was efficient, and there was no mercy in him.

Fight and take it. This young man was faithful to that simple principle. He might hesitate for a long time before he made up his mind. The blade might be dulled. But when he decided to do something, he would do it.

"Miss...Mari?"

At Shouryuu's query, Marielle bit her lip. Even the act of crushing one guild would place a huge burden on the Crescent Moon League, and the risk would be great. By that reckoning, she wouldn't be able to agree to Shiroe's proposal.

...But Shiroe had said he planned to change the whole town. That meant if they won this particular battle, the return would skyrocket.

That was the reason for Marielle's hesitation. In this case, the return would be a rise in status for the smaller guilds. However, that wasn't all.

It was also a problem of the soul.

"We're..."

"Please help me."

For the first time, Shiroe bowed his head.

"Master Shiroe? Where have your friends gone?"

Henrietta spoke up in an attempt to rescue Marielle, who was searching for the right words. By all rights, Naotsugu and Akatsuki could have been here as well.

"They're investigating and making preparations. I apologize for the late introduction: I've formed a guild, with myself as guild master. Its name is Log Horizon, meaning the horizon of all we've documented. Its members are Naotsugu, Akatsuki, Nyanta, and myself, and this mission will be its first operation."

"You...made yourself a guild."

"Yes. I'm sorry; after you invited us to yours…"

"No, no…"

Marielle shook her head. The gesture was almost childlike.

"No, that's nothin' to apologize for. …Well, well. Kiddo… Congratulations. You made yourself a guild. *You* did, kiddo. You made a home for yourself."

Marielle smiled. There were tiny teardrops at the corners of her eyes.

Shiroe, who'd always avoided joining a guild, had created a place for himself to belong. Henrietta couldn't accurately gauge the implications, but she understood what Marielle's tears meant. Henrietta's friend, with her simple, genuine tendencies, was wishing Shiroe the best from the bottom of her heart.

"Guild master. …Would it be okay if we at least heard him out? I'm interested. We do a lot around town, and I've felt the bad atmosphere Mr. Shiroe mentioned. I was worried Akiba might stay this way forever. It's been bothering me for a long time."

Shouryuu voiced his opinion briefly.

As the Crescent Moon League's combat team leader, he understood the circumstances, too. He knew he might make trouble for Marielle if he stuck his oar in unnecessarily. Still, in that sense, it spoke to how obviously torn Marielle herself was between wanting to help and wanting to protect the guild.

Henrietta put in a few words of her own.

"Yes, whether we can help or not will depend on the method. You know we couldn't commit ourselves to a plan with no real prospects, Master Shiroe."

Beaten to the punch by her two subordinates, Marielle—who must have felt that she should be the one to take the brunt of any unpleasantness—seemed a bit embarrassed. Almost immediately, though, she added her own encouragement. "Go on, kiddo. Talk."

At those words, Shiroe seemed to take half a moment to put his thoughts in order. Then, abruptly, he cut to the chase.

"We need capital. Five million gold coins, to start."

"That's an impossible sum!" Henrietta shrieked. As the person in charge of the Crescent Moon League's vault, she had a pretty accurate grasp of the guild's assets.

The funds in the Crescent Moon League's guild account came to about sixty thousand gold coins. If they sold off most of their stored items, they could probably pull together as much as 100,000 coins. If the individual property of each and every guild member was sold, they might be able to reach 500,000.

...But that was the limit. Even if they poured in all their members' assets, they couldn't scrape together more than 500,000 coins. Henrietta, a level-90 player, had about twenty thousand to her name. Considering the fact that an individual with fifty thousand was quite wealthy, five million gold coins was an astronomical amount.

"How're we supposed to pull together a fortune like that?! I know I shouldn't be sayin' stuff like this myself, but we're... We're a tiny guild, y'know?"

"M-m-money?!"

As expected, Marielle and Shouryuu groaned in despair.

If it was a question of combat power or labor, they could have given it their best effort. However, supplying funds probably struck them as an impossible demand from the start.

"What do you think, Miss Henrietta?"

"Me?"

"In the old world, you're an accountant with a master's in Management Studies, correct? I think it's possible. Everyone's still underestimating things in this world, you see. It isn't that big a deal. All we have to do is pull it in. Money is just the first step. It's nowhere near the biggest obstacle."

"......Pull it in...?"

Henrietta's consciousness expanded.

Ripples spread out from Shiroe's words.

We're not taking this other world seriously. We're underestimating it.

Why would Shiroe say a thing like that? What did he think they were underestimating? This was the world of *Elder Tales*. Yes, it was another world, but there was also no world they knew better.

"You don't need to think too deeply about what sort of capital it is or who it might belong to. The other guys have no intention of following the rules, either. Am I wrong? ...This is *a place with no rules*. There's no need to voluntarily straitjacket ourselves."

In a way, it was absurd.

However, for that reason alone, Henrietta understood. She was probably the only one who did. Right now, she and Shiroe were the only ones in the room. *I'm the only one who's really hearing Shiroe.* Henrietta was inexplicably sure of it. As that was the case, she needed to weigh decisions within that territory in Marielle's place.

What Shiroe was saying was:

"Make rules that will attract money"...

Henrietta felt dizzy. Shiroe had practically said they'd strike down all who opposed them. In other words, he was telling them to *take* it.

The word *take* wasn't limited to violence. Not only that, there was no need to act illegally or use atrocious methods. Even when the world was operating in perfect legality, this "taking" happened on a daily basis. Hadn't Henrietta felt the world was that sort of place when she watched her father?

On the contrary, she knew instinctively that it would be foolish to invite ill will. Illegal methods and methods that left mental discord in their wake were a card to be played only as a last resort, when there were no other options. Preferably, their "rules" would have people cheerfully handing them their money.

"...I think we...can."

Henrietta nodded.

"We can collect that capital."

"Huh?"

"What?!"

Henrietta answered Marielle and Shouryuu's startled cries with thoughts that were still a bit vague. She was currently making fine mental corrections to the plot she'd hit upon, fleshing it out.

"Pulling together five million coins won't be the end, will it? What do you plan to do after that?"

If Henrietta's instincts were correct, the young man in front of her had something truly stupendous in mind.

The feeling she was picking up from him was that of someone who'd burn down a house to get rid of the rats or buy up a garment manufacturer because he wanted a T-shirt.

No matter how preposterous a road it was, if that was the only road that led to his goal, Shiroe would take it.

"Collecting five million is the first step. The hardest part comes after that. It's…everyone's good will and hope. If many of the guilds that live here in Akiba don't care what the town turns into, then we'll lose. However, if that happens, there was no help for it. If that proves to be the case, I'll feel no regret over losing that sort of town. That said, I believe it won't. There must be more players who like Akiba than players who hate it. It's a bit late for me to say this now, but I have no intention of demanding your cooperation as payment for Serara's rescue. I came to you, the Crescent Moon League, because I need your help. I came because there are things I want you—Mari, and Miss Henrietta, and Shouryuu—to do. I'll ask again: Please help me."

Shiroe bowed his head deeply.

Shouryuu gave a small nod. On seeing it, Marielle examined Henrietta's expression.

Shiroe was serious. He seriously thought this could be done, and he seriously intended to try. That was what had made Shouryuu want to hear the rest of his idea and what had made Marielle hesitate to make a decision.

This young man was capable of risking himself for somebody else. However, wasn't it harder for him to say, "Please help me," than it was to put himself on the line?

Henrietta thought that will was noble.

If Shiroe was serious, then even if his opponent was all of Akiba, and even if the strategy was outrageous, he might be able to find a way to win.

Henrietta's severe financial executive's instincts were telling her so in a whisper.

"Yes, Mari. Do as you please."

"I, uh… The Crescent Moon League…"

Marielle squeezed her hands into fists, answering Shiroe with the expression of a guild master.

"The Crescent Moon League will cooperate with your plan, kiddo. …We'd like this town to shape up, too. It feels like, if this keeps up, we'll end up losing somethin' critical. B-but listen… We aren't a real prosperous outfit, so… Don't go pullin' a midnight disappearin' act on us, all right? Even then, though, I guess we'd have to help. If we just keep on pretendin' we don't see, we'll rot away inside; that's a problem of the soul, after all. So, we'll take that risk, too. …C'mon, kiddo. Tell us how. If there was somethin' we could do and we didn't, I think we'd regret it forever."

CHAPTER.
3

SUNFLOWER AND LILY OF THE VALLEY

► NAME: MINORI

► LEVEL: **6**

► RACE: **HUMAN**

► CLASS: **KANNAGI**

► HP: **447**

► MP: **458**

► ITEM 1:

[BELLED PRAYER STAFF]

AN ITEM FOR KANNAGI FROM THE RANGE OF EQUIPMENT FOR NEWBIE HEALERS. THE BELLS ON THE END OF THE STAFF MAKE A COOL, CLEAR SOUND. IF A COMPANION HEALER IS ON THE SCENE, IT WILL SLIGHTLY BOOST THE RANGE OF THEIR HP RECOVERY SPELLS.

► ITEM 2:

[WILLOW TIT BELL AMULET]

A REWARD ITEM FROM A QUEST IN WHICH YOU FIND A TINY, WOUNDED WILLOW TIT IN TOWN, PROTECT IT WHILE YOU CROSS A FIELD WHERE MONSTERS PROWL, HEAL ITS WOUNDS, AND RETURN IT TO ITS NEST. IT'S A BELL AMULET THAT FELL FROM THE NEST AFTER THE QUEST WAS CLEARED, AND IT'S A FAVORITE OF MINORI'S.

► ITEM 3:

[WHITE PAPER FIGURES]

ORIGAMI IN THE SHAPE OF PEOPLE. THIS CONSUMABLE ITEM SLIGHTLY ENHANCES THE EFFECT OF DAMAGE INTERCEPTION SPELLS BUT WILL BURN UP AFTER USE. FOR WHAT IT COSTS, ITS EFFECT IS RELATIVELY LOW, BUT MINORI IS CAREFUL TO ALWAYS HAVE SOME WITH HER IN CASE OF EMERGENCIES.

\<Tissue Paper\>
Has a fine, soft texture.
In this world, it's a valuable
level-90 item.

Starting the next day, they spent four days in planning, then began to implement the strategy.

Calling the schedule "tight" would have been a massive understatement. Still, miraculously, in spite of the sort of bustle that made heads spin and the fact that things proceeded at a reckless pace that pushed everyone to their limit and beyond, everything was completed on schedule.

The three who were behind the murderous schedule pinned its achievements and responsibility on each other.

Marielle—Kansai dialect–speaking big-sister type, Crescent Moon League guild master, and universally beloved busybody—puffed out her ample chest with pride. "Our accountant's a real hustler. I leave all the numbers to her, and she doesn't misread one in ten thousand. If Henrietta went and threatened 'em with a ledger, demon in hell or trumpet-wieldin' angel, they'd wet themselves right where they sat and apologize."

Shaking her abundant, wavy, honey-colored hair, Henrietta—the accountant in question—said, "My managerial abilities can only do so much. The really outrageous, earth-shattering thing is the craftiness of Master Shiroe's merciless, remorseless plan. Why does he even have a 'shiro' in his name? 'White'? Is that a joke? He really should call himself 'Pitch-black Kuroe.' If darling Akatsuki weren't around, I'd have to go ask to be held." With an evaluation like that, it was hard to tell whether she was praising or vilifying him.

As for Shiroe, who'd been so roundly disparaged, he adjusted his glasses as they were about to slip off and said, "Inasmuch as I'm aware I'm blackhearted, that's kid stuff. It's nothing compared to Mari's natural charm. When she cheers them on with that smile of hers, exhausted guild members decide to work a little longer. I think even a zombie might come back to life and go into service to win praise from Mari." He spoke with a straight face and seemed quite serious.

At any rate, according to the schedule those three had set up, Akatsuki, Naotsugu, Nyanta, and all the members of the Crescent Moon League were worked until they were dead on their feet. For League members who didn't yet have much experience, this was a life-or-death crisis. Spurred on by fierce encouragement from each other, the project participants were revived again and again, zombie-like, until they finished all the preparations and greeted the morning of the project's launch.

That morning.

In the streets of Akiba—where, at the beginning of summer, the sun steadily rose earlier and the temperature was inching up—temporary shops appeared in three locations. Although showy, they seemed a bit cheap.

The support pillar was made of bamboo, cut to a good size, and lashed together with lumber. Colorful valances swung from a big pavilion made from a sailcloth awning, so that it looked like an attraction or bazaar venue. There was a central platform that seemed to be a converted two-horse carriage and a wooden counter, which was the only truly splendid part of the whole outfit.

The shapes of the venues varied slightly from location to location, but the banners that fluttered in the wind all said the exact same thing in vivid letters: SNACK SHOP CRESCENT MOON.

In Akiba these days, it was rare to find any shop as lonely as a snack shop or dining hall.

All food tasted the same, after all.

As the settings in the *Elder Tales* game had dictated, there were pubs and taverns run by NPCs, and many inns would provide meals.

However, all the food provided by these establishments tasted exactly the same. From cheap bean porridge to ultra-premium roast chicken, everything tasted like flavorless soggy rice crackers. There was no fatty richness to the food, and although it was damp, the sullen flavor made it oddly difficult to swallow. The more one ate, the more discouraged they got.

It was the same with beverages. No matter what one ordered, although the colors were different, the smell and taste were just like plain well water. The one exception was alcoholic drinks, and even these tasted exactly like the others. They didn't even have alcohol's unique burn to them. One would just abruptly get drunk.

Under the circumstances, no one frequented taverns or dining halls.

Of course, there were a few people who'd visit in search of a place to sit down or take a break. There was potential demand for places with chairs lined up in the shade, as an alternative to standing and talking in the plaza. However, even those people didn't visit for the food.

They ordered the very cheapest food, and it was intended mainly as payment for the seat.

In the current Akiba, most players purchased food items from NPCs or the market.

Because all food items tasted the same, and apparently it was possible to get nutrients from them, cost had become the only basis of selection.

Since high-level food items had the effect of temporarily raising player stats, the combat guilds sometimes requested them. However, that demand was very slight, probably less than 1 percent of the whole.

To the overwhelming majority of players, food items were considered "universally disappointing livestock feed," and they only ate them because if they didn't their stomachs felt painfully empty. In that case, it was only natural that they'd go for the cheap stuff.

As a result, a fierce price-cutting war broke out.

The production of food items in this world was extremely fast. No matter how high-class the food item, all one had to do was select it from the menu and it would be done in ten seconds.

Provided one had enough material, it was possible to make three hundred meals in an hour. Chef wasn't a popular subclass, but even so, an explosion of cheap food items came into circulation on the market.

For their part, the producers didn't have to go out of their way to prepare high-level food items whose ingredients were hard to come by. In the current sluggish economy, it was possible to fill demand with low-level food items, and all they had to do was provide them at low cost.

That sort of market logic brought prices down. Even though "eating" was consumption related to one of the three primitive desires and therefore something everybody had to do, and even though there was a regular volume of food item transactions, prices were at rock bottom.

Why would anyone start a snack shop in a frigid business climate like that? The question was on the mind of every player in Akiba who happened to see the banners.

These days, even Chefs tended to put their items directly on the market. It was less work that way, and more to the point, over-the-counter sales brought unbearable stress. That was only to be expected: To the people who purchased them, the food items they'd made were nothing but cattle feed. No craftsman wanted to sell food to the general public that even *they* thought was bad. What the creators really wanted was to have customers delighted by their wares' delicious flavors, but no one saw that sort of smile anymore. At this point, there were no Chefs among the production classes who sold items from stalls.

However, when the sun had climbed to a certain height, and there was a bit less than an hour before noon, ripples of surprise began to spread.

They'd probably been made in the kitchen of some guildhall. A huge amount of parcels was delivered to each temporary shop, and an indescribably wonderful smell began to waft from them.

It was the fragrant smell of browning oil. The alluring scent of mixed spices.

At the same time, a woman with a gorgeous figure stepped forward and raised her voice, her long green hair swaying.

"Stop by and give us a try! We're Snack Shop Crescent Moon, open for business as of today! Is the flavorless yech of your everyday meals gettin' you down? Have we got news for you! Come rediscover *real* food! You're not even gonna believe how tasty this is! It's yum, yum, yummy!!"

Marielle delivered her spiel at the top of her lungs; she was already feeling pretty desperate.

The uniforms the guild's Tailors had put together featured pure white blouses, tight-fitting skirts with pink pinstripes, and bright salmon-pink frilly aprons with big bows—the sort of uniform family restaurant waitresses or fast-food workers had worn in the old world.

Serara, who was standing at the ready next to her, raised her small voice frantically, determined not to lose.

"Thank you! Thank you! Thank you for your purchase!"

She must have been incredibly nervous. They hadn't sold a single item yet, but she was already thanking people profusely and handing out flyers.

Crescent Burger: fifteen gold coins. Super Crescent Burger: thirty gold coins. Crispy Chicken (one piece): eighteen gold coins; (three pieces): fifty gold coins. Fish and Chips (small): ten gold coins; (large): twenty gold coins. Black Rose Tea (cup): five gold coins; (canteen): fifteen gold coins.

The flyers had a header that read "Grand Opening" and a menu.

Compared to a hamburger shop on Earth, the menu was pretty poor, but for the players of Akiba, it was more than enough to provoke nostalgia.

Spurred on by the savory smells and idle curiosity, several players made purchases.

Even the most diplomatic couldn't have called the prices economical. As a matter of fact, they were expensive.

In Akiba, a night in the cheapest room at an inn cost at least ten gold coins. One meal's worth of food items could be purchased for five. Viewed that way, the cost per meal here was three to six times higher than usual. This was not a minor expense.

However, at the same time, it wasn't an impossible amount.

Surviving in this other world didn't cost all that much. As far as places to sleep were concerned, provided one had a sleeping bag, if worst came to worst, they didn't even need to rent a room.

There were lots of ruined buildings. Simply taking shelter from the evening dew didn't cost anything. As far as food went, the market was overflowing with cheap items, and clothes and equipment didn't need to be replaced all that frequently.

Of course there were always more luxurious options to aspire to, but if one was frugal, it was possible to live on fifteen gold coins a day. The running costs that any endeavor incurred, such as guildhall maintenance fees and overhaul fees on weapons and equipment, made it difficult to save up large sums of money in this world, but it was easy to earn enough to keep oneself going from day to day.

A price of a thousand gold coins would have made players hesitate, weighing that cost against the cost of a magic item, but ten-odd gold coins was practically pocket money, an amount no one worried about spending.

Driven by that mentality, the onlookers purchased several items.

Marielle and Serara charmed customers who'd made purchases with smiling hospitality. The young male guild members who'd carried the parcels from the hall where they'd been prepared also smiled and yelled, "Thank you very much!" in chorus with Marielle and Serara.

When—half-hopeful, half-curious—the onlookers took the first bite, the shock nearly knocked them off their feet.

"Wha—?! Wha—?! What the heck is *this*?!"

It tasted. Put into words, that was all it was, but from the thrill that ran through the people who experienced it, the world might as well have turned inside out.

The meat tasted like meat.

The lettuce was juicy and refreshing enough to rinse away the grease from the meat, and the tomato added just the right acidity.

The sweetness of the lightly browned bread. The smoothness of the butter. The spicy bite of the mustard.

Each taste was novel and deeply moving.

The food was far from perfect. In the old world, it would have been closer to home cooking than restaurant fare, and the taste wasn't so

exquisite that it could have graced the first pages of a gourmet maga-
zine. However, in this world, it was easily the best flavor there was.

The players ate as if in a dream, fighting back tears.

This was, without a doubt, the best thing any of them had ever eaten
in their entire lives. Before that thought even had time to sink in, the
hamburgers were gone.

They even licked up the meat juice that had dripped onto the paper
wrappers.

No one thought it was embarrassing.

If they'd had the wherewithal to feel embarrassed, they would have
made themselves stop crying.

In less than an hour, the same shock they'd experienced had run
through the streets of Akiba.

The event was revolutionary, as if people who'd seen only in mono-
chrome had abruptly been given full true-color vision.

Suddenly, the people of Akiba seemed to realize just how dispirited
they'd been. Everyone had forgotten how important it was for food to
taste good. They'd given up on it.

Snack Shop Crescent Moon became Akiba's newest legend.

▶ **2**

Marielle's office looked like a battlefield in its own right.

A plain, solid conference desk had been set in front of Marielle's
grand work desk, which had been in the room to begin with, and the
fancy sofa had been exiled to a corner.

The conference desk held a mountain of materials and documents.

All the papers had been covered with fine figures, scribbled there
by Henrietta, the accounting supervisor, and Shiroe, the strategy
manager.

By the time the Crescent Moon League members returned to the
guildhall after winding up that astounding first day, it was already ten
at night. In the midst of a fatigue worse than if they'd spent all day
fighting tough monsters, many of the members collapsed where they
stood.

Physical stamina in this world seemed to be related to the ability values, or levels, of their *Elder Tales* characters. Since most of the Crescent Moon League members were midrange players, this sight was only natural, and the players deserved praise for lasting as long as they had.

However, sparing only a glance or two for the fallen sales team, Shiroe and Henrietta continued their battle with the paperwork, working as though they were running from the demons of hell.

. A corner of the room held stacks of paper and inkpots, generated through Shiroe's Scribe skills. Pulling several dozen sheets from the stack, Henrietta silently documented the latest figures. Then she heaved a great sigh and raised her head.

"I've finished the totals for today."

"Good work."

At her words, Shiroe looked up as well, letting his hand fall still.

"If you'd like to reward me, give me Akatsuki."

"...I won't give her to you, but you can cuddle her for an hour."

"My!"

Averting his eyes from Henrietta—who was wriggling with joy, her own eyes sparkling—Shiroe picked up a nearby sheet of paper covered in figures.

"The percentage wasted was lower than we expected, wasn't it?"

"That's because the customers never stopped coming. We sold the entire amount we'd planned on."

"...Meaning it's going to be an issue of laying in materials..."

"Yes, it will."

The figures in front of them were within the estimated range. As a matter of fact, they looked quite good, but that didn't mean there were no problems. This huge sales operation had harnessed the full power of the Crescent Moon League, but since they were dealing in food, they were bound to run through materials.

During the preparations period, they'd hunted monsters and animals that dropped items, building up their stores, and even today, the day the shops had opened, a party that had included Naotsugu and Shouryuu had been organized and sent out to gather materials. Still, if they kept burning through them at this rate, their materials would only last four days.

"…The materials really won't stretch."

"Shall we start buying?"

"We'll have to see what Mari says about it."

Shiroe and Henrietta fiddled with several more figures, running simulations of different models. What if they pared down the menu or increased their offerings? What if they raised the prices or lowered them?

No matter what combination they used, their stores of materials wouldn't last five days. The Crescent Moon League was a small guild, and apparently this was the limit of their storeroom and manpower.

"'Scuse the intrusion, you two. …Wait, it's my room anyway."

Just as the two of them finished their review and reached for their tea, the door opened wide and Marielle entered the office. She probably hadn't been drawn there by their conversation, but Marielle—elated and showing no signs of fatigue—approached them with her usual bright smile and ruffled Shiroe's hair.

"Well done, kiddo. You, too, Henrietta."

She hugged Henrietta tightly to her generous bosom, but Henrietta seemed used to it; she only greeted her with a nonchalant "Welcome back, Mari."

Without heading for her work desk, Marielle claimed a chair at the conference desk and filled their glasses, including one for herself, from a bottle of black-leaf tea she said she'd filched from the kitchen. When they sold it at the shop, they changed the name to Black Rose Tea, but it had nothing to do with roses. The name was just a reflection of Henrietta's tastes.

"And? How were our sales, y'all?!"

As she questioned them, Marielle's eyes sparkled.

At times like this, she really sounds like an Osakan… Well, it's cute, so I guess it's not a problem.

While Shiroe hid a sigh, Henrietta began to report their numbers.

"Our sales totaled 43,776 gold coins. We had 1,159 customers, and the average customer spent thirty-eight coins. We sold out of the Crescent Burgers and Super Crescent Burgers. Except for the Black Rose Tea, all other items sold out as well."

"Wow! That's fantastic! Forty thousand coins… Compared to our monthly budget, that's, um…"

"Forty times greater."

"Yep, forty!! What a haul! If we keep this up, we'll hit five million in no time!"

Marielle broke into a cheerful little dance, still facing the conference desk. Stealthily averting his eyes from her swaying chest, Shiroe checked her enthusiasm. "We won't make it in time, Mari. Not even close."

"Oh?"

"Think about it. That's a hundred and twenty days. It would take us four months."

"But we had to turn away so many customers! If we'd wanted to sell, there were plenty of folks who wanted to buy. If we just lay in more stock…"

Raising a hand to interrupt Marielle's words, Shiroe objected.

"We probably have tens of thousands of potential customers. There are over fifteen thousand players here in Akiba. That isn't the problem. The problem is in the number of Crescent Moon League members and how that affects the number of shops and the amount of merchandise we can arrange for."

"Is it?"

Marielle looked troubled, as if she hadn't completely understood. Henrietta explained in careful detail.

"Yes, he's correct. If it takes one salesclerk three minutes to hand the customer their merchandise and ring them up, that salesclerk can process twenty customers per hour. That's 160 customers in eight hours of business. Ten salesclerks could serve 1,600 customers. Even if we made every Crescent Moon League member a salesclerk, the most they could handle would be four thousand customers per day. Besides, that's if we focused exclusively on the selling aspect and completely ignored acquisition, preparation, cooking, and paperwork. It's a number we really couldn't sustain… In that sense, I think the plan we set up has the best balance of members assigned to sales, the kitchen, odd jobs, and procurement. And when we conducted sales with that balance, the results were…"

With a teacher's gesture, Henrietta pointed to the documents.

"Slightly over one thousand customers, an amount nearly equal to the number of visitors. …In other words, at the Crescent Moon League's size, no matter how much the users want the items, we won't be able to handle more than one thousand customers per day."

"Is that right…? Hmmm. And we could be makin' a killin', too…"

On having this pointed out to her, Marielle frowned, her eyebrows drawing together in disappointment. However, she recovered almost immediately and came back with a counter:

"Well, why not recruit more members? I bet we could at this point. I mean, we're the home of the miraculous Snack Shop Crescent Moon, Akiba's rapid growth stock. Right?"

"We can't do that."

Shiroe was the one to check her this time.

"Being suspicious isn't a very good thing, but if we recruit new members at a time like this, I think most of the people who join will be spies. We're already incredibly busy, and we won't be able to deal with them."

"Agreed."

"I see," sighed Marielle.

"Mari, money isn't the point of this strategy anyway."

"Uh-huh… That's right! The fortune right in front of my nose blinded me for a sec. …Still, we do need money, don't we? You said if this keeps up, it'll take us over three months. If we won't make it in time that way, then… Should we do that other thing? Will it work?"

Henrietta smiled at Marielle's timid question.

"Don't worry. No merchant worth his salt would refuse. I'm the one telling you, so rest assured it's true. Any simpleton that daft would qualify to be guillotined by Pareto optimality."

At Henrietta's beaming face, Shiroe gave a wry smile of his own.

The trajectory the project was following was almost exactly what he'd anticipated.

A team play by the two of them will probably be quite a sight…

Shiroe mentally ran through the plan in his head. Over the next few days, the three of them would have to successfully conclude three different sets of negotiations.

"All right, then, Miss Henrietta, please take care of those negotiations. I leave the details to you."

"Yes, sir. You can count on me."

Henrietta cocked her head to one side, smiling like a proper young lady.

"Mari, you handle product procurement."

"Roger that. …Although I'm not so great with numbers, y'know…"

"If you carry things through to a basic agreement, I'll help you explain the conditions. …In fact, why don't we conduct my negotiations and the product negotiations as a team? That should save time and trouble."

The sight of Henrietta encouraging Marielle relieved Shiroe.

Henrietta was far more capable than Shiroe had assumed. He'd gotten the impression that she was sharp from his previous dealings with her and from little things she said, but he hadn't expected her to be *this* good.

Marielle had great talent, but she was a little spacey; she probably needed companions like Henrietta and Shouryuu.

He thought of Akatsuki, who even now was running through the darkened streets on a special mission, and Naotsugu, who'd volunteered to organize the storeroom even though he must have been tired from the hunting he'd done during the day, and Nyanta, who was still doing basic prep work on the Crescent Burgers they'd sell tomorrow.

Everyone's performing their missions even better than I'd hoped. If we wipe out now, I'll have no choice but to claim total responsibility for it…

"What's wrong, kiddo?"

"Nothing."

Doubt as to whether he was a worthy companion for them skimmed through his mind.

…But only for a moment. It was his responsibility to become worthy. So that he wouldn't let down the companions who'd waited for him. So that he wouldn't make liars out of them.

Just as he'd promised Akatsuki that day. Just as he'd sworn in front of Naotsugu and Nyanta, Marielle and the others.

No, even the question of whether he was worthy or not was arrogant and pointless. The important thing now was to make the operation in front of him succeed. The path toward fulfilling his responsibility as the one who'd suggested this plan—a plan that required everyone's strength—lay, just barely, in doing this over and over.

"I'll lay the groundwork for the conference. Everything we're doing now is advance preparation. Let's move forward with plans for the festival without tipping our hand."

▶ 3

Kneading her fingers together nervously, Marielle sighed for the umpteenth time. In public, she smiled as though she was full of self-confidence, but she had absolutely no confidence when attempting something she had no experience with.

She knew why Shiroe had nominated her.

It was true that she had quite a lot of friends among the small and midsized guilds of Akiba. The person Marielle was about to meet was one of her acquaintances, and in that sense, he'd be easy to talk to. That said...he was one of the most influential of those acquaintances.

She tugged at her outfit here and there.

She'd dusted off some of her finest clothes for this, but she couldn't quite relax. That was only natural: She'd never taken part in a business talk in the game. She couldn't imagine that there were many people who had.

Clothes in *Elder Tales*—which, up until a short while ago, had been "equipment"—boasted a great deal of flexibility.

When exploring or hunting, equipment had to be chosen with an emphasis on practicality. In *Elder Tales*, unless the clothes were very unique, the basic design concept was medieval European fantasy costumes. In other words, vanguard warriors wore plate armor. The attackers, in the middle, wore chain mail or leather armor.

Healers differed widely from each other, but Clerics like Marielle could wear comparatively heavy equipment, meaning that a lightweight breastplate and leather armor, a tunic, and mantle were probably appropriate. Although it was possible to customize it by adding one's guild's crest or dyeing it a little, it wasn't easy to change the appearance of equipment that had been chosen to be functional.

However, spending time in town brought increased flexibility.

Elder Tales might have been a medieval European fantasy RPG, but its designs weren't strictly traditional. The artwork had been tailored to suit modern tastes. While medieval European-style fashions were the rule, it had a rather varied fashion culture that included Japanese and ethnic costumes, and even uniforms, maid outfits, and other otaku-esque designs.

Since the subcontracting developers and the operating companies for each of the regional servers had a lot of power regarding model and item data, this was probably only to be expected.

Apparently, the area that mapped to Japan in this world wasn't as hot and humid as real-world Japan. At this time of year, heading into summer, there was a wide range of fashion options and a huge variety of wearable outfits: casual options like capris and cotton tunic shirts; players in fantasy-style robes, ancient Grecian togas, and even casual Japanese dress; armor and haute couture suits.

Today, Marielle wore a white silk blouse and a long mermaid skirt. She had no jacket, but she'd tossed a cape loosely around her shoulders. The guild's Tailors had flashed her a V for victory, but she wasn't sure whether she'd worn the right thing.

"You mustn't act so nervous."

Henrietta spoke at her side, still looking straight ahead.

Henrietta wore a black ribbon in her honey-colored hair, which, as always, had a gentle wave to it. Her monotone dress was quite young and girlish.

Looking at her, Marielle thought, *It takes guts to have your own style.*

"Is this gonna be okay?"

"You mustn't be uneasy. You have to be aggressive when you go into negotiations. In any case, of all the needles' eyes that we need to get through, this is the easiest. Even if we fail, we can recover. These aren't last-ditch negotiations."

Marielle nodded, agreeing with Henrietta.

The first deal they had to negotiate today was for material procurement. Their material items had nearly run out already. Although they might be all right for tomorrow, the shortage would start to interfere with business by the next day unless they managed to replenish their stock.

Conversely, if these material procurement negotiations succeeded, the Crescent Moon League would be able to concentrate exclusively on cooking and retail sales.

And after that—

We'll think about that when we get there. Henrietta and Shiro are here, too. If I just stick to my post, he's bound to do something about it for me. I'll just give these negotiations everything I've got.

"That said… If we manage to make these negotiations a huge success, my next mission will be significantly easier. We'll have to stay focused going in."

"Yeeeeek… Quit puttin' more pressure on me…"

Just as Marielle had almost managed to become defiant, Henrietta's cool retort brought back all her timidity. There were certain things people were good at and certain things they weren't. She revised her self-assessment: She would never learn how to keep a poker face.

"Hi! Sorry to have kept you waiting."

The player who'd appeared was a human with hazel hair and keen hazel eyes. His name was Calasin. He was the guild master for Shopping District 8, the third-largest production guild in Akiba.

Calasin greeted them candidly as he closed the door, then took a seat.

They were in a private room in a tavern near Akiba's central plaza. These rooms could be rented for two hours for a few gold coins, and they were suited to confidential talks.

Marielle and Calasin knew each other.

There'd been a time when they'd gone out hunting together, back when they were both fledgling players.

Since both Marielle and Calasin had started their own guilds, they almost never went anywhere together anymore, but horizontal connections between guilds were surprisingly strong.

When, as with Calasin's Shopping District 8 and the Crescent Moon League, the guilds' fields were different, it was particularly convenient for them to cooperate and share information. As a result, Calasin and Marielle were still in contact.

"Wow, Miss Mari, that's a pretty scary face. What did you need today?"

Calasin spoke casually in a voice grounded in their relationship.

Although they were old friends, Calasin's Shopping District 8 was on a completely different level from Marielle's Crescent Moon League.

The Crescent Moon League had about thirty members, and while "mutual aid guild" sounded impressive, it really just meant that the guild was a jack-of-all-trades. It was a guild that midlevel Adventurers joined so they could train in their own ways and adventure with their friends.

Calasin's guild, Shopping District 8, was an artisan guild, a guild completely specialized to the production classes. It didn't provide support for combat or exploration. Its members traded materials with one another and exchanged finished items at wholesale prices, and commerce was at the center of its activities. Its enormous membership of seven hundred made it the third-largest commerce guild in Akiba, second only to the Marine Organization and the Roderick Trading Company in size.

Following the Catastrophe, battles had changed dramatically.

Players as experienced as Shiroe and Naotsugu could pick out all sorts of specific ways in which battles had changed, from the performance of individual special skills to the ecology of enemy monsters, but for the vast majority of players, the big change was probably the terror of having to fight for real.

Once a player fought them in person, even monsters of a level they could beat easily were terrifying. Swords, axes, fangs, claws, flames, and curses came at you. Even if they knew logically that they could handle it if their level was high enough, the terror and the smell of blood on the battlefield made more than a few players weak at the knees.

Even if they'd been locked into this other world and fighting monsters was the most efficient way to make a living, more players than one might imagine didn't want to fight any more than they absolutely had to.

Although she didn't know the exact number, Marielle estimated that, after the Catastrophe, nearly half of all players had become the type that wanted to avoid battles. With the winds of the era at their backs, the production guilds were seeing explosive expansion.

The Marine Organization, currently the largest production guild in

Akiba, had 2,500 members. The second largest, the Roderick Trading Company, had 1,800.

When the seven hundred members of Calasin's Shopping District 8 were added in, those three alone had a total of five thousand players, and no doubt there were many other small production guilds. This was yet another change the Catastrophe had brought about: There hadn't been that many players who specialized in production before.

"Well, we've got a favor to ask of Shoppin' District Eight."

"And what could that be?"

Even though Marielle's expression was more serious than usual, Calasin responded easily. He'd probably already given thought to what it meant for Marielle to call him at a time like this.

Marielle had made Snack Shop Crescent Moon a success.

To the production guilds, she was one step away from completely owning the food in this world. Just as people who'd grown used to full color couldn't go back to black and white, players who'd eaten richly flavored food would probably be unable to return to the former, flavorless food items.

As a matter of fact, Marielle had received reports that sales of food items on the market had experienced an abrupt slowdown over the past few days.

Elder Tales was no longer a game.

Whether or not there was a way to return to their former world, until that way was found, this other world was a second reality. They could avoid dying here, but no one could avoid living.

The approximately thirty thousand players on the Japanese server were unable to escape the curse of having to live there.

To exaggerate slightly, at the very least in this far eastern area, Marielle and the Crescent Moon League held the initiative in food provision. At any rate, it must have seemed that way to Calasin.

Wow… Calasin's got his merchant face on. I guess if you're runnin' a big outfit like that, you can't do things halfway…

That was the impression Calasin's determined face gave Marielle, even as she herself exuded tension. If Henrietta hadn't told her that they had the initiative in these negotiations, and to be aggressive, his expression would have given her cold feet.

"It's about procurin' supplies. Our guild is goin' through material items like nobody's business, and we're thinkin' about outsourcin' the procurement to somebody else. Specifically, we need young venison, lettuce, tomatoes, wheat flour, and potatoes. …Also haru-haru fish and ptarmigan meat. We'll have to discuss amount and pricin' details, but assume we're gonna need a lot."

"Procurement, hm?"

There was no hesitation in Calasin's response.

He'd probably seen this coming. To a certain extent, that was only to be expected.

The Crescent Moon League was small. Anybody could foresee that if they continued large-scale sales, they'd run through their stores in no time. If that happened, they'd be forced to stop supplying merchandise.

Both Marielle, who'd asked the favor, and Calasin, who'd just heard it, understood at once that the request took into account the number of members, the amount of materials they could acquire by hunting on their own, and the stores in their storeroom.

"…Amount and price, then. How much?"

In response to Calasin's question, Marielle took out a note and gave him several figures.

"I see…"

Calasin drew a slow breath; from his expression, he was considering something. He probably wasn't sure whether or not to accept the request.

Considered normally, this wasn't a bad deal. A major production guild like Shopping District 8 had vast stores of material items in huge warehouses. Recently, they'd been caught up in the price-cutting wars, and even if they prepared and sold their food items, they wouldn't bring in much. Selling these items off to someone else at a fair price would be a good way to adjust inventory.

If necessary, they could keep an eye on the market and buy the ingredients Marielle had requested at low prices, then resell them to the Crescent Moon League.

From a business perspective, there was no reason to say no.

That was the conclusion Marielle and Henrietta had reached.

However, that didn't mean he'd accept it easily. Marielle remembered what Henrietta had told her. *"We've got everyone's attention now. Even if it's a marvelous procurement contract, the other party won't jump at it. They'll try to find a way to get a bigger piece of the pie."*

After a short silence, Calasin broke into a sociable smile.

"These would be ingredients for use at Snack Shop Crescent Moon, correct?" he asked.

Marielle smiled. "That's right."

"I hear Snack Shop Crescent Moon is doing great business."

"It is, and thanks for sayin' so. Our Chefs are pleased as punch that it's goin' over so well."

"...You're using new recipes, then?"

"Our Chefs are real good."

Marielle fielded Calasin's probe with a smile.

Marielle had been beaming her sunflower smile since the very beginning, and to a bystander, it might have looked as if she understood all and was secure in her advantage. However, at this point, Marielle herself was pushed to the limit.

She'd broken out in a cold sweat at Calasin's question; she was worried she might have let something slip.

However, Shiroe had told her, *"No matter what happens, Mari, keep smiling. That's the most important thing. If you just keep smiling, the other person in charge will help with everything else."*

And so, feeling just a little desperate, Marielle kept right on smiling. It was a bargain sale on smiles. Her green eyes, which tilted down slightly at the corners, softened, and her smile seemed rapturous. Marielle wasn't aware that her generous bosom and maternal atmosphere worked together to create a natural barrier that allowed no further pursuit.

"We'll give careful consideration to the procurement proposal, but listen... In order to expand your chain rapidly, Shopping District Eight and the Crescent Moon League could work together to—"

"Excuse me. Calasin, I'm afraid it's nearly time."

Henrietta interrupted Calasin, addressing him in a clear voice.

"Time?"

"Yes. Our next contacts are here."

At Henrietta's calm voice, Marielle looked a bit guilty; she put her hands together in an apology.

"Sorry 'bout this, Calasin. You and I go way back, so I squeezed you in a bit early, but Henrietta says we really can't play favorites."

"Erm… What do you mean, Mari?"

"Uuuu…"

Marielle shot a sidelong glance at Henrietta. At this point, she wasn't acting. Marielle was never able to match Henrietta, particularly where financial outlay was concerned.

"We've set up negotiations with the Marine Organization and the Roderick Trading Company as well, with regard to a different matter…"

"A different matter?"

"Right. Y'see, it's… About fundin', I guess you'd say. About Crescent Moon sales."

"—!"

Shopping District 8 might have been the third-largest production guild in Akiba, but the Marine Organization and the Roderick Trading Company were even larger. The membership of the Marine Organization alone was triple that of Shopping District 8; it was an enormous guild. If big money like that was about to join the negotiations, Calasin and his guild would be left without a leg to stand on.

"We don't want to leave anybody out in the cold, and we owe Shoppin' District Eight, y'know? Like I said, we go way back. I'd love to have Shoppin' District Eight join the talks, too. …But Henrietta says we have to get the procurement business settled first or no can do."

"'Settled'…? Mari, you know we can't even advance to the next step unless we get our current supply environment in order."

Henrietta frowned at Marielle's words a moment prior, admonishing her as though she were a young child.

"Wait, Mari, Miss Henrietta. What is the Crescent Moon League planning? What do you mean, 'funding'?"

At Calasin's question, Marielle's lips parted slightly. Henrietta put a slender finger to those lips, then turned back to Calasin.

"How much is Shopping District Eight willing to pay for that information?"

Henrietta's enigmatic gaze pierced Calasin. The procurement deal wouldn't be a bad one for Shopping District 8 either way. He narrowed his eyes slightly, then made up his mind and spoke.

"Shopping District Eight will accept your request and the corresponding responsibility. We'll provide you with 3,200 each of young venison, lettuce, tomatoes, wheat flour, potatoes, haru-haru fish, and ptarmigan meat. The first delivery will be made early in the morning of the day after tomorrow. …Your cost will be fifty thousand gold coins."

"Forty thousand."

"…All right. I, Calasin of Shopping District Eight, accept this contract."

"Oh, *good*. It's better for you this way, too, right, Calasin?! C'mon, let's let him sit in on the next set of negotiations so he can hear what's goin' on."

"Yes, let's."

As Henrietta agreed, a bell-like tone sounded in Marielle's ear, signaling the arrival of their next visitors.

▶4

"Well, well! If it isn't two lovely ladies and the young gent from Shopping District Eight."

"……Hm."

As announced, the two who'd opened the door and entered were Michitaka, the general manager of the Marine Organization, and Roderick of the Roderick Trading Company.

"Pleased to meetcha! I'm Marielle, guild master of the Crescent Moon League. This is Henrietta, my head clerk."

"Would you refrain from using antiquated terms like *head clerk*, please? …As she says, I'm Henrietta. I'm in charge of the accounts."

The two delivered their greetings in turn. In the old world, Marielle had been nothing more than someone who took it easy at home and helped out with the chores, and Henrietta was a white-collar worker who'd graduated from the department of economics. Although she handled accounting duties and had learned a lot from her father, Henrietta was still just a rank-and-file office worker, and she didn't really know what sort of expression she should wear at large-scale negotiations like these. Still, both gave introductions that, while awkward, were impressive in their own right.

"Michitaka of the Marine Organization here. General manager."

The big man who greeted them jovially was built more like a warrior than a merchant. The arm he put out for a handshake was thick and had noticeable burn scars, probably because he was a Blacksmith.

"I'm Roderick, guild master of the Roderick Trading Company. It's a production guild."

In contrast, the young man who introduced himself as Roderick looked like a scholar. According to the information they'd received earlier, he was an Apothecary.

"Yes, we're ac...acqua... Um, we know! You're both famous."

Marielle beamed.

To Henrietta, it looked as though the burden on Marielle's shoulders had lifted ever so slightly. According to their preliminary meeting with Shiroe, her responsibility had been to contract with Shopping District 8 for short-term material procurement. In that sense, she'd completed her assignment during the previous negotiations.

The person in charge of this next round of negotiations was Henrietta.

In other words, this is my battlefield.

Henrietta smiled; there was an intelligent gleam in her eyes. The men in front of her were the leaders of Akiba's largest and second-largest guilds. The huge guilds were on an entirely different level, and ordinarily, they would have completely ignored the Crescent Moon League. Henrietta would have felt too daunted even to speak to them.

That said, all the preparations Henrietta and the rest of the group had made over the past week had been leading up to this moment. The days of hunting, the stocking up on ingredients, the energetic sales under the blazing sun, the trench warfare–like document filing—it had all been in order to set the stage for this moment.

This step was grounded in the previous one, and the step before that had been drawn from the one before it. In addition, it had been Henrietta's companions who had drawn it out, not Henrietta herself.

If I back down now, I'll never be able to face the others. Besides, this pitch-black plan came courtesy of Master Shiroe. ...If we can't win with this, we'd never win with anything else. Fu-fu-fu-fu. And here I am, right in the middle of it...

Henrietta considered herself a second-rate *Elder Tales* player. Up to this point, she had never tackled any large-scale battles nor high-end content. And yet, incredibly, she was sitting right at the center of what was probably the largest strategy since the beginning of this world.

Her strength was useful to someone.

It was all right for her to use her power.

That knowledge brought her elation and a firm feeling of resolution.

"Yeah. We know you, too. You're the manager of Snack Shop Crescent Moon, right? You've turned into the talk of the town over the past few days. I ate some, too. I've only had it once so far, but still."

Michitaka laughed as he spoke.

Marielle responded with her usual smile; she seemed completely self-assured.

"...What's caused you to assemble production guilds, particularly major ones like ours, Miss Marielle of Crescent Moon?"

As Roderick spoke, he sneaked a glance at Calasin's expression. He might have been trying to deduce the reason Calasin had been admitted early by himself.

"Hm, why? You want to know why. Well, 'course you do. Let's see..."

"Before we begin, let me explain why we invited Shopping District Eight to come early."

Henrietta began to explain, counting her own breaths.

Slowly, bit by bit. Being careful not to go too quickly. Speaking in such a way that she would sound relaxed and at ease. She chose her words carefully, modulating her tone as she explained.

"We've asked Shopping District Eight to supply us with ingredients."

At her words, tension abruptly flickered across Michitaka's cheery face and Roderick's keen eyes. Those words alone had been enough to tell them how the situation was trending.

Shopping District 8 had seven hundred members.

The Marine Organization had 2,500 members registered. The Roderick Trading Company had 1,800. While there were differences in the orientation and level distribution of their artisans, the balance of power was roughly equal to their member ratio. However, if, in addition to the ingredients procurement, Snack Shop Crescent Moon were to team up with Shopping District 8 in earnest, the power relationships were likely to flip on them.

Crescent Moon had triggered a food item revolution.

However, its scale meant that its supply system was small as well. Delivering meals to one thousand players every day wouldn't come close to satisfying the demand: There were more than fifteen thousand players in Akiba.

That said, if the seven hundred members of Shopping District 8 mustered all their strength, they would be able to fill that demand. No doubt the profits would be enormous.

After all, this was food.

Unlike clothes and furniture, weapons, armor, and accessories, food was needed—and consumed—on a daily basis. Once one ate it, it was gone. Even if each individual item was cheap, the total sales were bound to be astronomical. On top of that, since it was consumable merchandise, these sales would be continuous. It was as plain as day to them that with the food supply under its control, Shopping District 8 would turn its power to personnel expansion, and before long it would have upset even the numbers ratio.

Henrietta understood Michitaka and Roderick's thoughts perfectly. Depending on how it was used, food could become a nuclear weapon able to destroy the balance between the production guilds at a stroke.

"You're saying you're partnering with Shopping District Eight?"

It was Michitaka who made the first move.

Apparently his personality was as straightforward as his appearance indicated. There was no telling whether it worked this way with real-world managers, but in guilds in online games, surprisingly, this type of player was the sort who won popularity.

"No. If that were the case, they wouldn't have needed to call us. Is it something else?" Roderick murmured.

Roderick wore delicate glasses. Between his gender and the glasses, he looked a bit like Shiroe, but he seemed slightly neurotic, and Henrietta thought it counted against him somewhat. Even if he were more blackhearted than Shiroe, she doubted he had the audacity to make people swallow that blackness.

Up until just the other day, Henrietta had assumed Shiroe's introspective, reserved character was something similar to Roderick's, and so the difference felt particularly marked to her. Any resemblance between the two was purely superficial.

"Yes, as you say, it's something else. This other matter is something we want to ask of the Marine Organization, the Roderick Trading Company, and Shopping District Eight equally."

Henrietta tilted her head slightly.

Negotiations were all about reading each other's cards.

In that sense, Henrietta had been placed in a very dangerous position.

Henrietta's group had brought up this topic. That meant that unless they disclosed their information to a certain extent, the talks couldn't advance. However, the very act of giving up information meant showing their cards.

One of her advantages was that the other parties wanted profit. To them, Snack Shop Crescent Moon looked like tasty, lucrative bait.

In addition:

As long as we hold the initiative in these negotiations, we'll always get to decide what information to release and what to conceal.

Almost as if she were playing chess, Henrietta organized their information into "can reveal" and "shouldn't reveal" at high speed.

Shiroe had given Henrietta one condition with regard to these negotiations: She was not allowed to lie.

Since they were all trying to read one another's cards, and she wasn't allowed to bluff, this was a significant handicap. When she thought of future developments, she could understand that this condition was absolute, but she couldn't deny that it placed her at a slight disadvantage.

Master Shiroe certainly does make unreasonable demands. ...I'll have to have him lend me sweet Akatsuki to make this worth it. Aah, darling Akatsuki! That jet-black, glossy, beautiful hair... She's just like a doll!

Beside Henrietta—who'd started fantasizing, her cheeks faintly flushed—Marielle had a small warning coughing fit.

"...Oh. I beg your pardon. The topic at hand, then: The Crescent Moon League is currently planning a large-scale operation. You may consider it a—a type of challenge. However, the Crescent Moon League doesn't have enough power to carry out this challenge. To that end, we'd like to ask for your support."

"Hm... A quest, is it?"

Henrietta didn't answer Roderick's words with either yes or no. She only lowered her eyes slightly, curving her lips into a crescent of a smile.

I do believe he's been kind enough to misinterpret me...

Quests were a type of mission in *Elder Tales*. They were sequential adventures that could be triggered by a request from a non-player character, or by a book or clue, and their content was quite diverse.

For example, an old villager might ask one to go find his daughter in the woods and bring her back. Or to clear a certain cavern of goblins. Or to bring back a manticore spine from the swamp. The term *quest* spanned nearly every possible type of mission.

In *Elder Tales*, which didn't have a clear story the way ordinary off-line RPGs did, quests *were* the game's story. The decision of which and how many quests to accept was left to individual players. However, *Elder Tales* had encompassed several hundred thousand, or even several million, quests since the days when it was just a game, and no player had a clear grasp of the full picture.

Just as there were many different types of quests, the rewards given for quests were diverse, too: They could be experience points or gold coins, items, knowledge of magic, or a right of some sort. Rare rewards included training in magic or recipes for the production classes.

Roderick had misinterpreted Henrietta's "challenge" to mean "quest." Not only that, but from the words *large-scale operation*, he assumed that the quest couldn't be completed by an individual player; it would require multiple players or possibly even a huge group larger than a party.

The operation that was currently under way was the sale of the knowledge of the new cooking method in exchange for funding.

However, to Henrietta, the new cooking method seemed more like a type of idea or realization.

If they let even a little bit of information slip, the sharp production guild leaders might pick up on the method, even without being told anything specific. In fact, there was no telling when someone from another guild might catch on, at least to some of it.

In light of these circumstances, Henrietta had chosen to use this "guidance" strategy. She'd use her negotiation partners' suspicions and rivalry to get them to say the words she wanted them to hear.

…She wouldn't lie. But, with this trick, Henrietta wouldn't let them reach the truth, either.

"What sort of support does your group need, Mari?"

Calasin's question was another assist Henrietta had foreseen. Without answering right away, she gazed into the eyes of the three men.

Making it seem as though she was having trouble making up her mind was another necessary part of negotiations.

Beside her, she knew her ally Marielle was spreading around that brilliant sunflower smile of hers. The three young men seemed to be looking at Marielle's and Henrietta's faces in turn.

Well, Mari's gorgeous. She really is. If only she weren't so very tall, she'd be just my type, and I'd take her home and hug her like a body pillow… Oh there, see? He's blushing. Master Calasin is sweet on Mari. How adorably innocent…

Actually, all three were looking at, then averting their glances from, both the sunny Marielle and the moonlike Henrietta, but Henrietta didn't notice the attention directed at herself.

Several moments after she'd organized what she needed to say, Henrietta opened her mouth.

"Before I tell you what we need, let me explain our system. Unless I clarify the forces we have lined up, you may not trust me. The director of this large-scale progressive operation is Master Shiroe."

Henrietta had taken a gamble.

This dialogue hadn't been part of her instructions from Shiroe, and she didn't have Marielle's permission. Henrietta didn't know how much significance Shiroe's name would have. She'd heard that he was a veteran player with a long career in the game and that he had some very unexpected acquaintances, but in that case, she didn't know why Shiroe was on friendly terms with a small guild like the Crescent Moon League or, for that matter, why he wasn't affiliated with a guild.

Henrietta had spoken with Shiroe personally, and she thought he was an extraordinary player. However, was that really all he was?

Henrietta had heard about the griffins from Serara. From what Henrietta knew, those were items that an ordinary veteran player shouldn't even have had access to.

"Machiavelli-with-glasses is running it?"

Although he'd muttered it in a very small voice, Michitaka had definitely said it.

"We've asked Master Naotsugu to hold the front line, Miss Akatsuki to act as the attacker, and Master Nyanta to be the point guard. Incompetent as we are, Marielle and I will form the rear guard. In addition to these, we intend to execute the operation with the Crescent Moon League members and other interested persons."

Henrietta let her words end there. Surreptitiously, she watched for Michitaka's reaction.

She was certain he'd responded to Shiroe's name and to a few of the others. However, he'd repressed the reaction, and she didn't know what it had meant. Yet even so, he had reacted. She was sure of it.

In other words, Master Shiroe really does have a chance at victory.

Shiroe's name had meant something.

"I've just given you an outline of our core members. We would like to request your support in order to make up the remaining shortfall. …That shortfall is capital. At present, we are in need of five million gold coins."

The three men sucked in their breath audibly.

It was an enormous sum indeed.

There had, of course, been previous quests whose accomplishment required money. It might have been bribes during a mission or payment for training. If one included quests whose missions required a certain item to accomplish—which meant that players needed money in order to purchase said item at the market—in a broad sense, "expenditures" were necessary in about a quarter of all quests.

However, five million gold coins was far too much. It would have been an unthinkable sum for any quest meant for individual players. …On the other hand, if this were a type of legend-class or wide-ranging quest, the amount wasn't impossibly large.

Taking into account the fact that they hadn't heard rumors of such a thing, was it a completely unknown quest? There was a good possibility that it was. It might be a brand-new quest, one introduced with the *Homesteading the Noosphere* expansion pack, a quest no one knew about. They didn't yet know exactly what sort of content *Homesteading* had included, but they'd heard reports that the current level-90 maximum was being raised, and that meant it might have been aimed at characters above level 90.

If it was a long quest, would it be the sort of large-scale quest in which a sequence of multiple quests formed a story? If that was the case, in long quests such as those, each time an individual quest ended, players could expect to gain a certain reward.

In long quests, it was normal for players to be given small rewards at each important point, to keep their motivation up.

…That was probably what was going through the three men's heads.

People tend to assume that information they want to believe is true. She'd heard this often from her stock-trader father. The three were gravitating toward the desire to believe in this tale of an absolutely unknown quest.

Henrietta asked Marielle to take out what they'd brought.

What she took out was black tea and custard pudding.

"Go ahead, help yourselves! That's our new offerin'. It's nice and sweet! It's made with Roc eggs."

Marielle urged the three men on with a cheerful smile. They were astonished, both by the delicious flavors and by what they'd just heard.

Rocs were monsters whose levels were 85 or higher. A recipe made with their eggs… That would be a completely unknown recipe, most certainly higher than level 90, wouldn't it?

"Of course, we aren't asking you to give us the money for free. After the completion of this large-scale operation, we are prepared to give detailed information regarding the operation to all three of you. We have also asked our Scribe to copy the cooking method we currently employ and the methods we have learned while making our attempt, and we intend to provide you with these as well."

To Henrietta and Marielle, the "operation" was a sort of neighborhood watch initiative with the goal of improving the atmosphere in Akiba. They didn't yet know the details about where it would touch down—Shiroe was keeping that part vague.

However, with an initiative like that one, there would be no detailed information to reveal. Once things were over, it would be—and would *have* to be—as clear as crystal. Shiroe himself had declared that politics conducted behind closed doors could not maintain any kind of public order. There would be no disadvantage to revealing information, and at that point in time, the value of that information would evaporate.

However, to the three production guild leaders, the story sounded completely different. If what the Crescent Moon League intended to challenge was an unknown long quest, everything about that quest—its starting point, its terms, the puzzles along the way—would be S-rank confidential information. Now, when they couldn't turn to solutions sites, it might well take them years to discover the same quest.

On top of that, Henrietta had clearly said, "The cooking method we currently employ and the methods we have learned while making our attempt." If it came with that sort of reward, the quest probably involved production. From the activities of Snack Shop Crescent Moon, it could only be a new—and groundbreaking—food item recipe. Even if it was only a reward for Chefs and had nothing to do with the other production classes, it would be invaluable.

The three of them had begun to believe the story they'd invented.

Henrietta was sure she'd made it over the pass.

That was how unprecedented these terms were. It would be strange for them *not* to accept.

If they did refuse, it would be because they doubted some aspect of the tale, but the three men were completely caught up in the story of the unknown quest they'd imagined.

It's about time I threw them a life vest...

"We're working with everything we have to raise funds. Including asset disposal and the Crescent Moon sales, we've managed to raise

500,000 gold coins. We still need 4.5 million. We thought that asking any one guild would drastically change the current balance. In that case, 1.5 million gold coins from each guild... How does that sound?"

In a single stroke, Henrietta cut the amount she was requesting by two-thirds.

In this world, a level-90 player could have anywhere from ten thousand to forty or fifty thousand gold coins on hand. In other words, those 1.5 million gold coins could be covered by contributions from about one hundred members.

If the Marine Organization, the largest of the three guilds, took up a collection from its 2,500 members, the contribution would only be six hundred gold coins per person.

Six hundred gold coins was no more than the cost of a suit of mid-range armor. It was only natural that the three players' expressions shifted into determination.

"The Roderick Trading Company will participate."

"Shopping District Eight is in as well."

"All right. The Marine Organization will set you up with capital. Heck, if you want, we'll fund the whole thing on our own."

"I'd have a problem with that. ...Are you planning to monopolize the profits?"

As the three began to argue, Marielle said, "Oh, now, don't be like that, y'all. Okay? C'mon. Play nice, for my sake."

At these words from Marielle, who'd smiled through the entire talk, the three had no choice but to back down. After all, the Crescent Moon League held the initiative in the discussion.

"In that case, we'll expect your payment in... Will four days be sufficient?"

"Fine. And when will you deliver the recipe?"

"It depends on our Scribe's schedule, but if possible, we'd like to give you the cooking method upon receipt of the funds. You'll have it by the day after at the very latest. The Scribe is Master Shiroe, you see."

With those parting words, the three left the rented room. After they'd gone, Marielle and Henrietta were exhausted. Henrietta had controlled the initiative and set the pace from beginning to end, but the pressure had been greater than she'd expected.

Although it hadn't taken long, she felt mentally fatigued. Her back seemed to have gone limp and weak; unable to sit up properly, she slumped forward onto the table.

"Sorry, Henrietta…"

Marielle seemed listless and apologetic.

"Whatever's the matter, Mari?"

Henrietta's well-bred speech had also grown rather careless.

"I wanted to help with the negotiatin', but there wasn't much I could do… Negotiatin's hard, isn't it…?"

Marielle sounded sincerely miserable. Even though Henrietta was completely worn out, she couldn't fight back a giggle.

"What are you saying, Mari? If you hadn't smiled like that, we wouldn't have had a chance in these negotiations."

The smile Henrietta gave Marielle was filled with deep gratitude. Without Marielle's beaming sunflower smile, they'd never have been able to separate those three veteran players from their money.

…And so Henrietta and Marielle acquired five million in campaign funds.

▶ **5**

It was a bright moonlit night.

A dry wind, still warm with the afternoon's heat, blew across a crumbling station platform over which lightning bugs flitted. It was a concrete plateau about two hundred meters in length, mounted on an elevated structure, and it commanded a view down over Akiba's central plaza.

In the real world, it had been a platform at Akihabara Station.

The rails and support posts had rusted away long ago, and it was covered with unidentifiable weeds and moss. The buildings to the right and left of the platform bore what could have been the scars of a great crash: They seemed to have been struck with terrific force partway up, and their tops were broken and jagged.

The moonlight threw the dark spearhead shadows of the buildings across the platform's marbled green and concrete surface, and in the midst of it all stood two tall shadows.

Shiroe and Nyanta.

"I think the wind's picked up a bit, don't mew?"

"Yes, it has."

Shiroe looked up at the moon, shading his eyes with one hand.

Possibly because the wind ruffled his hair, making a few strands catch on his eyelashes, he narrowed his eyes behind his glasses and spoke slowly.

"It's still a little while before midnight, I think… We've probably got a bit of time left before Soujirou comes. Captain Nyanta, do you want to sit down somewhere?"

"No, no. Thanks for meowr consideration, but I'm not quite such a run-down oldster."

"I didn't say it because I thought you were old." Shiroe shrugged.

"Are mew not looking forward to seeing Soujicchi, Shiroechi?"

"Um. Mm…"

The question made Shiroe think a bit.

"It's not that I don't want to see him. I just feel a little guilty. When Soujirou formed his guild, he invited me to join, so… It's awkward."

"He did, did he?"

"He didn't invite you, Captain Nyanta?"

"If memory serves, I wasn't logging in regularly back then. I don't remember getting an invitation."

"I see…"

They were waiting for Soujirou Seta.

He was an old friend of Nyanta, Shiroe, and Naotsugu.

He was also a Samurai and Master Swordsman, and one of the eight former Debauchery Tea Party members in this world.

In a way, Soujirou was one of the players who'd been most influenced by the Debauchery Tea Party. Not only was he hardworking and earnest, he was kind. When the Debauchery Tea Party had decided to disband, it might have been Soujirou who missed it most.

Samurai were skilled with a variety of Asian weapons, but the essence of these was the katana. The term *katana* covered many varieties: *Tachi*, the traditional longsword. *Kodachi*, smaller short swords. *Wakizashi*, or side swords, meant to be worn in pairs, and the main Samurai weapon—the *uchigatana*, or "striking sword." In *Elder Tales*, generally speaking, swords made of steel that emphasized superior attack power were called *tachi*, and lighter swords that emphasized speed and handling and were easy to swing were called *uchigatana*.

Soujirou was an *uchigatana* master.

His techniques, which hid their strikes in elegance instead of speed, were nearly impossible to follow, even if one strained their eyes. Soujirou could parry an attack from a giant who could snap great trees in two, and even Sand Cricket Armor, which could block an attack from an iron hammer, was useless against him.

"There's a knack to it, sir," Soujirou had said with a slightly bashful smile.

Naotsugu had left the game, and at the same time, due to a variety of personal circumstances, several of their other companions had left *Elder Tales* as well. By all accounts, Captain Nyanta had also nearly stopped playing for a while or had at least not logged in frequently.

In the midst of that, Soujirou had headed the list of members who had stayed in *Elder Tales*. "I don't want to let the Debauchery Tea Party go to waste," he'd said and started his own guild.

Of course, as a prerequisite, he'd invited the remaining members of the Debauchery Tea Party to join. However, the Tea Party hadn't been a guild, and many of the players who'd "belonged" to it had been free spirits.

There had been several players who'd joined Soujirou's guild, but several others had refused. Shiroe had been one of the latter.

"I don't think mew have anything to feel guilty about. Mew were following different paths. Soujicchi isn't the type of boy who'd be upset about something so trivial."

"That's true, but...," Shiroe said evasively.

His refusal to join the guild wasn't the only thing that was worrying him. The issue was *why* he'd refused.

Shiroe didn't think it was Soujirou that he'd turned down.

He'd refused to let himself be bound by a guild.

Yet now here he was, going all the way to Susukino to help the Crescent Moon League guild, then, becoming irritated by the growing silent power of the big guilds in Akiba, he was seeking out Soujirou's guild, the West Wind Brigade, for help to change the situation.

Simply time had passed, and Shiroe had changed with it.

He was already different from the Shiroe who'd been merely fastidi-
ous and prejudiced against the human relationships known as guilds.
However, he didn't think his current feelings would get across to
Soujirou if he only defined them in the negative, as "different."

In addition, he thought that Soujirou, who'd started his West Wind
Brigade immediately after losing the Debauchery Tea Party, might
have understood quite a lot more than Shiroe had.

The West Wind Brigade…

While not large, it was a guild with great influence in Akiba.
Although its official membership was 120, its active membership was
said to be sixty, and yet even with small numbers like that, it competed
on equal terms with D.D.D., Honesty, and the Knights of the Black
Sword, the famous guilds of Akiba.

While it could never have won on size, it had competed with the big
guilds to hold first place in large-scale battles that had gone down in
the server's history, such as Radamanteus's Throne and the Nine Great
Gaols of Helos.

In terms of military achievements, its record might be even more
splendid than those of the big guilds, which had hordes of reserve
members.

"Don't worry about it too much. Mew've decided to conquer, Shiroechi, so mew need to walk tall. Mew're already the landlord of my
veranda, mew know."

At Nyanta's words, Shiroe changed his mind. *Come to think of it, he's
right.*

Just as Soujirou had created a place for himself and defended it,
Shiroe had built a new place for himself. He couldn't afford to spend
forever worrying.

"Good evening. I haven't seen you in a while, Mr. Shiro. Sage Nyanta."

The approaching shape hailed the two of them while it was still a
good distance away. On seeing Soujirou's boyish expression, Shiroe
remembered, *Oh, that's right. He was younger than me, wasn't he?* It
had been almost a year since they'd spoken.

"It's been a long time, Soujirou."

"Long time no see. How have mew been, Soujicchi?"

At their greetings, Soujirou ducked his head, looking a bit embarrassed.

Smiling together like this made it feel as though they'd gone back in time.

Soujirou came over to them, lightly dodging the countless vines that hung down over the platform as he approached. The lightning bugs seemed to dance out of the way of his hands.

As Soujirou came closer, they saw he was dressed in Japanese *hakama* and had two swords hanging at his waist, like a patriot from the last days of the Tokugawa shogunate. Of course, in a full-scale battle, he'd probably wear armor; this was how he equipped himself when in town.

"I hear mew started a guild. How goes it?"

"I did; thank you for asking. It was going pretty well, but then the Catastrophe hit, so..."

Soujirou shrugged.

His expression made Shiroe realize something unexpectedly.

Now that he thought about it, he himself, Naotsugu, Nyanta, Soujirou—none of them seemed to be the least bit discouraged by the Catastrophe. This way of taking things as half sightseeing and half adventure, no matter how bad the circumstances were, might have been in the genetics of the Debauchery Tea Party.

"Are Nazunacchi and Mistress Saki still with mew?"

"Nazuna is. Saki's part of the guild, but... It looks as if she wasn't logged in at the time of the Catastrophe."

The names Nyanta had brought up belonged to skilled healers who had been part of the Debauchery Tea Party. The question reminded Shiroe of another reason he hadn't joined Soujirou's guild.

"Are you still as popular as ever, Soujirou?"

"Huh? Ah... It's not like that..."

Soujirou abruptly looked flustered. Nyanta narrowed his already threadlike eyes even further in a smile and asked, "Ah, youth. How many do mew have now?"

At his question, Soujirou quietly raised one hand and folded down just the thumb.

He still *has a harem...? Not that I'm jealous or anything, really... but. But. Four is incredibly hard to swallow...somehow. I mean,* four *of them? What's with that? Nazuna, Saki, and two others... Talk about a deluxe lineup...*

Shiroe felt his energy draining away.

"—But never mind that! What's going on, Mr. Shiro? I didn't expect you to summon me. I thought you didn't like me."

"Huh? Why?"

The unexpected words made Shiroe answer the question with a frank question of his own.

"Well, I... Um. Because I tend to attract harems."

Soujirou faltered, red-faced. Shiroe had no way to respond. Beside him, Nyanta burst into loud laughter. If Naotsugu had been there, he would have promptly delivered a physical comeback in the form of a karate chop.

"That's definitely a serious problem, but there's no way I'd hate you for it. We were in the Debauchery Tea Party together, remember?"

"I see. I suppose that's true... But then, what brings you here?"

At Soujirou's question, Shiroe straightened, psyching himself up again.

"I'll get straight to the point: I'd like your help."

"What sort of help might that be?"

"...What do mew think of the way Akiba is now, Soujicchi?"

"This town? That's a pretty abstract question... Well, I think it's painful in several ways. It isn't just this town. I mean, depending on how you look at it, this entire world is a prison, isn't it?"

"A prison, hm?"

Soujirou combed his hair up with his fingers. His Samurai-style ponytail fluttered in the wind that crossed the platform.

"Yes. We were abruptly pulled into another world. We don't know how to get back home. We can't die, either. That's simply how the world works, and on top of that, there are monsters prowling outside the town. Leaving us aside, I can understand how players who hate fighting would feel as if they've been locked in."

"That's right. Now that mew mention it, that's exactly right," Nyanta agreed.

Soujirou had taken a vague thought that was on everyone's mind and stated it clearly. Shiroe agreed: If one thought of it that way, it was only natural that they would feel trapped.

"So it is painful, you know. I don't think it's good. Under circumstances like these, people tend to resort to bullying the weak. As a matter of fact, my guild has been talking about leaving town."

"You're leaving Akiba?"

"No, I just meant the idea has come up," Soujirou said. "We haven't made specific plans or anything. Besides, it's convenient to be head-quartered in town. It's just that it's hard to watch things get worse and worse. Especially when there's nothing we can do about it."

"There's nothing we can do about it." He'd said the words easily, but it certainly wasn't because he'd relinquished responsibility. Soujirou had thought of doing something and had properly examined the possibilities. As a result, he'd concluded that there was nothing he could do, and he was saying so honestly. That was all.

As proof, his voice is bitter...

"There is something we can do."

"Do you mean that, Mr. Shiro?!"

"...I think there is."

Shiroe honestly avoided making a positive statement. He did want to do something, and he intended to try, but he had no guarantees. In any case, in Tea Party terms, anyone who refused to follow without a guarantee was a coward, not a friend.

That meant that if one wanted someone to be a friend, they didn't give them guarantees.

"In order to do it, I want your help."

"What would you like me to do?"

"...It isn't just you, Soujirou. I'll have to borrow the West Wind Brigade's name."

Shiroe stared Soujirou right in the eye.

If, as Nyanta had said, birth and death were constants for all things, and effort was necessary to ensure long life, then as the one who'd created and protected the West Wind Brigade, Soujirou had nourished it properly with love and paid for it through hard work. If he was going to borrow that strength, Shiroe couldn't avert his eyes.

And even more so, because he himself hadn't tried to cultivate anything.

Soujirou looked mildly startled, but then he nodded, seeming satisfied. Shiroe continued.

"First, I want you to talk to the people around you about how the current atmosphere in Akiba is bad. Tell them that if this keeps up, things will go to seed. If you'd let that travel to the other major guilds as well, I'd really appreciate it."

"Yes, that's fine. That's something everyone already feels, though, on some level."

"Still, I think it's important to put it into words. If you can make them aware that the West Wind Brigade thinks this and might even take action, it will have enough of an effect. Second, you should be getting an invitation in a few days. If possible, I'd like you to stay in Akiba until that day. It's an invitation to a conference. I'd like to settle things at that conference somehow."

"I understand."

Soujirou agreed easily with a nonchalant smile.

"You're sure you don't need to ask about the particulars of the operation?"

"Well, you're busy, aren't you, Mr. Shiro? I'd hate to take up your time with things like that. Besides, I'm a vanguard lunkhead, and you're the Tea Party's top strategy counselor. Even if you told me, I'm sure I wouldn't understand half of it."

The words were so warm that Shiroe flinched.

He'd never thought that Soujirou would trust him this much, after they'd been apart for over a year and after he'd shrugged his hand off once already.

"Mew're a good boy, Soujicchi."

"Only because you praise me for it, Sage Nyanta."

Soujirou smiled as he spoke. Then his expression tensed, and he looked at them both squarely.

"On a completely different note: Mr. Shiro, Sage Nyanta... Would you join the West Wind Brigade? It would make Nazuna happy, too, I think. We're all pretty good-natured. Right now we're taking turns exploring the outlying areas, working to uncover information about the new expansion pack. I know this may sound forward, but... That strategy you're putting into action, Mr. Shiro. Wouldn't it be more efficient if you worked under the auspices of the West Wind Brigade?— Or is that out of the question?"

Soujirou had straightened up, standing formally. His suggestion made sense, but Shiroe couldn't agree to it now. Last week, he might have been able to. At this point, though, Shiroe already had a home.

"You really do dislike me, then?"

Soujirou sounded dejected. Shiroe had shaken his head.

Even as he thought, *That's the second time I've turned down an invitation from Soujirou*, Shiroe touched his shoulder.

Nyanta's words had finally given Shiroe a clear picture of what it was he needed to do. It was what he'd kept his eyes turned away from.

By taking advantage of Naotsugu and Akatsuki's kindness and by letting Nyanta protect him, he'd managed to go without saying it until now.

"It really isn't that, Soujirou. …Listen. I realized it was about time I made a place for myself. I've been running away from tiresome things that happened years ago, and I ran all the way here, but I finally realized I need to be one of the people who protects things, too. I've formed my own guild. It doesn't have many members yet, and we've just barely begun, but… I finally realized that the place where I belong can't exist until I make a place for other people to belong."

As Soujirou gazed at him as though he were meeting him for the first time, Shiroe slowly told him about his resolution.

CHAPTER.

4

KNIGHTS OF CAMELOT

▶ NAME: HENRIETTA

▶ LEVEL: **90**

▶ RACE: **HUMAN**

▶ CLASS: **BARD**

▶ HP: **9696**

▶ MP: **9845**

▶ ITEM 1:

[POWDER SNOW BLOUSE]

AN ELEGANT, PURE WHITE BLOUSE WITH A SUMPTUOUS TEXTURE. IT PROTECTS AGAINST COLD, BUT SINCE IT HAS NO PHYSICAL DEFENSIVE POWER, IT'S USED AS NONCOMBAT EQUIPMENT. ALTHOUGH THE MATERIAL IS THIN, IT'S SURPRISINGLY WARM; HOWEVER, THAT ALSO MEANS IT'S EXPENSIVE. THE BUTTONS ARE CRAFTED FROM COCOA OPALS.

▶ ITEM 2:

[COMPOUND BOW]

A MIDSIZED BOW EQUIPPED WITH A PULLEY. THE STRUCTURES INSIDE THE BOW ARE RELATIVELY COMPLEX, WHICH RAISES THE BOW'S ACCURACY. THE BOW ITSELF IS A PRODUCTION-CLASS ITEM, BUT IT CAN USE EVERYTHING FROM MASS-PRODUCED ARROWS TO TREASURE-CLASS ARROWS AND IS VERY VERSATILE.

▶ ITEM 3:

[AKATSUKI DOLL]

A DOLL AKATSUKI HERSELF GAVE HENRIETTA TO ACT AS HER PROXY, IN ORDER TO ESCAPE HENRIETTA'S AFFECTIONS. IT ISN'T SUPPOSED TO HAVE ANY EFFECT, BUT AKATSUKI SOMETIMES GETS THE SHIVERS, AS THOUGH SOMEONE IS PETTING HER ALL OVER. ALTHOUGH HENRIETTA SAYS, "THE REAL ONE IS CUTER," SHE LIKES IT A LOT.

<Tea Set>
Famous designer brands,
including Arita and Imari.

Following the opening of Snack Shop Crescent Moon, the town of Akiba grew livelier.

Although it was just food and drink, it *was* food and drink.

Up until this point, the people of Akiba had eaten food that had absolutely no flavor, and these new delights captivated them in the blink of an eye. For the most part, Crescent Moon meals were takeout fare, and they certainly weren't lavish by the standards of the old world. In this other world, however, they were welcomed as the finest delicacies.

The original three-shop supply system wasn't able to keep up with demand, and a few days after the initial opening, a fourth shop opened. Slices of pizza—kept warm on an iron sheet heated by a Salamander that was conjured by one of the Crescent Moon League's Summoners— and custard pudding made with sweet cream had been added to the menu, and these proved wildly popular as well.

The citizens of Akiba had known from the very beginning that Snack Shop Crescent Moon was run by the Crescent Moon League, which was only a small guild. Some were critical of the fact that a minor guild was monopolizing the new recipes, but in the game world, justice was considered to be on the side of the one who achieved results fastest, and the criticisms were ignored.

As a practical problem, the Crescent Moon League received threatening letters telling them to publish the new recipes, but even the people in question knew they had no real grounds for complaint.

About the time the fourth shop opened, a rumor began to spread through town.

According to this rumor, the Crescent Moon League had joined forces with the three biggest production guilds in Akiba: the Marine Organization, the Roderick Trading Company, and Shopping District 8.

The total membership of these three big production guilds was over five thousand. This was nearly a third of the entire population of Akiba, and it made for an enormous force. In fact, as if to corroborate that rumor, transactions for some of the food items on the market had picked up, and Shopping District 8 seemed to be buying up materials.

Although there were now four shops and the new menu items had increased the rate of customer turnover, demand far outstripped the Crescent Moon's food supply. Even working together, it was all the shops could do to handle a bit less than 1,500 customers per day.

Most of the people in Akiba had experienced the flavor of Crescent Moon's delicious take-out hamburgers, and those who had wanted to repeat the experience. Now that they'd been reminded of the flavors they'd been used to in the old world, it was agony to return to a life of sodden, flavorless space food.

It grew common for lines to begin forming at the Crescent Moon shops before dawn, and the shops started handing out numbered tickets to customers.

This completely unexpected Crescent Moon boom had influenced several things for the better.

First, Crescent Moon food was rather expensive. The cost of one meal was between three and six times the cost of a meal purchased at the market. Of course, there was no entertainment or anything else on which to spend money in Akiba, and very few users hesitated over spending an amount like that. However, although they didn't hesitate, they needed to have the money to spend.

Eating Crescent Moon hamburgers three meals a day, every day (if any player was lucky enough to be able to buy that much!), would cost 1,350 gold coins a month.

Since it had hardly cost anything at all to live in Akiba up until now, there had been players who'd sat huddled in the ruins day after day, lost in the sorrow of being unable to return to the old world. The fact that even *they* now felt like earning a few coins was a huge change.

For the first time in a very long while, public recruiting began in Akiba's central plaza. This was a method of recruiting in which participants gathered and looked for companions to join them on temporary hunting expeditions, and it had nothing to do with any guild. This type of recruiting was rare in this other world, and it drew lots of attention in the plaza.

When it was time for the parties to depart, all the clerks of the Crescent Moon shop located in the plaza waved and loudly chorused, "Have a good trip!"

This probably had at least a little to do with the fact that the members of those temporary parties had bought canteens of Black Rose Tea before they left.

Still, it was an odd, heartwarming sight, unlike anything witnessed in the era of the *Elder Tales* game. As they left Akiba, the members of the temporary parties had tickled, flattered smiles on their faces.

In addition to that sort of individual economic activity, there were market trends as well. The prices of several food items, such as young venison, potatoes, and ptarmigan meat, had begun to rise.

This was the result of careful buying up on the part of Shopping District 8, but there were always people who were sensitive to the rise in prices and would respond by attempting to fill the demand. Several guilds that had picked up on this information organized voluntary material procurement teams and began to put items on the market. No doubt they predicted that prices would rise and envisioned vast profits. However, Calasin of Shopping District 8 had already anticipated this situation, and at an earlier stage, he'd directly approached several dozen small adventuring guilds of his acquaintance and proposed a large-scale expedition team organization.

Schedules for hunts that spanned several days were put together, and alternate members were found and dispatched. The guilds organized teams to hunt on location and other teams to bring the spoils back to town, creating a system in which the production guilds supported the material supply line on their own.

This was the first time—not only since the Catastrophe, but in the history of *Elder Tales*—that a production guild had established a direct support system for a combat guild. The method proved successful, and Shopping District 8 managed to obtain vast quantities of materials at a set price without leaning too heavily on the market.

When players who had never left the town began to go out on excursions, it triggered varied consumption activity regarding expendables and repairs, and this in turn increased the opportunities for artisans to work. Although the transformation was still subtle, little by little, the town of Akiba was changing.

Was Snack Shop Crescent Moon the source of these changes?

If the Crescent Moon League had completely joined forces with Akiba's three largest production guilds, the group would have encompassed one-sixth of all the players on the Japanese server. It would have meant the birth of the largest force on the Japanese server at the very least. Recently, there had been many inquiries from other cities via telechat regarding the Crescent Moon League. There was also no end to the players who hoped to join the guild, but Marielle kept turning them down, telling them, "Hang on till the end of the month, 'kay?"

Even the members of the combat guilds, which ordinarily didn't interfere with the production guilds and seemed to inhabit a completely different world, were taking an interest in the situation.

In this world—which had no Internet or WebTV and was, in other words, almost completely without entertainment—rumors provided a lot of the fun.

The citizens of Akiba gathered here and there, tirelessly discussing their predictions and guesses. Mentioned in these rumors were the names of Marielle, the cheerful, caring guild master of the Crescent Moon League; of Henrietta, who was rumored to be quite accomplished; and of Shouryuu, the young combat team leader. However, at the same time, some of the veteran players and people who were well-informed about the situation whispered Shiroe, Naotsugu, and Nyanta's names, and that of the Debauchery Tea Party, as if they'd just remembered them.

That said, almost no one realized that the players—the Adventurers—weren't the only ones discussing the rumors.

▶ 2

Ten days had passed.

Snack Shop Crescent Moon, which had more business than it could handle every day, was already an established part of the town, and its endless lines were a local attraction. Even today, in the clear summer weather, the four shops were doubtless serving their jostling hordes of customers as fast as they could.

However, this was a wide space far from that tumult.

It was the enormous conference room on the top floor of the guild center, the building that was the cornerstone of Akiba.

The conference room was open to any Adventurer who used the guild center. However, in a world with no electricity, elevators were nothing more than iron boxes, and very few people were eccentric enough to climb sixteen ruined floors' worth of stairs.

In the center of this vast, high-ceilinged space sat a large round table. The individuals seated around it could have been said to represent Akiba.

"Black Sword" Isaac, the leader of the Knights of the Black Sword.
Ains, the guild master of Honesty.
"Berserker" Crusty, D.D.D.'s commander.
William, the young leader of Silver Sword.
Soujirou, the harem-prone guild master of the West Wind Brigade.
Michitaka, the iron-armed general manager of the Marine Organization.
Roderick, the guild master of the Roderick Trading Company.
Calasin, leader of Shopping District 8.
Marielle of the Crescent Moon League.
Woodstock of Grandale, Animal Trainer.
Akaneya, the shrewd Mechanist of RADIO Market.
...And Shiroe, who wore the guild tag "Log Horizon."

Since many of the twelve who sat at the round table had several close associates standing behind them, there were nearly thirty players in this vast space.

The members of the gathering wore a variety of expressions. Some were uneasy, some suspicious, some expressionless, and some seemed self-confident. All had been summoned to this gathering by an invitation that had arrived the previous evening.

The title of the invitation had been "Re: The Town of Akiba."

It had been sent jointly by Shiroe of Log Horizon and Marielle of the Crescent Moon League.

Almost all the assembled members were in charge of huge guilds. The Marine Organization, the Roderick Trading Company, and Shopping District 8 were all major production guilds. The Knights of the Black Sword, Honesty, D.D.D., Silver Sword, and the West Wind Brigade—all combat guilds—were either large or had a track record of impressive achievements. The Crescent Moon League, Grandale, and RADIO Market were small, but they had been central to the attempted former liaison committee for small and midsized guilds, an alliance that had failed.

Only one guild, Log Horizon, was unfamiliar to everyone present. No one had even heard of it.

However, guilds as large as the ones assembled here had their own diverse ways of gathering information, and less than a quarter of the members looked puzzled by Shiroe's presence.

As the seated players eyed one another, sizing each other up, Serara of the Crescent Moon League appeared and served them chilled fruit tea. This wasn't a beverage that Snack Shop Crescent Moon sold, and a few of the members looked a bit startled, but the silence continued, seeming to swallow up that slight confusion.

Shiroe sat quietly.

It didn't mean he felt calm.

To Shiroe, this conference was a battlefield.

It was a battlefield of clashing swords and flames, no less than any of the large-scale battles he'd taken part in before. Shiroe felt simultaneously hot, as though he was delirious with fever, and cold with nervous tension, but he bore them both. Almost all the players gathered here were enemies from whom he'd have to extract compromises.

The remaining few were allies who were counting on him. He couldn't let either camp realize how hard-pressed he felt.

I chose to start this war, after all.

As Soujirou had said, this world was a prison. Everyone in it was spellbound by the curse of struggling to survive. The despair of having no way to get home. The monster-haunted wilderness. The shackles of apathy.

Shiroe himself had spent the days since the Catastrophe being hounded by the situation. He'd responded to the circumstances in front of him, gotten his plans in order, and lived with the sole purpose of increasing his chances of survival.

However, this operation was different. Saving Touya, saving Minori, bringing some sort of order to Akiba... Ultimately, these were all self-indulgence on Shiroe's part. He wanted them, and he intended to get them, even if it meant starting an unnecessary war. That was all.

He did think there were merits, of course. He believed there would be not only for him, but also for the people important to him and for Akiba.

However, that didn't change the fact that this had its beginnings in what was essentially selfishness.

In that sense, Shiroe had gained the first freedom he'd had since the Catastrophe. This war had begun with his self-indulgence; he'd started it in order to make his own wish come true, and he was going to fight it with everything he had. Although this did make him feel very tense and put him under enough pressure to make him cringe, at the same time, it gave him fierce joy.

"Shiroechi? Are mew all right?"

Nyanta, who was standing behind and to his right, spoke to him. At this point, he could accept those words honestly. Nyanta wore the guild tag "Log Horizon" now, as did Naotsugu and Akatsuki, who weren't at the meeting. They were going into this first battle as a guild of four, and although they might be on duty at different posts, they were on the same battlefield.

Bring my friends victory.

That was Shiroe's fervent wish.

At last all the participants were seated, and the tension in the room built.

Shiroe stood and delivered the opening remarks.

"Thank you for taking time out of your busy schedules to attend this conference. I'm Shiroe of Log Horizon. ...I've invited you here today to discuss a certain matter with you and to ask a favor. It's a rather complicated matter, and it will probably take some time, but please bear with me."

Shiroe paused, looking around the room.

...Well, at any rate, they all came. That's good. It's probably because Soujirou laid the groundwork, but even so. That saves me the trouble of going around and persuading each of them individually. ...Although it also makes this conference that much more of a decisive battle.

"You can keep the pleasantries brief, Shiroe of Debauchery. It's not like we don't know each other."

It was "Black Sword" Isaac who'd raised his voice. He was a seasoned soldier and one of the leading high-level players on the Japanese server. He was a true warrior who'd led the charge in countless large-scale battles. Shiroe had been invited to several of these battles as support. Enchanter was a bottom-of-the-barrel class, and he'd assumed Isaac wouldn't remember a player like that, but apparently he'd been wrong.

"What's going on here anyway?"

The irritated voice belonged to William, the young leader of Silver Sword. The youth's flowing silver hair was tied back, and he looked like a typical elf lord. He seemed to be a very impatient type: He kept crossing and uncrossing his legs.

"As you say. I'll get right down to business, then. The matter I would like to discuss—*propose* may be a better word—has to do with current conditions in Akiba. As you know, since the Catastrophe, we've been stranded in this other world. We have absolutely no idea about how to get back to our old world. To the best of my knowledge, we don't even have a clue. This is incredibly painful, but it's a fact. Meanwhile, under these circumstances, Akiba's atmosphere is souring. Many of our companions have lost their motivation, while others have grown desperate. The economy is in tatters, and our exploration rate is stagnant. I'd like us to do something about the situation. That is why I've called you here."

Shiroe spoke with his eyes half-closed.

He was fine. He'd gone over the words he needed to say in his mind, again and again, until they seemed so real he could practically feel them.

"What are you planning to do by getting us all together?"

"Pain in the butt…"

"Why does stuff like this have to be said now?"

"I know what you're trying to say, but what on earth can we do?"

As if to quell the murmurs that rose here and there, Ains, the young guild master of Honesty, asked a question.

"Will this be something like the earlier alliance of smaller guilds?"

"Similar. However, I hear that did fail."

Shiroe glanced at the guilds in question, Grandale and RADIO Market. The two representatives went pale and nodded. These guilds—and actually, the Crescent Moon League as well—were far too small to be at this conference. In terms of numbers, several of the groups here were over fifty times larger.

"True, that plan did collapse. However, I think it was because it had several unreasonable aspects. The plan at the time was for the small and midsized guilds to band together and oppose the big guilds. …In other words, the small guilds would come together and fight to protect their own interests. Our plan failed."

Akaneya, guild master of RADIO Market, was also a master-class Mechanist, a subclass that created mechanical clocks and devices. Marielle picked up where he'd left off, supplementing his words.

"That's right. We said we'd cooperate, but we ended up just chasin' after our own guilds' interests…which meant we couldn't agree, which meant things broke down."

"Are you planning to speak to every force—or at least, all the leading forces in Akiba—and coordinate their interests this time?"

"…They couldn't even bring the small guilds together. With the big guilds' egos involved, it'll never work. This is insane!"

The members began to react to Marielle's words.

Marielle's name—in other words, the Crescent Moon League's name—had been on the invitation as well. As a result, the participants had probably thought, in the backs of their minds, *Is the real purpose of this conference to continue the small guild alliance that failed?*

That's a natural assumption…

However, even if his name was familiar to a certain set of people, it would have been difficult for Shiroe to convene the conference on the strength of his name alone.

Marielle's name value and the Crescent Moon League, alias "Snack Shop Crescent Moon"—the notoriety of those two names had carried him to the beginning of the conference. However, he'd need to clear up that misunderstanding as soon as possible.

"My purpose this time is a bit different. I want to improve current conditions in Akiba."

The sound of a chair scraping back interrupted Shiroe's clear words.

"In that case, count us out."

The player who'd stood was the one who'd been fidgeting irritably, William of Silver Sword. He adjusted the saber at his waist and tossed back his mantle.

"We're a fighting guild. The atmosphere in town is no concern of ours. We just come back here to exchange items. In other words, it doesn't matter to us whether the atmosphere gets better or worse. The lot that cares about the town should carry on here. I'm not saying discussing it is a bad idea, although I do think it's a waste of time. We just aren't interested, that's all. Leave us out of it."

Flinging that remark over his shoulder, William left the conference room.

The room began to buzz.

The people in charge of Grandale, RADIO Market, and the Crescent Moon League looked particularly pale. Shiroe had heard that in the last days of the small guild alliance, members had dropped out this way one after another.

However, Shiroe, who was steering the discussion, had anticipated developments like this one.

Silver Sword is out, then…

Shiroe analyzed the fact's influence on the tide of battle, updating a mental scorecard.

Silver Sword certainly was a large combat guild, but it wasn't vital to this conference. If the biggest fighting guild (D.D.D.) or the biggest production guild (the Marine Organization) made a motion to leave, he'd do something to stop them, but he'd assumed from the beginning that one or two guilds would storm out.

More importantly, the departure of William and his group had unsettled the atmosphere at the conference, and he had to do something about that.

"There are eleven of us now, but I'll continue. The reason I've called you here, as Silver Sword said a moment ago, is to advocate for the formation of an organization to discuss the self-government issues in Akiba: the 'Round Table Council.' Roughly speaking, there are two pressing objectives. First, to improve the atmosphere in Akiba. More specifically, to set it on a track toward revitalization. Second, to improve public order. For now, I will focus on these two points, with the ultimate goal being an organization which will be able to resolve issues with Akiba's self-government."

The assembly answered him with silence.

It was the type of stillness that occurred because participants were gauging one another's responses.

Now it really begins.

In the awareness that he was finally standing at the starting line, Shiroe examined the expressions of those around him.

True, the players gathered here could influence about 80 percent of the population of Akiba. The membership of the assembled guilds alone was more than six thousand. That was 40 percent of the players living in Akiba.

On top of that, guilds this large had friendly ties with many other guilds, as well as numerous quasi-subordinate guilds. Arranging for materials and going hunting with other guilds also gave them wide-ranging horizontal connections.

The players assembled here held great influence over all the Adventurers in Akiba. Consensus at this conference would be nearly equivalent to consensus among everyone living in Akiba. Of course, Shiroe had chosen which guilds to invite to the conference with this result in mind.

However, in equal measure, it would be incredibly difficult to get guilds this enormous to come to an agreement. It would be many times harder than crushing a single guild. Shiroe had been fully aware of that going in.

"Before that, could we hear your criteria for member selection?"

It was Ains who first broke the silence. The guild master of the major combat guild Honesty, he spoke in a calm voice that meshed with his middle-aged appearance.

"Of course. First, I chose the Knights of the Black Sword, Honesty, D.D.D., and the West Wind Brigade because they are large-scale combat guilds or because they have achieved great things. Silver Sword, which has bowed out, was selected for that reason as well. The Marine Organization, the Roderick Trading Company, and Shopping District Eight were invited to represent the production guilds, as they are the three largest. The Crescent Moon League, Grandale, and RADIO Market were called as representatives of the smaller guilds. So that there will be no misunderstandings, I would like to make one thing perfectly clear with regard to these last three: These three guilds were selected in order to incorporate the opinions of players unaffiliated with a guild and of smaller guilds, which I was unable to invite to join us, rather than as single guilds in their own right. Just because a guild is small, that doesn't mean we should ignore the weight of what they have to say. In addition, if this council is formed, I will probably request that they perform these tasks."

He'd anticipated some backlash from having invited three smaller guilds to participate, but the assembly accepted it more calmly than he'd expected.

It was true that, in all, over six thousand players were affiliated with the major guilds he'd summoned. However, conversely, that meant that the number of other players in Akiba—in other words, the unaffiliated players and the members of small and midsized guilds—was close to nine thousand. They seemed to have accepted that the smaller guilds had been invited to represent these players.

Of course, Shiroe observed, there was a large possibility that they'd let it slide because they assumed there would be no council.

"And you?"

The taciturn question came from "Berserker" Crusty, the leader of D.D.D. Belying his name, he was a dandy who wore glasses.

"I'm attending as organizer and as the one who came up with the idea," Shiroe said firmly.

He was hosting a conference regarding Akiba's self-government. If the qualifications to participate in that conference were guild size or fame, then Shiroe himself technically wasn't qualified to be there.

If the guild master of a guild formed just the week before—a guild with only four members, so tiny one hesitated even to call it "small"—began to talk about the future of Akiba, no one would listen.

Even from the perspective of the criteria Shiroe himself had used to select the guilds, he would have been out.

Still, that's neither here nor there.

Was he qualified to participate? No, probably not. Well, then, had the big guilds that *were* qualified made the town any better? Had they done anything for the whole community since the Catastrophe? No, they hadn't.

They've already demonstrated that things won't go the way I want if I just sit around and wait. …Sure, it's arrogant. I'm just indulging myself. I won't stand on ceremony anymore. I won't hold anything back. I'll do what I want to do. And in order to do it, I'll lay groundwork, and I'll even convene a conference.

"Hm… In other words, you sponsored this conference and sent out invitations just to qualify yourself to participate?"

Crusty's question was grounded in an accurate perception of Shiroe's intent. Since that was so, Shiroe held his head high and answered, "Yes, that's correct."

"Say that council is formed. How exactly would you maintain public order? And actually, in this case, what deterioration in public order are we talking about specifically?"

At "Black Sword" Isaac's question, Shiroe braced himself.

"I believe it's common knowledge that a few guilds are keeping newbies under what amounts to house arrest on the pretext of protecting them. That isn't a healthy situation."

Directly confronted by these words, "Black Sword" Isaac flinched.

"…You mean the EXP Pots, right? But you couldn't call that illegal…"

EXP Pots. The room buzzed at the abrupt mention of that noun. More than half the reactions were something along the lines of "Ah, I thought that would come up." No doubt it was a fact that, questions of legality aside, the others had also felt vaguely guilty, at least to some extent.

"Right now, no law exists for the players. Saying that no law has been broken when 'law' doesn't even exist is mere sophistry. I'm certain everyone here is aware of that."

Isaac's expression was grim. Shiroe continued.

"This is about more than EXP Pots. The problem lies in the fact that we, the players, have no law. As things stand, anyone can do anything at all, no matter how reckless. Even so, there's almost no disadvantage to us, provided we're the only ones we care about."

"Now *that's* an exaggeration. We have law. Any player who fights in a noncombat zone pays with their life."

"That's a result. It isn't law. It happens because of a simple principle. …Let me put it more clearly: The act of fighting in a noncombat zone is the cause, and it carries the effect of an attack from the guards. That's all. You can't even call that a rule. It's just a phenomenon. It isn't something we approved. It wasn't even created. How could something like that be law?"

At Shiroe's words, Isaac shut his mouth.

The Knights of the Black Sword was one of the major fighting guilds rumored to be buying EXP Pots. His obstinate arguments were probably intended to cover up his own feelings of guilt. However, the arguments were an obstacle on Shiroe's road to victory, and Shiroe cut them down with all his might.

"For example, I visited the town of Susukino the other day. In Susukino, a guild called the Briganteers had gone into business kidnapping young female NPCs and selling them to players as slaves."

The conference attendees turned shocked faces to Shiroe.

"In terms of the conversation we've been having, since they weren't attacked by the guards for it, it wasn't 'illegal.' But is that what law is? In this world, it could be. At the very least, the specs make it possible. If asked to say whether it's possible or impossible, it is possible. But that isn't what law is. The question I want to ask you is, 'Are we going to let that be a possibility with regard to ourselves?' Isn't that fundamentally what law is? It's the question of where we put the rules by which we ourselves are governed."

There were any number of possible excuses.

For example, the newbies were being penned up for their own protection. The EXP Pots were being confiscated to supplement the newbies' living expenses, which they couldn't completely cover due to their poor combat abilities.

With regard to the NPCs, it could be argued that they were just

AI-powered dolls and so had no human rights. At the very least, one couldn't prove that they *weren't* AI-powered dolls and *did* have human rights. At any rate, real-world history showed that human rights were something that generally had to be won, instead of proven.

For that reason, Shiroe's tactical objective wasn't to take down these excuses one by one. At the very least, his short-term objective was to make everyone present admit that it was necessary to govern themselves in this lawless other world.

In reaction to the question Shiroe had tossed at them, some of the conference participants shut their mouths, and others loudly voiced their opinions. It wasn't just the formal members, either. Their staff members also joined in, and tumult filled the conference room.

The responses seemed to be roughly split into two camps.

One held the opinion that it was indeed necessary to make rules of some sort.

The other held the view that that sort of consensus building would be impossible.

"Silver Sword said they wouldn't participate in the conference and left, but they seem to have approved of the conference continuing. Suppose a force that doesn't approve of the council's very existence appears in Akiba. In other words, a force that defies the council's aims. What will you do?"

Crusty directed his question at Shiroe. The question was as calm and to the point as ever, but he asked it as if he was voicing the second of the two views.

"Fight. Specifically, I'll exile them from Akiba. Even if they manage to infiltrate, they'll have a very difficult time doing anything. Of course, the option of forcing them to disband is also on my radar."

Shiroe's answer raised a great clamor, mostly from the combat guilds.

It was the same sort of startled cry that Marielle, Henrietta, and Shouryuu had given in the Crescent Moon League conference room two weeks earlier.

"Disband a guild," "exile a guild"... These were easy things to say, but nearly impossible to accomplish. In this world, even death wasn't much of a deterrent. After all, resurrection existed. With death no deterrent, being arrested lost much of its effectiveness. For example, if a player was arrested and detained, ultimately they could escape by committing suicide.

Under circumstances like these, it was incredibly difficult to do any lethal damage to guilds.

However, the baffled silence wasn't rooted in a feeling of faltering helplessness, as the Crescent Moon League's had been: The conference room held top players with influence over nearly 80 percent of the population of Akiba.

There were many things that, while impossible for the Crescent Moon League, would be possible if the members of this conference agreed to them. For example, they could set guards on all of Akiba's gates, and if a player who had a warrant on them tried to enter, they could obliterate them with a PK. The production guilds could also refuse to sell articles of any kind to a wanted player.

Of course, such a move would take massive amounts of time and money. Even so, it would be possible to exert material and immaterial pressure that way.

"You couldn't do something like that without the help of combat guilds like mine, though."

"Black Sword" Isaac tossed those words at Shiroe. He'd regained his composure.

"And anyway, if there were, say, ten or twenty people, it could work. We could punish 'em that way. But if a guild like the ones gathered here didn't go along with the council, ignored its decisions, flipped the bird at the law… If one started talking like that, we'd have a war on our hands. Even if the council got off the ground, there's no guarantee we'd reach an agreement on every single matter. Heck, under those circumstances, *could* we reach an agreement? If we try to forge an agreement between opposing views but end up with a war instead, there's no sense in having a council."

Isaac had a very good point.

The assembled players began to mutter their agreement, and the murmur spread.

For example, his Knights of the Black Sword had 190 members. If that many level-90 members rose up in revolt, it would be hard to oppose them practically. Since the town was a noncombat zone, they'd have to arrest or PK them in other zones, and even if they succeeded there, it wouldn't do any decisive damage to the guild.

For a guild with more than a certain number of members, refusal to do business and other types of economic pressure wouldn't have much effect: Guilds of that size could fill most types of internal demand through members who held production subclasses.

Of course, it depended on the level and ratio of subclass holders, but fifty of them would probably be able to create a self-contained system.

Based on these facts, even if the council Shiroe proposed were established, it was very likely that matters the big guilds were opposed to would be unable to get the council's support. In other words, the big guilds would have veto power, which meant that conditions would be exactly the same as they were at present.

Shiroe lowered his gaze and adjusted his glasses.

All developments up to this point have been about what I expected. Certainly, under normal circumstances, if we established a council, infighting is probably the best we could manage. ...But this time, I can't settle for that.

"I'm afraid I have to admit this doesn't feel plausible. Don't you agree?" Crusty asked.

His profile was as delicate and graceful as ever. It was a bit hard to believe that a man who looked so much like an intellectual was feared as a Berserker, but it was a fact. As proof, he continued to deliver relentless words in a calm voice.

"I do think there is meaning in establishing that council. However, it would be...no more than a type of posturing. I can't imagine it would have any real power to restrain."

At that remark, Shiroe quietly raised one hand.

As if his gesture had captured their attention, all eyes went to him. A momentary silence fell in the conference room.

"Today...about four hours ago now, I purchased the guild center."

A stunned atmosphere hung over the members.

Every one of them needed time for the meaning of those words to sink in.

"Naturally, I hold the right to change the zone settings, including entry and exit permissions. In other words, anyone I blacklist will be unable to use the guild center. That is to say, they will be unable to use the guildhalls, or the banking facilities, or the safe-deposit boxes."

As everyone stared at Shiroe with odd expressions, as though they'd gotten something stuck in their throats, Henrietta sighed deeply. In this vast conference room, she alone had seen through Shiroe's scheme. At her sigh, Shiroe gave a wry, fleeting smile.

"There, what did I tell you? He's pitch-black."

Henrietta's murmur was simultaneously appalled and filled with pity. Beside her, Marielle, who'd been watching the conference with bated breath, nodded.

Shiroe's words had rung out like a death sentence.

▶ **3**

In the morning, when she woke up, she washed her face in water from the trough.

The crude trough was really meant to be used in a stable as a manger. She washed her face in the cold water that filled the dingy trough, then dragged her dirty mantle around her shoulders.

This was one of the rooms set aside as a group sleeping area for newbies at the Hamelin guildhall. It held shabby furnishings and the bare minimum of facilities required for day-to-day life.

I have to get to the kitchen...

Morning preparations were always hectic. Each of them began to work according to the roles they'd been forced into. Minori's job was to serve breakfast, and she had to go to the kitchen to pick up the meal.

Please let me get through the whole day without any trouble, Minori prayed.

Today was a special day.

Minori dressed hastily and headed for the kitchen.

A player with Chef skills who'd woken early would be there, making black bread. Minori didn't consider this a poor meal. In this world, even the most luxurious food tasted the same, which meant that, conversely, even this meal of black bread and water could be called a feast. …She'd been telling herself so for the past two months.

Minori greeted the Chef girl in a small voice, then hastily dragged out a large tray. In addition to the Chef, who was also a newbie, the kitchen held an executive member on guard. Doing her best not to meet his eyes, Minori hurriedly began to fill a pitcher with well water.

There was enough for thirty-five people in all. She set the water and the black bread on a big wooden tray.

"Hold up."

At the man's voice, Minori shrank back reflexively.

She felt a nasty, greasy sweat break out on her palms.

Why?! …I'm not doing anything. I'm behaving the way I always do, so why…?

She *had* to act normally, no matter what, but apparently she'd already tripped up, first thing in the morning.

"Y-yes, sir?"

She squeezed out a response, thinking even as she spoke that her voice was so faint it might as well have been a mosquito's whine.

"Hah! That's one gloomy face. …Well? Can't you even greet folks properly?"

The guard snorted as if she bored him, then criticized her.

Holding herself in check, Minori greeted him.

"Of course. Good morning, sir."

"Whatever. …You're a Tailor, right? How high?"

"I'm level thirty-two now."

"You can sew rank-thirty leather armor, then. Boost your skills with leather aprons and leather gloves today."

"Yes, sir."

Bobbing her head to him again and again, she left the kitchen. Minori's heart was pounding so fiercely she thought it might break.

Since that night, Shiroe had contacted her several times.

It was always after sunset, when the guild had gone to bed.

She'd wrap herself up in her mantle on the cold concrete floor, holding her breath, and then a bell only she could hear would sound in her ear. That was the signal that Shiroe was requesting a telechat.

Of course, she couldn't have much of a conversation in the silent Hamelin bedroom late at night. Mostly she gave small coughs or sent little signals by knocking on the floor lightly. When there was no guard, she said two or three words. She had to keep her voice very small, so he wouldn't notice how pitiful and tear-filled it was.

Most of the things Shiroe contacted her about were trivial.

Once a day or once every two days. The telechats were short, too—about ten minutes.

They talked about things like where he'd gone today or whom he'd met.

Apparently Shiroe had companions now: A Guardian named Naotsugu who cracked weird jokes constantly but was reliable. A lady Assassin named Akatsuki who was small and sharp-tongued. Then there was Nyanta, an elderly Swashbuckler that Shiroe called "Captain." She also heard names from the Crescent Moon League: Marielle, Henrietta, and Shouryuu.

Shiroe told her about the things he'd done and the things he was doing. In exaggerated terms, it was the world he saw.

Shiroe and I are in the same world. …It's the same world, but to me, it looks so tired and dingy… Shiroe says it's wide and pretty…

That was painful to Minori.

She didn't think it was unfair. She was sure that if the world looked this shabby to her, it was because her eyes and soul were clouded.

Shiroe was surrounded by cheerful, fun, kind people, but she wasn't. She knew she envied him that. Shiroe's world was bright and warm, and her own was dingy and cold. It seemed to her that, in other words, the grime inside her heart was seeping out into her surroundings and that hurt her.

Shiroe told her things, bit by bit.

That he'd never settled down in any guild before.

That he'd traveled around providing support, like a mercenary.

That he'd destroyed everything he built and had never tried to help it grow. That even so, he'd finally decided to make a place for himself to belong. That even now, he was a little afraid of working with others, of asking for things, of issuing invitations.

To Minori, these were just groundless fears on Shiroe's part. Needless worry.

After all, he'd been kind to Minori and Touya. Maybe to Shiroe that kindness had been too small to count for much, but it was still saving her and Touya, even now.

The world Shiroe lived in was a world he'd won for himself. If she didn't have the world Shiroe did, it was because she hadn't been able to win it.

Minori thought she'd probably lost it during those few days after the Catastrophe.

I spent those days after the Catastrophe crying because I wanted somebody to save me. That's why I lost it...

That thought was accompanied by bitter pain. Minori had joined Hamelin for the same reason: She'd wanted someone to save her, hadn't felt like saving herself. She'd lost it because she'd foolishly thought that someone would rescue her. She and Shiroe had been given the same chance. It was just that Shiroe had made good on that chance, and she hadn't.

In that sense, then, the situation wasn't unfair.

If the shining things that surrounded Shiroe didn't surround her, it was in no way Shiroe's fault.

Besides, if I thought like that, this time I'd really... I'd be too worthless to even talk with him.

If Shiroe had begun working to secure a place for himself now, even she ought to be able to do that... She might have lost all her property, but as a newbie player, she'd barely had anything to begin with.

She had Touya. She still had her precious family.

No matter how lonely or scared it made them, they could leave the town and live in hiding, in the shadows of the ruins. If they'd only managed to steel themselves for that in the days after the Catastrophe, they never would have found themselves in a situation like this.

She rallied her feelings by main force and started for the living room, where the other beginners would be waiting.

Shiroe really did seem to be working to rescue Minori and Touya. Not only that, but from the odd word here and there, she'd sensed that he was working not just to rescue Minori, but to free all the newbie players who belonged to Hamelin.

Shiroe is an amazing person. …He's calm and collected, and mature, and cool, and he knows everything, and he's tall, and he's kind…

Noticing that her thoughts were tending to fall into a loop, Minori's cheeks grew hot.

Someone like that was trying to save her.

Shiroe still thought Minori was an acquaintance worth helping.

Of course Minori herself couldn't believe she was worth anything of the sort. She thought Shiroe's kindness had probably made him feel responsible for the two of them, even though they'd only played together for a little while.

But Touya was different. Touya had muttered, "He's really awesome." Then, after falling silent for a very long time, he'd continued, "…Wonder if I could be like that."

Minori was really proud of her little brother.

If Touya was thinking that way, Minori had to, too. In the future, she would have to prove to Shiroe that he hadn't been wrong to save them. If she didn't, she'd lose the right to accept Shiroe's calls now.

For that to happen, she couldn't let herself think underhanded things like, *It's not fair.*

She could be jealous. She could also let that envy make her suffer.

If that pain became the strength she needed to move forward, Minori thought, she'd welcome it. However, she didn't have time to waste on pessimistic feelings like "It's not fair."

After handing out bread to the other kids, Minori went to the west corner, her usual place, and nibbled at her own black bread. It didn't taste good, but it wasn't terrible, either. As she swallowed down the rather vague, unstimulating food, she waited with bated breath.

There were no key members of the guild in the living room.

The newbies who'd gathered around her sent searching glances at Minori. In response, Minori nodded, whispering things like, "Hang on just a little longer."

Most of the commonsense things Shiroe had taught them were very general knowledge, the sort of rudimentary information that formed the foundation of all game play in *Elder Tales*. However, in this other world, where they were cut off from online solutions sites, these knacks and scraps of knowledge gave Minori and Touya a big advantage. Before they knew it, this broad, shallow knowledge that wasn't limited to their main classes or subclasses had elevated Minori and Touya to something slightly above ordinary newbies.

The two of them had tried to use this modest knowledge to alleviate the impossible demands Hamelin placed on them, and somewhere along the way, that attitude had earned them trust from the other newbies.

Minori gave one of the players who already seemed to be in bad shape some hot water she'd snitched especially for her, then went back to thinking.

Shiroe had said he'd contact her today. Once his call came, she'd have to act.

She'd already told her roommates a little bit about it, and she knew Touya also knew what they were going to do today.

Minori wasn't sure when the call would come, but she thought it would be either in the morning or that night. During the day, Touya and the others were out hunting. Any strategy would be harder to implement if the targets that needed to be rescued were scattered.

After they finished their bread, Touya and the other players who were going out to hunt began drifting to another room to get ready. The newbies who would be hunting would gather and be given the day's destinations, party members, and formations. After that, the chosen members would change, check their equipment, and depart.

Just then, a faint bell sounded in Minori's ear.

That's it! It's Shiroe!

Tension over the uproar that was about to break out made her heart begin to pound like a trip-hammer. Even if she was killed, she wouldn't die. Logically, she knew this, but if someone were to turn a weapon on her, she'd still shrink back.

Minori didn't know what sort of operation was about to play out, but there could very well be violence. The possibility that there'd be a battle was not a small one. Still, Minori had thought it through carefully, and she'd resolved that, no matter what, she wouldn't disgrace herself.

When the telechat was connected, Shiroe's voice, a voice only Minori could hear, began to speak.

"Good morning. Minori? …I know this is sudden, but we're about to begin the operation. The signals will be the same as always. …Are you in your bedroom right now?"

Koff. She gave one small cough, answering in the affirmative.

"Is Touya in the other room getting ready?"

Another cough.

"All right. When Touya leaves the guildhall, you leave, too. … All of you, the new players. Just walk right out the door. You don't have to worry about anything. I've taken total control of the guild center."

Total control?

Minori didn't know what he meant, but she responded in the affirmative anyway.

"Next, if anything happens inside… If you fall and resurrect, after you wake up in the temple, run for the guild center. The guild center entrance hall is the headquarters for the rescue operation."

Minori struggled desperately to remember everything exactly.

"I have an important battle to fight on another front, and I can't be there. A young guy named Shouryuu is commanding the operation. Aside from him, there's an Assassin named Akatsuki; you can count on her. She'll be either at the hall or nearby."

She was so nervous the strength had gone out of her knees, and her chest hurt. Even so, fighting hard, Minori managed to return a single small affirmative cough.

"Naotsugu is camped at the temple. If the worst happens, you can count on him as well. All right: This is it. …Let the escape begin."

▶4

Touya had received a similar telechat.

So the operation's starting, huh, big brother Shiroe?

Touya gulped. He was putting on his battle armor, and his hands felt unusually tense; he breathed slowly and deeply, scanning his surroundings. It was still too early to tell his nearby companions.

Shiroe's order had been to get all the new players to flee into the guild center. The Hamelin guildhall, where Touya and the others were now, was linked to the guild center zone by a single door.

If they all made it through that door, he would have achieved the objective Shiroe had given him. If it had just been him, Touya was confident that he could have gotten away in less than ten seconds.

However, Minori wouldn't do a thing like that.

Minori would wait to make sure that Touya had gotten completely away before she made her escape. No, if he knew his sister, she'd let all the other new members besides Touya go as well and be the very last one out.

In that case, I can't just run, can I?

He knew Minori tended to punish herself.

It was the flip side of having a sense of responsibility, and Touya suspected he might be the reason that responsibility had taken root in the first place.

Touya liked his big sister.

His classmates said that siblings tended to fight whenever they got the chance. He'd heard that habits and ways of thinking that one could have forgiven in a stranger turned into a source of stress when one had to live with them, and he remembered thinking, *That makes sense.*

Still, Touya thought the pecking order was what caused the stress. There was an age difference between normal siblings; between one and three years in most cases. In children, an age difference like that created a disparity in abilities that was too big to ignore.

To older siblings, their younger brothers and sisters probably seemed like badly made copies of themselves. To younger siblings, older brothers and sisters were tyrants.

If things were like that, and they had to live together, of course it would be stressful.

On that point, twins had it easy. Minori always did her best to look after Touya because she thought of herself as his big sister, but she was only a few hours older than he was, and Touya didn't consider her to be any kind of guardian.

He thought of her as a great person to have as family and as a friend.

The fact that they were twins made them excellent playmates and opponents for each other. In a world where it was normal for there to be an age difference between siblings, that sort of pecking order was completely foreign to the two of them. As far as Touya was concerned, they were lucky.

However, even though they were the same age and on equal footing with each other, his sister was a bit timid. He was a guy, and so at times like that, it was his job to protect her. Touya had thought so for ages.

"Hey, it's time to move out. I'll go tell the guild master. You lot line up in front of the guild center."

The speaker—the leader of the hunting team, that arrogant Summoner—left the room, tossing those words back over his shoulder. He'd probably headed for the guild master's room.

Touya shoved his cheap sword into his belt and, starting for the door, called back to his companions.

"The rescue I've been telling you about is on. Let's get to the guild center hall right away. Hurry!"

He felt them catch their breath. On some level, the others had probably sensed it in the air, too. A flurry of motion broke out. Some hastily tried to grab their belongings, but he checked them. "Leave that stuff. It's not like we've got anything anyway."

It was true. Touya and the others didn't have any property to speak of. All they had were all the clothes and sundries they could pack into the ready-made bags they always used, the cheap kind that didn't even have weight cancellation spells on them.

When Touya glanced back, keeping his ear pressed to the door, several of his companions nodded. Touya opened the door, stepped into the hall, and ran straight to the other group bedroom.

As he approached the door to that room, he heard a small shriek and the sound of a struggle behind it. When Touya flung the door open without even thinking about it, he saw Minori struggling with a regular guild member.

What, they're onto us?!

Touya gulped. Then he gestured at the frightened newbie girls who were watching the struggle from the fringes, motioning for them to leave. In nearly the same motion, he rammed the short-haired bandit who was leaning on his sister, trying to hold her down.

"Wha?! What are you kids planning—"

There was a wheezing sound as the man filled his lungs. The short-haired bandit was probably going to yell. His sister's frightened face. That face alone was enough to set Touya moving again before he was even aware of it.

He dropped into a crouch, and his left arm snaked around smoothly.

The sword leapt from its sheath with such force that it seemed to have been launched rather than drawn. The shining silver light became a straight line that struck at the man's throat.

It was a special Samurai attack skill, Rania's Capture.

Its effect crushed the target's vocal cords, preventing them from chanting spells. In this case, the player wasn't chanting a spell, but the effect seemed to work anyway. The short-haired bandit choked soundlessly, holding his throat.

Normally, guildhalls were noncombat zones. Any act of aggression would summon the non-player guard characters instantly, even if they hadn't been nearby.

However, the noncombat zone settings were determined by the owner of the zone, and they could be lifted. In Hamelin's guildhall, combat had been legalized because it was necessary to "manage" the newbies.

The regular members had used those settings to hurt their new recruits.

—At least they had until today.

"Get them to safety!"

At Touya's call, Minori leapt up as if she'd been stung and pushed the other girls toward the guildhall's entryway. Now that things had gone this far, there was no time to dawdle. All she could do was encourage her frightened companions and lead them away.

Meanwhile, Touya squared off against the bandit.

The man's face was hard, and hatred blazed in his eyes. His throat had been crushed by one of the newbies he'd held in contempt as little squirts, and the rage it had whipped up inside him was unbelievable. There was a difference of more than twenty levels between Touya and him.

The bandit whipped out a scimitar with a blade that had to be fifty centimeters across and swung it at Touya.

The effect of Rania's Capture only robbed players of the ability to chant spells and speak. It was very effective on magic users and healers, but it wouldn't drain any of the combat ability from a physical fighter like the man in front of him.

The bandit's sharp sword overcame Touya's defensive stance easily and slashed into him. The fundamental difference between their skill levels was far too great.

Touya's surprise attack had only succeeded because, in his arrogance, the man had assumed that no newbie would turn on him and because the attack had been Rania's Capture.

Many Samurai special techniques had long recast times. Most skills were so-called "one-shot tricks" and could only be used once every five or ten minutes. As if to compensate for that, the techniques were designed to be powerful, and their hit rates were incredibly high. That was how Touya had managed to affect a midrange player who had a twenty-level advantage.

The certain-kill techniques were powerful and varied, but there were very few convenient midrange techniques that could be used to bridge the gaps between them. That was the fateful characteristic of the Samurai.

The effect of Rania's Capture lasted fifteen seconds.

He only had about ten seconds left. Touya stomped down his panic as he took blows from the bandit's sword.

I don't have to win! If I can just hold out here until the other guys have gotten away—

Red sprays of blood were spreading across the area. Touya didn't even have to look to know they were coming from him. His whole body ached and prickled painfully. He could feel his hands and feet getting colder and heavier.

"Touya!"

An effect like a shining, sky-blue mirror blocked the bandit's attack. With the level difference, the man's attack shattered the mirror in an instant, but it had been Minori's damage block spell. He saw the bandit click his tongue in annoyance.

"They all left for the entryway. Let's get into the corridor!"

"Roger that! Let's move."

After checking the man with a large attack, Touya left the bedroom with Minori. The corridor wasn't even two meters wide. Out here, he could protect Minori without letting anyone capture his side or get behind him.

"Gepluh! Gah!"

However, just then, the effect of Rania's Capture ran out. The bandit clutched his throat, gave a cracked cough, then screamed at Touya.

"Do you have any idea what you're in for after pulling a stunt like this?! I'll kill you a hundred times, you damn brats!!"

Just as Touya had feared, the man's rough voice echoed through the guildhall. Several of the doors in the corridor opened and the bulk of Hamelin's forces stuck their heads out, then hastily grabbed for their weapons.

The guild master with a face like thunder. The Summoner, who wasn't even trying to hide his irritation. The production-class men, who turned coarse stares on the new girls.

As one, they roared threats, then drew their weapons.

"What can the two of you do?!"

The Summoner brandished his arms, and a black wind whirled up. It was Deadly Swarm, a cloud of winged insects about the size of ants. The spell had the side effect of clouding the target's vision, and it went straight over Touya, attacking Minori directly.

Minori desperately chanted her damage block spell, but the level difference was too great. As the evil black insects slammed into it and were smashed, one after another, the shining wall cracked, then shattered like glass.

Even in the corridor, I can't block direct magic attacks on the vanguard! I'm an idiot!

Even as Touya told himself off, he threw the sword in his right hand into the false, swarming darkness with all his might. What he saw was the shape of the Summoner, waving his staff deep in the darkness.

"Touya! *Touya!!*"

"Just a little longer, Minori! Keep your head down!!"

Touya's arms had already taken so much damage they were bluish black, but he flung them around his twin sister and charged at the zone door as if he meant to ram it.

CHAPTER 5

GRAB YOUR FUTURE

▶ LEVEL: **19**

▶ RACE: **HUMAN**

▶ CLASS: **MONK**

▶ HP: **15142**

▶ MP: **4453**

▶ ITEM 1:

[HAMMER OF THE RAGING EARTH]

A SECRET-CLASS ITEM AWARDED AS A PRIZE IN THE FIFTH CONTEST QUEST BETWEEN THE CYCLOPS AND A BLACKSMITH. ALTHOUGH IT CAN ALSO BE USED AS A WEAPON, IF USED IN FORGING, THIS EXCELLENT ITEM CAN RAISE THE DURABILITY OF THE ITEMS BEING PRODUCED.

▶ ITEM 2:

[ARTISAN'S APRON]

PROTECTIVE GEAR FOR BLACKSMITHS. IT'S PRACTICALLY USELESS IN BATTLE, BUT IT HAS THE FANTASTIC EFFECT OF ENDOWING ITEMS THE WEARER MAKES WITH ABILITY VALUE BONUSES AND HP-BOOSTING BONUSES. HOWEVER, IT'S PROTECTIVE GEAR FOR THE UPPER BODY ONLY, SO PLAYERS NEED TO BE CAREFUL WHEN WEARING IT.

▶ ITEM 3:

[BLACKSMITH'S SEVEN TOOLS]

KEY ITEMS USED BY BLACKSMITHS IN PRODUCTION. THESE ITEMS ARE NECESSARY TO ALL BLACKSMITHS, ACROSS ALL LEVELS. SOME ADVENTURERS HAVE A DEDICATED TOOLBOX FOR THEM.

<Frog Figurine>
An item that brings you luck
with money. Buy it as a set
with a bear figurine.

►1

"But that's blackmail!!"

Meanwhile, in the vast conference room on the top floor of the guild center, the participants' discussion had grown heated.

Shiroe's declaration—"I own the guild center"—had been a bombshell.

The only players who had not been shocked were Shiroe himself; Nyanta, who stood behind him; the members of the Crescent Moon League; and Soujirou of the West Wind Brigade, who hadn't known exactly what would be done, but had dimly suspected something of the sort.

The guild center was one of Akiba's core facilities.

The functions of the center itself included guild formation, joining or leaving guilds, and the receipt of bonuses for high-level guilds— practically every guild-related, system-level clerical procedure.

However, in Akiba's case, that wasn't all it did. The guild center's entrance hall housed the service counter for the bank. The bank was a commonplace facility in the world of *Elder Tales*, and players used it to store money (in accounts) and items (in safe-deposit boxes).

In this other world, death resulted in no more than a slight drop in experience points and equipment durability, but at the moment of death, there was a set probability that ordinary items that hadn't been equipped to the player would be scattered across the area.

If the player was lucky, they could retrieve them, but if they'd been killed in a PK attack, the items would almost certainly be stolen. Even without that, it wasn't prudent to carry lots of money around. Ordinarily, almost all players kept most of their property in the bank, and if they wanted to purchase an expensive item at the market, they'd withdraw money for a small fee.

To the players, the bank was the most familiar, most important commercial facility in the *Elder Tales* world, and they used it every day.

The only bank window in Akiba was in the guild center. The fact that Shiroe, an individual player, could restrict entry to the guild center carried staggering implications.

Of course, every town had a bank. The accounts were the same, which meant that money—and even items—could be withdrawn from any bank, no matter where the original deposit had been made. For example, a deposit made in Akiba could be withdrawn in Minami.

That said, right now, with the intercity transport gates dead, the long journey between cities was very risky. Shiroe and his group had gone to Susukino, but they were part of a very tiny minority. Since the Catastrophe, it was likely that less than one-tenth of 1 percent of all players on the Japanese server had gone to a town other than their own.

Considering the current environment, the rights Shiroe held were equivalent to the authority to freeze bank assets at will. It was no wonder that the conference members were aghast.

Shiroe had announced this strategy—of an entity controlling the bank to control players—to the Crescent Moon League when they had nearly earned the five million in funding necessary to acquire the guild center, and even Henrietta had murmured, "Compared to Master Shiroe, devils are far tamer. Devils are fully aware that they're bad, but not Master Shiroe. That byname, 'Machiavelli-with-glasses,' is too cute for him."

"Freeze the assets in the bank?! If that isn't a threat, what the heck is?!"

Woodstock, the guild master of the small guild Grandale, spoke in a shaking voice.

"I simply answered Isaac's question. The question was, 'Even if the council is formed, depending on the matters presented to it, won't the big guilds exercise their right to veto and start a war?' The answer is no: There will be no war. Warring forces will lose the right to use Akiba's guild center."

"And I'm telling you that's blackmail—"

Shiroe responded to the obstinate claim.

"It may very well be. However, if what I've done is blackmail, what of what Isaac and the other big guilds have done? Isn't it blackmail to threaten to start a war if a proposal inconveniences you? How is that different? All I'm saying is that I want to establish a council and discuss things. I don't plan to ignore remarks that strike me as inconvenient. Think about which proposal is more sensible."

A subdued silence fell.

To the conference attendees, it may have seemed as if they were having an ugly nightmare.

"Where did you get that kind of money?! The guild center is a common zone!! A huge amount like that—"

"We financed it."

The speaker was "Iron-Arm" Michitaka, general manager of the Marine Organization. He seemed to have been one of the first to recover from the shock; the energy was starting to return to his voice.

"Then, Shiroe, the challenge you were directing was…"

"Yes. The establishment of this council."

"Well, that figures."

In the midst of a storm of questions as to why they'd put up the money, Michitaka nodded. Technically, only the eleven seated around the table were conference participants, but the shock of Shiroe's proclamation had sent their followers and advisers into a panic as well.

"Quiet down! What a ruckus!" Michitaka barked, then let his eyes fall to his documents.

The documents held the secret of the cooking method Nyanta had discovered, and the preparation method for the hamburgers currently being sold by the Crescent Moon League. It was a *cooking method* in the truest sense of the word, not a special "recipe" game item of the sort that could be registered as a new, complete item in the item creation menu.

Early that morning, the leaders of the three production guilds—the Marine Organization, the Roderick Trading Company, and Shopping District 8—had been called to this room before the conference and received these documents directly from Shiroe.

Once the structure was revealed, it was far too simple. The new food items at Snack Shop Crescent Moon weren't the result of a new recipe.

In chasing the fantasy of a new recipe, the production guilds had been tricked by the Crescent Moon League. Each had lost their investment of 1.5 million gold coins.

However, Shiroe hadn't given them anything that remotely resembled an apology.

Instead, he'd posed a question to the disgruntled trio: "What makes you think those documents are worth less than 1.5 million gold coins?"

"Isn't there something you still need to say, Shiroe?"

Michitaka urged him to continue. Although he'd steeled himself, his expression was something between a wry smile and dissatisfaction.

"He's right. No matter how you try to gloss it over, Mr. Shiroe, there's no denying that you're currently in a position where you *could* threaten us. Humans are wired to lose their composure, and possibly even feel that they've been threatened already, just by realizing that someone could do it. Surely you know that."

It was Soujirou who'd chimed in.

"It's just as you say. Even I don't think a town where a single person holds this much plenary power is ideal. On that note, let me return to the first matter I discussed. Do you think the Adventurers in this town—or, in larger terms, this world—really want things to stay this way? I have two policies to propose. One is that we revitalize everyone living in this town and, by extension, this world. Second, that we create and implement laws to govern the Adventurers who live in Akiba, at the very least. Is anyone opposed to any of what I've said so far?"

There was no answer.

Of course there wasn't.

In the first place, considered individually, none of the things Shiroe was saying were bad ideas. Bringing life back to the town was a good thing in and of itself, and it would benefit combat and production guilds alike.

Of course, if the burden from specific measures were to prove a harsh one, things would be different. If only a few participants were made to shoulder a heavy burden while all the others regained their footing, the question would be, "Which of us is going to draw the short straw?"

However, at this point, that wasn't a concern that opposed the topic of betterment itself.

The same went for establishing law. Some might feel that it was a nuisance and would only make things stuffier. However, all the players gathered here were Japanese and had originally been playing on the Japanese server. As such, they all knew the importance of "law."

Here as well, of course, there was a possibility that problems could arise, depending on the content of that law. There might also be bad laws they couldn't agree to. However, if it was a simple question of establishing law, there didn't seem to be anything to object to.

"All right."

"Black Sword" Isaac, who'd struck the conference table with his thick palm, broke in as if he was shouldering the confusion of the entire assembly himself.

"If you're going to go that far, tell us the specific policies of this proposed council of yours—of Log Horizon's."

The black-armored warrior kept his steely glare fixed on Shiroe, and it naturally drew the eyes of those around him. Shiroe held his head high and began to speak with even more enthusiasm.

▶ **2**

There was something unique about moving from one zone to another.

For example, in the case of the guild center and guildhalls, one moved between the zones by using a specific object shaped like a door.

On the guild center side, the second- and third-floor guildhall corridors held countless such doors. These corridors, with their ranks of doors and not much else, were linked to many separate guildhall zones.

In reality, there were no physical rooms behind the doors. There wouldn't have been any space for them. The doors themselves were right next to each other, and the wall behind the doors was only a meter thick. These floors held seventeen of these door-filled corridors, and no matter how hard one looked, they wouldn't have found the space to build a room.

It was easiest to picture if one thought of the doors in the strange guild center corridors as devices that transported them to another dimension (in this case, a guildhall). Conversely, using a door that acted as a guildhall exit would put one in front of the corresponding door in the guild center zone.

Was it Minori who'd touched the doorknob, or was it Touya? To the very end, neither of them knew. They'd simply jumped back to protect themselves from the black, smokelike swarm of poisonous insects, and as a result, they'd tumbled out into the guild center corridor.

"There's two more!"

Unusually, there were several players standing at the ready in the corridor. By the stairs, a boy in leather armor and a girl equipped with a katana were directing the newbie Hamelin members back and away.

Minori coughed, over and over.

It felt as if those poisonous insects had gotten inside her through her mouth, and the disgust made her retch. In reality, the insects had been a magic-generated effect and had only existed temporarily. Now that they were out of sight of the spellcaster, the insects ceased to exist, but the memory of the vivid physical sensation kept her from believing that.

"You okay, Minori?"

Touya was rubbing her back; he sounded worried. Since she was kneeling on the floor, Minori couldn't see Touya's whole body, but she did see the red stain that was spreading across the floor in front of her.

"You're the one who's... Hang on, Touya, I'll cast Small Recovery..."

"Nah, I'm fine. ...Only..."

Feeling Touya look up, she looked that way, too. Standing there were a young swordsman in blue leather armor, equipped with two Chinese-style straight swords, and a girl dressed all in black.

"What are your names, guys? Are there any others on their way out?"

Although he was a "young" swordsman, the player who spoke to Minori was probably still older than she and Touya were. He had black hair and looked as if he might be in high school.

Are we...safe...?

She didn't understand why the Hamelin members weren't leaping into the guild center corridor, but they certainly did seem to have been saved. Minori felt relief drain the strength from her knees.

Minori took the hand the young man held out to her and stood.

Touya had made it to his feet before she did, and he answered the question posed to them a moment earlier.

"I'm Touya. This is my big sis Minori. We should be the last two newbies."

"You are? That's great." The swordsman smiled as though a weight had been lifted from his shoulders. "I'm Shouryuu. Pleased to meet you. ...Okay, let's get you to the entrance first; your friends are already waiting there. We'll get you patched up, do a head count, and then ask you a bit about the situation for future reference..."

"Hey, Minori~. Quit doing that wet noodle impression. It's lame."

"Oh, honestly! Touya, you're such a meanie!"

Even as he teased, contrary to his words, Touya's voice was gentle with relief. Now all they had to do was follow this Shouryuu swordsman, and they'd see Shiroe. Just as Minori thought this...

——!

Something was wrong behind her. The feeling made her sick. She didn't even have to turn to look; she could feel that someone was in the process of materializing there. She was about to glance back, but even as she moved, deep down, she knew: Now wasn't the time. She should be flinging herself toward the stairs instead. Even so, her body had already begun to turn, and it wouldn't stop.

Just as she registered that a man's palm had filled her field of vision and was about to grab her roughly, Minori felt something ram into her. It was Touya.

The man's hand had been grabbing for Minori's collar, but when she was sent flying, it missed its mark and reached for Touya instead. Even though the arm wasn't thick, it squeezed Touya's wrist with such monstrous strength that Minori turned pale. The steel framework of Touya's gauntlet creaked ominously.

The Summoner—*that* Summoner—had moved between zones.

"You little…!"

His face was brick red with rage. True, the Summoner was a magic user. However, with enough of a level difference, his physical strength could surpass even that of a Warrior like Touya. In this gamelike world, physical strength was not proportionate to appearance. From the way Touya gritted his teeth, it was clear how much destructive power those thin arms held.

"What did you do?! What *are* you?!"

"Shut up! *Shut—yer—trap!!*"

But Touya's voice was strained.

As if to push aside their levels, that insurmountable difference in strength, through sheer willpower, Touya shoved the man with all his might. The Summoner didn't take any damage from the attack, but Touya had drawn his second blade, his katana, and was barring the way, posed as if to protect Minori.

"Don't try to act tough, brat! As if there's anywhere you could go!"

Those words awakened deep pain in Touya and Minori.

They were burdens, and even now, in this instant, it was hard for them to stand against the man's violence.

Even so, Minori screwed up her courage and was about to retort when, in that instant, a jet-black shadow swooped in like a swallow from the opposite direction.

The shadow sent the big man flying with a kick that had all her weight behind it, then stood between the twins and the Hamelin Summoner who'd come through the door.

Oh my… That lady's incredibly pretty.

The girl, who was as beautiful as Minori's admiration indicated, cut the man's knees out from under him in a motion so smooth she seemed to have practiced it thousands of times. It was so fluid, it looked more like a kind of dance than an attack.

However, the words that fell from her pale pink lips were sharp.

"I thought so. What a weak-looking face," the girl muttered. The expression she turned on the Summoner was filled with deep disdain.

"Who're you?! Akatsuki?—Log Horizon? Never heard of 'em."

The magic user, who'd frozen momentarily, seemed to have checked his mental menu. When he read the girl's—Akatsuki's—guild tag, he looked at her with clear contempt.

However, his words didn't seem to affect the girl in the least. She tilted her head slightly, with her usual too-serious expression, then responded.

"Really? I would imagine you'd be more embarrassed, with a tag from a third-rate guild like Hamelin. When you walk around town, don't you ever get snickered at and want to run back to your guildhall…?"

Her words infuriated the man; he seized her by her shirtfront. Combat was forbidden in the guild center, but from experience, the members of Hamelin were well aware of what constituted "combat."

Attacking with a drawn weapon or casting a hostile spell would immediately (and mercilessly) be recognized as fighting. However, unless it was accompanied by severe pain, contact with bare hands wasn't considered "combat."

Just as real-world yakuza had near-perfect knowledge of how far they could go before an act became illegal, these players knew just how much they could do before their actions were deemed "combat" by the system and the guards punished them.

"*What* did you say, girl? You know about Hamelin and you're still spouting crap like that? Little runt!"

It was bone-chilling intimidation, but even then, Akatsuki didn't flinch. The man, who was sturdy for a magic user, had lifted her light-weight-class body by the collar, and even her toes weren't touching the ground. From that position, Akatsuki murmured.

"…Ah, my liege? I'm sorry. There's one we hadn't registered yet. His name is Shreida. He's a big man who looks like he'd have smelly breath, and as you'd guess from his name, his face looks like it's been run through a shredder. …Yes."

"*What* was that?! Let's you and me go back to my guildhall, and then you'll get what's—"

The man's voice cut off.

As a matter of fact, it wasn't just his voice. He'd ceased to exist.

As Akatsuki dropped to the floor with a light noise, there was no man in front of her.

"Thank you for registering that one, my liege. Elimination complete. It looks as if when players who are in a zone are added to the 'no entry' list, they're ejected from that zone. I couldn't say whether he's in Akiba or whether he's returned to his guildhall.—Yes. That's right. Understood. We've just secured a girl named Minori and a boy named Touya. They say they're the last ones. I'll continue to watch the Hamelin guildhall door."

The transparently lovely girl turned, her face still far too serious, and went over to Minori and Touya, who had slumped to the corridor floor as though their legs would no longer hold them.

"You're Minori and Touya, right? My name is Akatsuki. I serve my liege Shiroe as his ninja. Your safety and that of your comrades is assured. My liege is fighting valiantly on another battlefield at the moment. For now… Why don't you come take a bath?"

Minori was so relieved that this time she did start to cry.

▶ 3

"I have two basic policies I'd like to propose. Revitalization of the area and improvement of public order are as I explained earlier. As far as specific policies are concerned, let me begin with an outline of the revitalization. I've already run this by several of the parties concerned. …Mari?"

At Shiroe's words, Marielle steeled herself and stood.

"I'm sure some of y'all already know, but Crescent Moon started runnin' a shop called Snack Shop Crescent Moon a little while back. We're gettin' lots of customers, and business is real good."

Behind Marielle, who had her hands on the conference desk and was leaning forward as she talked, Shiroe noticed Henrietta silently cheering her on.

"Snack Shop Crescent Moon is a take-out place whose main product is real, good-tastin' hamburgers, like nothin' we've ever had here. We're well aware that all sorts of rumors are croppin' up all over the place. Such as, for example, the secret's a completely new recipe, level ninety-one or higher, from some unknown zone. ...It isn't."

Aside from the production guilds, who already knew this, the news caused another significant stir in the conference room.

"I'm gonna disclose that secret here. This is how it works. You get your ingredients ready the usual way, and then you cook just the way you'd do it in the real world. Only the person doin' the cookin' has to be a Chef. That, and if their cookin' skills are judged to be too low, they'll fail. That's all it is. I guess the fact that there aren't any tricks or strings is the trick."

As the listeners gradually registered the meaning of those words, the murmur grew louder.

The preconceived notion that cooking was something made from a creation menu had had everyone fooled. Once spelled out, it was very simple, but it was also revolutionary.

As the room buzzed, Marielle sat down. Shiroe jumped in before another debate could start.

"The one who discovered that cooking method is Nyanta, the Chef standing behind me. With his permission, I taught it to the Crescent Moon League, and we launched Snack Shop Crescent Moon."

"I see. That's why the Marine Organization backed them..."

"But doesn't that mean they were tricked?"

As the hum of conjectures continued unabated, Shiroe ignored the comments and kept speaking.

"To my mind...it's a discovery that holds quite a number of suggestions. The discovery itself was made by Captain Nyanta here, but without it, I doubt I could have set up this conference, and I wouldn't even have considered doing so. Michitaka. Did you get results?"

"We did," Michitaka replied in a deep voice. At first glance, the leader of the gigantic guild seemed calm, but his expression was suffused with profound astonishment.

The reason the three production guild leaders had kept their silence ever since the conference began lay in the words Shiroe had just spoken.

"Our guild… Well, us and the Roderick Trading Company and Shopping District Eight, working together… We've just successfully developed a steam engine."

This announcement was also met with surprise, but the surprise didn't cause a stir the way the others had. On the contrary: The participants who'd heard the words doubted their ears, and they kept their attention riveted on Shiroe and Michitaka's conversation, so as not to miss the rest of what Michitaka said.

"To be completely accurate, it's a prototype. There are lots of issues, but the theory's been verified."

"That didn't even take half a day. That's fantastic."

"Basic components can be created from the creation menu. So can tools. The idea of diverting components was a masterstroke."

Michitaka and Shiroe were nodding in agreement.

"Hey… I mean, a steam engine, that's real impressive. Bottom line, though: What's going on?"

"Black Sword" Isaac sounded completely staggered.

"Don't you see, Isaac? It means this: That discovery isn't limited to cooking skills and Chefs. It's been demonstrated that if players who've acquired production-related skills actually work with their hands, without using the creation menu, they can make items that don't appear on the menu. Not one item related to steam engines exists in the original *Elder Tales* specs. There was no new food item recipe; however, the fact that it doesn't exist brought us a whole new dimension instead of a single, superficial new recipe. Things have gone far beyond the realm of fine food."

It was Roderick of the Roderick Trading Company who answered Isaac's question. His answer was so logical that it might have come from a scholar, instead of a merchant.

"From now on, it's going to be possible to make items that aren't on the creation menu. There's going to be an inventing boom for a while. We should be able to recreate a few of the things we had in the real world. Such as, let's see... Televisions might be out of reach, but it's quite possible that we'll be able to make radios."

Calasin of Shopping District 8 picked up where Roderick had left off.

His words drew a nod both from the intellectual-looking Roderick and from Michitaka, who was smiling heartily. Their guilds had witnessed the success of the steam engine experiment.

"More new inventions should arouse new demand. Naturally, methods of earning money will increase, as will the need to earn it. In other words: revitalization. I think we'll need a few safeguards here; it's possible that the economy may get out of control. Still, that's a chaos we should be able to master. It isn't stagnation drifting toward depression, is it? In this world, basic medieval items and handheld tools can be made from the creation menu. Since we have tools and models, I predict that progress will be rapid."

Michitaka carried on following Shiroe's prediction.

"Our three production guilds have confirmed those things, and we've got our eyes on both the earnings they may bring in and the new enthusiasm that will well up. ...To the point where I wouldn't mind supporting Shiroe over just this one thing."

"Then the production guilds are..."

"Yeah. We support the establishment of the Round Table Council."

As a matter of fact, even the small-scale Snack Shop Crescent Moon had achieved sales of fifty thousand gold coins per day. The arrival of competition would probably bring the price of the new food down as well. The average cost per customer might fall from the thirty gold coins it was at Crescent Moon until it was only a few gold coins. Still, even then, the potential customer demographic—in other words, the number of players—was more than ten times the number Crescent Moon had served.

It wasn't difficult to imagine generating an incalculable economic effect.

The combat guild members could only sit there gasping.

If the three major production guilds could declare it that categorically, the others seemed to be left with no choice but to believe them about the revitalization.

"The lack of energy is at least partially due to feelings of despair and apathy, but we think a large part of it is the fact that there isn't anything to do. It takes very little money to live in this world, to the point where it's a problem. It's healthier to use a certain amount of money, and to earn it so you can then use it. I think, from here on, we should see a wider variety of jobs begin to appear. For example, in the case of Snack Shop Crescent Moon, you wanted salesclerks badly enough that you would have paid for them, correct?"

"That's right. Since things were the way they were, we kept the work in the family, but it would've been nice to hire clerks."

Marielle shook her head several times as she answered Calasin, and no doubt she meant what she said.

"There should be more jobs for the members of the combat guilds as well. This goes for material discovery and acquisition, as well as guard duty, but once the council is established, don't you think we should set aside a budget and commission a complete investigation of the Fairy Rings? Once that investigation is complete, there's accumulation of zone information, followed eventually by compilation of historical records, and then publication of newspapers and other media… As long as we find the budget for it, there are lots of things we should do."

They knew that the Fairy Rings—teleportation devices that linked zones—were functioning. However, the Fairy Rings were influenced by the movement of the moon, and their destinations changed. The odds that a Fairy Ring was connected to the place one wanted to go were slim, and now, when it was impossible to check solutions sites, there was no telling where a player might be sent. As a result, players steered clear of them.

Investigating them was certainly possible, but it would take massive amounts of time and effort. In addition to the twenty-eight-day lunar cycle, destinations changed every hour. The fact that one Fairy Ring's destination information was completely different from that of a Fairy Ring somewhere else was also a big factor. Even if they limited themselves to the time when the moon was out, the connections between the Fairy Rings in all the zones were bound to yield an enormous number of combinations.

It wasn't as if no one had wanted to investigate them, but it was far too ambitious a task for any single guild to undertake.

However, if they could establish a backup system like the one Shiroe had spoken of, it certainly wouldn't be impossible. It would also send big missions to the combat guilds.

"Next is the issue of public order. Some people will probably feel that the establishment of law cramps their style. Still, I don't think there's any sense in making it all that strict. This other world feels like the Middle Ages, and I believe it has the sort of culture that will do well even if it isn't bound tightly by laws. People have monopolized hunting grounds, true, and there are turf wars. However, if we think of those acts as being a type of competition, they aren't anything we should unilaterally deny."

Several of the conference participants nodded. "Black Sword" Isaac was one of them.

"That said, there are few actions that go overboard, and we'll need to deter them to some extent. For one, I'd say we really should ban PKs in low-level zones. There's no point in bullying our companions who are level fifty or under, is there? They don't have all that much property anyway, which means that hunting them is simply killing for pleasure. We can decide on the specific places later, but I think we should ban PKs in the low-level zones near Akiba."

There were no comments here, either.

This was only natural: No guild as large as the ones that had been invited to the conference would assiduously PK as an organization. Most of the guilds that player killed were oppressive midsized groups.

"Next, the issue of human rights. Let's guarantee the right to liberty. In our current environment, where death isn't absolutely final, kidnapping and confinement are arguably more serious crimes than they were in the real world. The decision of whether to join or leave a guild should be left to the individual in question. We should ban and institute penalties for threats and talent hoarding that ignores the will of the affected player. I shouldn't even have to say this, but forcing a member of the opposite sex into sexual activity will carry the maximum penalty."

"Well, yeah, sure..."

"I guess we'd have to include those, huh?"

The atmosphere in the venue was beginning to shade toward agreement. In the first place, it wasn't as if the participants had thought there were no problems. The issues had struck everyone present as detestable, and they'd thought they should probably be gotten rid of.

That said, although the act of fighting in a noncombat zone was subject to an automatic penalty, in this world's system, there were no such automatic penalties for other violent acts, confinement, or threats. They'd also assumed that penalties that were not automatic—in which someone shouldered the responsibility of monitoring things, handed down decisions for each individual case, and occasionally meted out punishment—would take so much time and effort that implementing them would be impossible.

However, with the card Shiroe held—the ability to freeze players' savings—things became much simpler. If a player was causing trouble of some sort, the Round Table Council could investigate and suspend the player's use of the guild center. Problematic players would find it difficult to live in Akiba and, in practical terms, would probably be forced to relocate to another town.

To most of the participants, Shiroe's proposal seemed quite reasonable.

The invention of the steam engine and the production guilds' declaration of support for the Round Table Council had startled them, but once they'd heard the explanation, they found they agreed with a lot of it.

Shiroe had presented specific measures because he wanted participants to decide whether they agreed or disagreed with the establishment of the Round Table Council after they'd heard the content of the proposal.

Having done so, even if not all present approved of the proposal wholeheartedly, they did seem generally satisfied with it. The atmosphere of the conference itself seemed to be gradually shifting to a discussion of what should be done after the Round Table Council was established.

"In closing, these human rights issues should be applied to the People of the Earth, as well as to Adventurers."

A few of the participants began to open their mouths. A quick-witted listener could probably have foreseen this development from the mention of the slave trading in Susukino.

However, what Shiroe began to talk about was something else entirely.

"I don't know yet what the results of this conference will be. At present, I'm not sure whether or not you'll approve the outline I've presented and establish the Round Table Council. However, there is one thing I want you to recognize, and I think it's high time you did. We are in another world, and somewhere, this world is warped in a very strange way. It's true that it's influenced by *Elder Tales*. However, as you can tell from the Chef discovery I mentioned earlier, this isn't simply the world of the game. It's another world, one with more sophisticated physical laws. Has anyone here really talked to the People of the Earth?"

"But they're NPCs," said someone's attendant.

"They aren't non-player characters. They're people with their own individual personalities. They have their own worries and dreams and ethics and lives, and they're living them. They call themselves the People of the Earth... At least, in contrast to their term for us, the Adventurers. Let me make this clear: They are the natural residents of this world, and we are parasites. The town of Akiba has always been an Adventurer town, so there are comparatively few People of the Earth here, but in terms of the world as a whole, they must outnumber us by far. Adventurers and People of the Earth have different roles with regard to this world, but if things keep on like this, we won't be able to build proper relationships."

"Relationships...?"

They could agree with part of what Shiroe had said—it did make sense, now that they thought about it—but even so, it tended to rely too heavily on logic. "In *Elder Tales*, which has become a different world, they are citizens of the world, not non-player characters." Stated plainly like that, even if it didn't completely go without saying, it wasn't something entirely incomprehensible. However, for the majority of the players, emotionally, it still didn't register.

"Uhm... I have a little bit to add to that."

In the midst of that bewilderment, Marielle timidly spoke up.

Possibly she got nervous every time she spoke in front of these dignitaries: She faltered, but even then, she maintained her natural cheerfulness and spoke clearly.

"So, Snack Shop Crescent Moon is real popular, and that's a fact. But listen, the players—the Adventurers, I mean—weren't the only ones who came and bought from us. The People of the Earth came, too. In other words... I dunno how to say it. I don't really get it myself yet, but... They want to eat stuff that tastes good, too."

This time, the conference room went so quiet one could have heard a pin drop.

The shock that had struck the participants seemed to have crumbled the very ground they stood on.

To many of the players, the NPCs had been nothing more than non-player characters. The Briganteers of Susukino might have gone too far, but even the completely ordinary, well-intentioned players assembled here had seen them as a type of talking vending machine. At the very least, in *Elder Tales*, that hadn't been wrong. When this was a game, that was what they had been.

However, for that very reason, to players with as much experience in *Elder Tales* as the ones who'd gathered in the conference room, Marielle's report felt like an attack that destroyed something fundamental.

"I'm not saying we should give up on returning to our old world. I don't even want to say it... But let's admit that this *is* another world. It's been nearly two months since we were sent here. We've been 'demanding guests' for long enough. You're free to think that the People of the Earth don't have feelings, but as a matter of fact, they do. As in the official *Elder Tales* scenario, we seem to be Adventurers, a type of privileged class. That makes us something like mercenaries, with special abilities that allow us to attack monster strongholds. However, the vast majority of people in this world are People of the Earth. Let me repeat myself for clarity's sake: Without the People of the Earth, we can't live in this world. They provide all sorts of services, including the bank. However, the People of the Earth could probably survive without us. If we keep living like this, doing just as we please every day, unable to govern ourselves, we will do irreparable damage."

When Shiroe finished speaking, he sat down in his chair heavily, without waiting for a response. He was tired, but he felt good.

Even after Shiroe had delivered his entire proposal, the conference room was silent.

No one moved. It was as if they'd all become statues. What Shiroe had said had been that strange and that shocking. Most of the conference participants had thought they'd been pulled into the world of *Elder Tales*. They'd felt as if the world of the game had become real.

Even now, they couldn't exactly deny that.

However, the facts Shiroe had set before them today—the method of creating articles without using the item creation menu, for example, and the idea that the People of the Earth had actual personalities and were the main force in the world—had been more than enough to take what knowledge of the world they'd managed to scrape together over the past two months and smash it to smithereens.

"—Are you suggesting that there's a possibility of war with the People of the Earth, Shiroe?"

Crusty's quiet question was delivered in the tones of a fair-skinned philosopher.

"I understand that it's something for the Round Table Council to consider, not for me to think about now," Shiroe tossed off irresponsibly.

The die had been cast. Shiroe had played every card he had. He'd disclosed all the information he held. He'd shown them the world he wanted in a shape that was easy to understand.

Shiroe had begun this war out of self-indulgence, but he'd only wanted to win; he hadn't wanted to make anybody lose. He'd wanted to win a victory, not steal it.

Although he didn't intend to sound trite, if possible, he'd wanted them all to reach that goal together. "All" meaning all the people of Akiba.

Even so, if an overwhelming number of people still don't understand, after hearing all that... We may have a war on our hands.

When Shiroe glanced to the side, his eyes met Marielle's.

Marielle's face was slightly troubled, but she still wore the same artless sunflower smile. Henrietta, who stood behind her, shrugged. Her expression seemed to say, "Do as you please."

Time passed. It felt like a very long time and also like the space of a few breaths. Everyone in the conference room sat in total silence. The first player to open his mouth was "Berserker" Crusty, leader of D.D.D., Akiba's largest combat guild.

In a calm voice that held no tension, he spoke to the assembly.

"D.D.D. approves the establishment of the Round Table Council as a body to govern Akiba and intends to participate."

The next words came from Soujirou, who sounded quietly entertained.

"The West Wind Brigade also approves. I haven't seen you dominate like that in a long time, Mr. Shiro... I really do wish you'd joined my guild."

"Well, we can't bust up Akiba. The Knights of the Black Sword are in."

"Honesty approves as well. Let's work to better relations with the People of the Earth."

"Black Sword" Isaac and Ains, the guild master of Honesty, gave their answers, too.

"As I said earlier, our three production guilds support Shiroe and the Round Table Council. We hope the decisions made there will be fruitful ones."

Roderick and Calasin nodded their agreement to Michitaka's words. They had already inferred several possibilities from Shiroe's report and had instructed their guild members to run various experiments.

After that, the declarations of approval came one after another, as if carried along by a swift current. Grandale and RADIO Market, smaller guilds, expressed their intent to participate as organizers of the former small- and midsized guild alliance.

Marielle, who had apparently been pushing herself very hard, slumped facedown onto the conference table with the smile still on her face, as if she had no energy left. Smiling wryly, Shiroe slowly unclenched his hands, which were slippery with sweat, under the conference table, so that Marielle wouldn't notice.

On that day, the town of Akiba witnessed the birth of the Round Table Council.

▶4

"Commander Marielle! The cupboard is all packed, ma'am!"

"None of that 'commander' business, 'kay? I really can't take it."

There were people working busily, and people numbering packages, and people dithering around with no idea what to do.

A week had passed since the assembly that had resulted in the Round Table Council, and the Crescent Moon League guildhall was buzzing with noisy activity.

"You're the guild master, Commander Marielle, so please sit there, ma'am!"

"Nope. No can do! We're a small outfit, and as I keep tellin' you, the guild master doesn't get treated like a big shot around here!"

"*Mari.* You're scatterbrained, and you are in the way. Sit in the corner and have some tea or something, please."

Henrietta scolded Marielle, who was arguing with the newbies. At her words, Marielle teared up a bit and, with a clearly dejected "What am I, useless?" removed herself to a corner of the office.

The Crescent Moon was right in the middle of a move.

The entire guild membership was bustling around, cleaning and packing up the furnishings that were originally theirs. As she looked around at her companions, whose number had grown, Marielle was lost in thought.

The day the Round Table Council had been established was also the day Hamelin had fallen. In the same building where Marielle and the others had been meeting, Shouryuu and Serara of the Crescent Moon League and Akatsuki and the other members of Log Horizon had safely taken Hamelin's escaped newbie members into protective custody.

Very few people were aware that while he'd been conducting the proceedings of that complicated conference as its initiator and chairman, Shiroe had also been quietly directing the operation to destroy Hamelin.

Even Marielle might not have noticed if she hadn't been told about it beforehand.

With their names added to the blacklist of people barred from entering the guild center, the members of Hamelin hadn't even been able to follow the escaping newbies.

From what they'd heard, Akatsuki had tracked down the names of all the members of Hamelin beforehand. Apparently, Akatsuki's absence during Snack Shop Crescent Moon's creation and operation wasn't because she was avoiding being used as Henrietta's dress-up doll.

Having been evacuated to the guild center, the newbies had promptly completed the procedures to leave their guild under Shouryuu's supervision. Approximately thirty-five low-level players had been kept under what practically amounted to house arrest by Hamelin. They were a sorry sight, dingy with sweat and grime.

Just about the time Serara and volunteers from the Crescent Moon League were getting food and fresh clothes ready for the newbies, the members of Hamelin finally realized what was going on.

Since they were unable to enter the guild center and the guild center was the only zone that their guildhall was linked to, the members of Hamelin were prisoners in their own building.

Of course, as Shiroe had predicted earlier, there were ways to escape. One was Call of Home. This was a spell that transported players who were registered in Akiba back to Akiba. Ordinarily, it was used to return from distant field or dungeon zones. However, there were no rules against using it from within a town or building. Using Call of Home would return them to the entrance of Akiba.

Another way was to end one's own life in the zone. In that case, a player would lose some experience points as a penalty, but they would resurrect in the temple. Since the temple was in the center of Akiba, this equaled a move by default.

By the time the members of Hamelin discovered these methods and used them, the sun had set. The council's course of action had been established, and the discussion of the laws that would be implemented had entered its final stages.

The situation had already progressed to the point where Hamelin couldn't do a thing about it. On top of that, although they'd escaped their guildhall-turned-prison, they would never be able to enter the guild center again.

The outcome of the game had been decided several moves earlier.

Something unexpected had happened as well.

Marielle and the others had planned to introduce the rescued newbies to new guilds or support them until they were independent, whichever they preferred; they'd already reported their intentions to the Round Table Council and had the topic placed on the agenda.

In fact, every guild that attended the conference had volunteered to accept newbies and take responsibility for supporting them.

However, on closer examination, only sixteen of the thirty-five low-level newbies wanted to enter the assembled guilds. The remaining nineteen all wanted to join the Crescent Moon League.

According to Serara, Shouryuu had been a bit too visibly "gallant" while conducting the rescue. He'd come off as such a reliable leader that he'd increased the number of players who wanted to join the League.

In Henrietta's words, it was "a type of imprinting, like showing a toy 'mother' to chicks," and it was something even Marielle hadn't seen coming, either.

That said, the Crescent Moon League was already a solid part of the Round Table Council. The council had already declared its intent to provide support, so they couldn't toss them out on their ears like unwanted kittens. In any case, the League was a homey kind of guild that was able to accept both midlevel and low-level companions with open arms. Knowing that the other members were happy about it, Marielle decided to accept the newbies.

With that, the Crescent Moon League's headquarters developed several disadvantages.

Now that the guild's membership had nearly doubled in size, its current guildhall was cramped.

There was no rule that said guild members had to sleep in the guildhall, and no matter which guild they were part of, players could rent rooms at inns as individuals. Rooms could be rented by the night or reserved for a month or a year, and many Adventurers had their own private spaces.

However, for low-level players, even that expense was hard on the wallet. The members of the Crescent Moon League got along well with one another, and many of them did sleep at the guildhall.

In the first place, Marielle, the guild leader, used the guildhall as her own house, so it was only natural that the people below her would imitate her.

"Mari. Mari? We're ready; stand up. Here, these are yours."

Hugging the stuffed teddy bear and cushion Henrietta had handed her, Marielle left her familiar old office. Almost all the furniture had been carried out already, and the room was wide and bare. Not even a shadow of its former self remained.

"Commander Marielle~. We've gotten the office at the new guild-hall ready, ma'am."

Smiling and saying, "Thanks much!" to the guild member—who was bouncing up and down—Marielle set off.

And so, unable to make do with its old guildhall, the Crescent Moon League found itself facing a move. Like the old hall, the new hall was located in the Akiba guild center.

Even though Marielle had started off carrying her belongings, the move was a very short one: She stepped out of the old guildhall into the guild center, then teleported to the new zone through another door in the next corridor over.

However, the rank of the hall they were renting had changed. They'd leveled up from a seven-room guildhall to a hall with thirty-one rooms. The rent had gone up as well, of course, but they still had some of their earnings from Snack Shop Crescent Moon left over.

Henrietta, who was strict about balancing income and expenses, had given it her guarantee—"I don't see why not"—so Marielle felt secure in her decision to move.

They now had nearly fifty guild members, but with the new hall, they'd be able to manage quite well. Each individual space—the kitchen, the conference room, the workrooms, storerooms, and hall—was larger, so above and beyond the fact that there were more rooms, the guildhall felt more spacious. Thirty-one rooms: It seemed almost like a castle.

One surprise was that the guildhall was two stories, which meant it even had a staircase.

"It's so *big*, ma'am!"

"Whoa. It's huuuge."

"I bet we could fit a dragon in here!"

Marielle grinned at the excited guild members. The business of placing the furniture they'd brought over around the guildhall, undoing packages, and jotting down notes regarding new equipment they'd need seemed to have begun.

Thinking of the expenses for tables and carpets was giving her a headache, but their artisans would probably be able to make the minimum of what they'd need. Besides, if it turned out they didn't have enough of something and had to save up for it, it would be a good excuse to go adventuring.

Akiba had begun to come to life again. Just thinking about it made Marielle feel warm and happy.

There's lots we need to do. …There're so much I want!

The area of her spacious new office was about three times the area of her old one. It was so big she was having a hard time relaxing. The desk and chairs she'd used at the old guildhall had been brought in, along with the sofa and cushions, but in the huge office, the compact desk-and-reception set only served to emphasize the vast coldness of the room.

"This is rather…large, isn't it? It might even be bigger than the conference room at the old guildhall."

Henrietta, who'd come in with some documents, also seemed a bit nonplussed. When they'd come to inspect the hall before moving in, there hadn't been any furniture, so she'd been able to say, "It's nice to have so much space." However, now that the room actually held furniture, all that extra space made it feel much too lonely.

"What'll I do? Am I really gonna live in a place like this?"

In spite of herself, Marielle sounded miserable. This was going to be quite a problem in its own way.

"I think it would be good to put up some dividing screens. Single-leaf wooden screens and some ornamental plants."

Henrietta jotted down the necessary items one after another in a nearby notebook. That would work, come to think of it, and in an office this spacious, it would be entirely possible to set up a reception corner. If they split it into three rooms, Marielle thought, she could probably even use the innermost one as her bedroom.

"This is gonna cost us quite a bit."

"Very true. …Still, I believe that's a good thing."

Henrietta smiled faintly, her eyes still on the notebook. The lovely smile made Marielle happy. She knew Henrietta was feeling the same thing she was.

"I love ya to pieces, Henrietta~."

In an attempt to express those feelings, Marielle hugged her hard.

"Now how did that conversation lead to *this*?! Honestly, Mari!"

Startled, Henrietta struggled. On top of that, they were spotted by a newbie—"I-I'm sorry, ma'am!"—and so by the time Marielle finished tidying up the room, chuckling the whole time, she was worn out.

"You are something else, you know that...?"

"I said I was sorry. Forgive me, 'kay? Please? Pretty please?"

"I only said that since it will contribute to the town's economic development, buying a few pieces of furniture would be a good thing."

Marielle's attitude had made Henrietta blush bright red, and her shapely eyebrows were bristling. Marielle couldn't stop smiling at the sight of her friend's face: Although Henrietta was always visiting hugs upon Akatsuki, apparently she wasn't skilled at being on the receiving end of things.

"I swear, it's like the sun came out all of a sudden."

Marielle wasn't talking about the approaching summer.

She meant the town of Akiba ever since the establishment of the Round Table Council.

That night, several dozen flyers had been promptly posted in Akiba's central plaza to spread the word of the Round Table Council's establishment. The news spread with terrifying speed, and by the time dawn broke, there was no one in Akiba who didn't know.

...Not that there hadn't been any backlash.

After all, the Round Table Council was not a self-governing body made up of members selected by democratic vote. To the standard Japanese mind, this council had practically been forced on them from higher up, and it must have seemed as if the big guilds were behind it, pulling the strings.

However, having anticipated this, the flyers also listed the intent behind the council's establishment, its short-term goals, and its methods in detail.

In a magnanimous gesture, they also gave the secret of the completely new cooking method made famous by Snack Shop Crescent Moon.

In the space of a night, the town of Akiba was flooded with food of all kinds. Food that tasted like it should—the sort that had only been available from Snack Shop Crescent Moon—could now be made by any Chef.

Of course, with the new cooking method, the knowledge and techniques of the person doing the cooking mattered just as much as cooking skills. Some of the dishes, made by amateurs, couldn't have been called "good" by the most diplomatic player. However, even these were much better than the former dull and uninteresting food items.

Several hasty Chefs opened stalls one after another. Some baked bread and sold it, while others sold sweet juices. Some simpler stalls made and sold baked potatoes. Some even made meat or fish soups in big iron kettles over open fires by the roadside and sold it by the bowlful, as if they were doing impromptu business in a disaster zone.

Everyone was able to satisfy their previously unfulfilled appetites for food. Delicious foods became the subject of rumors and sold out almost instantly, and the town of Akiba developed a luxurious pastime that no one had even imagined could exist the day before: "eating and strolling."

The townspeople welcomed the change.

Among those who met it with cheers were a fair number of People of the Earth, as well as Adventurers.

The revitalization of the town, maintaining public order through the establishment of law, improving relations with the People of the Earth, and the introduction of a tax to support these initiatives were announced in a public address given the following afternoon.

At the address, which took place in Akiba's central plaza, several notables from Akiba—including "Berserker" Crusty, the leader of D.D.D., and Michitaka, general manager of the Marine Organization—assembled to talk about the intent behind the establishment of the Round Table Council.

The idea of a tax drew some skeptical comments, but when they were told that collection would be nearly automatic and that it wouldn't be very much, they accepted it with passive agreement. The tax would be instituted in the form of a fee for guild center use, with one coin per day collected from any player who entered or left the guild center.

This was one of the entry- and exit-related items that could be set by the owner of the guild center zone. According to Roderick's calculations, the revenue would earn the Round Table Council a monthly budget of slightly less than 400,000 gold coins.

Everyone, and particularly players who didn't belong to one of the big guilds, had sensed the importance of establishing law, and by now everyone understood what revitalizing Akiba would mean.

The revolution that had been sparked by a single evening meal had brought life back to the faces of all the townspeople.

The upshot was that the Round Table Council was widely accepted by everyone who lived in Akiba. A governing body like this one would have been created eventually, and in that case, it was dozens of times better to have a competent self-governing organization than something dictatorial—something controlled by the big guilds, for example.

When the representatives from the eleven guilds that made up the Round Table Council addressed the crowd from the platform, each drew loud applause. That said, it felt more like the reaction of amiable onlookers at a large-scale party than support for a political assembly.

Everything was colored by the sunset, and people thronged the central plaza. Players who hadn't been able to find a place in the plaza looked down over the platform from various floors of the surrounding mixed-use buildings.

Many of them held bread, sweets, or shish kebabs in their hands as they watched this first event in a very long time. Some of those present had a bit of alcohol in them, and the proceedings were more like a policy announcement given in the midst of an uproar than a public address.

In any case, Crusty, the Round Table Council's representative, explained that they would work to reorganize the town of Akiba on a new system; that they had several projects, including investigating the Fairy Rings; and that the cooperation of the townspeople would be vital in order to achieve these things.

Abruptly, as the townspeople met that declaration with cheers, an astonishing number of artisans began to bring in food and alcohol. Representatives of three production guilds—headed by the Marine Organization—proclaimed vigorously that they'd make that day the first of the auspicious festival days and yelled that they were bringing out all the delicacies their storehouses held. At that, the excitement in Akiba reached fever pitch.

"If that racket keeps up, my head's going to turn into a cream puff."
"Yep, it just might."
Marielle giggled. Henrietta looked put out.
The night grew later and later amid endless calls of "Cheers!"
One week after that night...
Sunlight continued to stream into the town of Akiba.
New dishes were supplied almost every day, and they heard that the production artisans who weren't Chefs were also trying various things in order to create new items.
The thing that currently held Marielle and Henrietta's interest was a bathing facility. When *Elder Tales* was a game, bathtubs had been mere background objects. However, now that this was another world, one they were actually living in, bathing suddenly took on a different meaning. The humidity was lower here than it was in real-world Japan, and the summer heat wasn't quite as sweltering... But, as women, there was no way they wouldn't be interested.
From what they'd heard, the West Wind Brigade had promptly gained the cooperation of Mechanists, Blacksmiths, and Carpenters and begun to build a large public bath in their guild castle.
News of advancements flew in almost daily—reports that somebody somewhere had used some new device—and this really did bring energy back to Akiba. The young man who'd planned it all had received no attention whatsoever at the speeches on the night of the raucous festival, but he'd seemed satisfied.
When she thought of Shiroe and his companions, Marielle felt a mixture of happiness and gratitude, but she also felt something very strange.

Hamelin had decided to disband not long ago.

He really did *take down a whole guild. Wow... Shiro's a pretty scary kid. Talk about dangerous...*

Marielle sat on her luxurious chair at her work desk, hugging her knees and ducking her head low. She remembered the strong eyes behind Shiroe's round glasses. When Shiroe had led that conference with that fiery will of his, he'd done so with so much force that she'd been a little afraid of him.

The Shiroe Marielle knew was the veteran player who was always mulling something over privately, who tied himself down with all sorts of bad premonitions, and yet was kind and trustworthy even so.

He was more good-natured than anything, a homeless wanderer, oddly mature for his age, evasive but reliable, a lone Enchanter. That was all.

Marielle didn't know the steely youth who'd used his intense will to drive his opponents into a corner, as if he were at a duel or a chessboard.

But he did save us, didn't he...?

With her face still buried in her knees, Marielle gave a mischievous little chuckle. Shiroe, Akatsuki, Nyanta, and Naotsugu. Her reliable friends had brought Serara back to the Crescent Moon League, and they'd brought energy back to the town of Akiba.

They could have said it wasn't their problem and left everyone out in the cold, but even then, they'd kept up their relentless pursuit of the "greatest good." In her head, Marielle still couldn't quite mesh those four with the four who'd relaxed at the guildhall drinking tea, but that didn't change the fact that they were their benefactors.

"...Hm. Come to think of it, I haven't seen Shiro's crew today. What're they up to?"

Abruptly curious, Marielle checked with Henrietta.

"My. Hadn't you heard? Master Shiroe's group is moving today, too."

▶ **5**

At about that time, on the edge of the outskirts of Akiba, Shiroe and the others were in the process of taking up residence in one of the mixed-use buildings closest to the northern boundary.

Log Horizon, which Shiroe had founded just the other day, had a current membership of four.

Shiroe, the Enchanter who, in spite of his mild demeanor, would carry even the most reckless plan through to the end once he'd set his mind to it. Byname: Machiavelli-with-glasses. (…Although, personally, Shiroe had several objections to that name.)

Naotsugu, the Guardian, a rock-solid vanguard tank and panties evangelist, who was always ready with flippant banter and bad jokes.

Akatsuki, the pretty-girl Assassin, slight and black haired, always dead serious and the resident straight man.

Finally, the quiet and restrained Swashbuckler Nyanta: adviser and guardian of the group's collective stomach.

With four members, the guild was so tiny it would have seemed presumptuous to call it "small."

In the first place, as Michitaka of the Marine Organization had commented, everyone had thought Log Horizon was a temporary guild, formed just to launch the Round Table Council. The guild couldn't shed the image that it had been established in haste.

Shiroe had spent so much of his game life steering clear of guilds that this sort of profiling was only natural.

On the morning after the night when he'd looked up at the white moon hanging over the Kanda River, while the streets were still hazy with mist, Shiroe took Akatsuki and Naotsugu into Akiba.

The dawn sunlight held a growing premonition of summer, and the cicadas were already starting to cry. After thoroughly stressing himself out over how to begin, the words Shiroe settled on were completely commonplace: *I'm forming a new guild. Would you join it?*

Rats, he thought, barely a moment later. *I should have come up with something better.* Even as Shiroe began to regret his approach, the other two readily agreed to join up.

"What, you're finally ready to go for it, Shiro? I was starting to think I'd just keep hanging around with you like this, like some guild without a guild tag."

"Ninja follow their lords wherever they go. Command as you see fit, my liege."

Along with Nyanta, whom he'd already invited, Shiroe's guild, Log Horizon, now had four members. In this way, the tiny guild—which, in terms of numbers, should have been called Log Minimum instead of Log Horizon—got its modest start in the streets of Akiba.

"Will our wallet be all right, my liege?"

Akatsuki's question came as she was cleaning the floor. The only words to describe the high-ceilinged space were *enormous* and *completely empty*.

Her worry was well-founded. Guilds as small as Shiroe's didn't generally bother with guildhalls the way normal guilds did.

In most guilds with memberships in the single digits, individual members might rent their own rooms at inns, but they very rarely set up a guildhall.

With only a few people, there weren't many possessions or guild trophies that needed to be put somewhere, and people could be met in the plaza or at taverns. There was no problem with conducting strategy meetings on the side of the road, and in any case, the telechat function kept them nicely connected.

Smaller guilds with a few more members would rent guildhalls at the guild center and use these as their headquarters.

The guild center was close to the center of town, and since it was also economical and clean, it was quite popular. It also held halls of all sizes, from affordable three-room suites to halls that had thirty-one rooms and could accommodate guilds with a hundred members. It was close to shopping at the plaza and to the bank, and since it was so convenient, most guilds used it.

But for even larger groups, the "big" guilds, even the halls at the guild center began to feel cramped.

The largest guildhalls available for rent at the guild center had thirty-one rooms. Marielle of the Crescent Moon League had considered hers a castle, but although this might be true for guilds with thirty or forty members, guilds with memberships of over two hundred found that even that wasn't enough space.

For that reason, guilds as large as the Knights of the Black Sword and the West Wind Brigade often chose buildings that could be purchased in Akiba proper, bought the whole zone in which the building lay, and established their headquarters there.

Production guilds like the Marine Organization, which now boasted five thousand members, divided their artisans into several departments by category and housed each department in its own ruined building. In cases like that, the entire guild overall had several headquarters.

Headquarters like these were known as "guild houses," "guild towers," or "guild castles."

At 90, Log Horizon's average member level was high, but it had very few members. Ordinarily, keeping a whole building like this one would have been inefficient; if they'd needed headquarters, they could have just borrowed a guildhall from the guild center. This expense was what was worrying Akatsuki.

"…It's all right. We'll manage."

Even as he responded, Shiroe was scrubbing the walls with a deck brush. This ruin had been a warehouse and a large-scale store, and it had an enormous old tree growing up through its first six floors.

There was a big hole in the center of each floor, and a mossy tree trunk, which must have been several centuries old, had threaded its way up through them. The great tree pierced every floor from the basement on up, heading for the sky, and at the roof, its great branches spread out into a green dome.

The entire town of Akiba seemed to have been swallowed up by a sea of trees, but it was rare to see the growth of a tree overlap with a building so completely.

"This building's cheap because it's like this. There aren't any stairs, you know, and it's hard to use."

"Hm… Is that right?"

Shiroe was clearing rubble while they talked. The general cleanup had been done over the course of a few days with the help of the younger Crescent Moon League members, but the ruin was still far from livable.

Originally, it was likely that the place had been a big home electronics store or something similar: This first floor was almost unbroken by walls, and the ceiling must have been four or five meters high.

Of course it was hard to imagine that this building had been stairless ever since the old era, when it had been built. The well that had held stairs, and the elevator shaft that had doubtless been next to it, had probably been where the trunk stood now.

After this building had been abandoned and damaged, the old tree that had grown in the stairwell (or elevator shaft) had most likely pierced through the floors and eroded them.

The fact that this building had been ignored when it was being sold for such a low price was probably due to its distance from the center of town and its sheer inconvenience.

"Still. Akiba's not a big town, and this is prime real estate. I mean, heck, stairs can be built."

As Naotsugu, who'd come down from the second floor, pointed out, the first and second floors were now connected by a steel stairway. The stairs looked rough and bleak, but they were sturdy enough and large enough to be used without a problem.

"But listen, when this was a game, there was no option to 'Repair Facility with Hole in Floor,' was there?"

Shiroe's words seemed to satisfy Naotsugu: "Oh yeah. Guess not."

The impact of the new cooking method Nyanta had discovered hadn't stayed in the culinary world. By now, all the production guilds had begun to develop new items. It wasn't limited to the production subclasses, either; even the role-playing subclasses had begun experimenting to see what changes their skills could bring to this world.

The stairway had been the result of one such experiment.

Interfering with basic objects such as the walls and floor would have been an unimaginable act in the *Elder Tales* game, but in the past week, it had been demonstrated that even that was possible.

At this point, the stairway only linked the first and second floors; if they wanted to go to the third floor or higher, they had to shimmy up a rope. If they wanted to expand, though, all they had to do was call on the artisans again.

Compared to the rest of the market, the cost of this zone had been cheap, but even so, it had been a pretty sizable amount. That had been something they'd planned on, but they'd also had to pay the artisans a reasonable sum to build the stairway. Tiny Log Horizon didn't have the funds for a complete overhaul of the building.

They'd commissioned the installation of the stairway and reflooring of the second story—where they'd be sleeping for now—from the Marine Organization. Michitaka, the guild master, had accepted cheerfully. "Yeah, if you use work-arounds like that, I guess you could find new ways to use ruins that weren't good for living in before. Building a stairway's an interesting idea."

Michitaka himself had stopped by the site of the remodel several times, and when Naotsugu had called, "Hey! If the idea's so interesting, cut us a deal, wouldja?!" he'd actually seemed to worry about it, which had tickled Shiroe.

Even when they knew it was likely to lead to new sales, in this other world the processing of various materials was so different from what it had been in the real world that it was hard to calculate prices that would bring in a decent profit.

Henrietta had explained this using jargon like "optimization of supply and demand" and "full employment" and "minimum wage." Shiroe understood the broad theory—the structure—but he really couldn't slot in figures and run actual simulations.

In any case, the economic system in this other world was full of holes, and it was tough to say just how far real-world common sense could be applied.

For now, as Michitaka put it, "Well, we'll just bill what looks good. Good market prices should work themselves out with time, once things settle down," and there seemed to be nothing for it but to make do with slapdash accounting.

On that day, too, Shiroe and the other three had been cleaning since early in the morning.

However, there was no way four people could completely clean a building with six aboveground floors and a basement. In any case, this was a ruin: The window glass was broken, and the farther up one went, the bigger the hole in the ceiling grew.

The four of them had soon abandoned the idea of overall repairs, and they were concentrating on making the second floor—their temporary living quarters—comfortable. At present, the second floor only held two large halls that had been made with flooring material, but they planned to make about eight private rooms there as well.

With that many, they wouldn't be troubled for rooms for a while.

They weren't sure whether they'd be able to finish during the summer or if it would take until autumn. Mainly due to concerns about temperature and sleeping outside, Shiroe hoped they'd be done by winter.

However, even as Shiroe and the others worked to create their home, they had a variety of visitors. Shiroe had set the zone's entry restrictions to "unrestricted," so nearly every acquaintance they had came to the first floor of the ruined building and yelled their names.

Henrietta, who was in the middle of a move herself that day, conscientiously brought by an assortment of fruit to congratulate them on the establishment of Log Horizon's headquarters. Upon nervously accepting the gift, Akatsuki was captured in the blink of an eye and very nearly forced to wear a "special present" or some such thing, but it's probably best not to discuss that.

Soujirou of the West Wind Brigade stopped by for a visit, accompanied by Nazuna, a beautiful healer and fellow former member of the Debauchery Tea Party. It wasn't clear which of them had liked cherry liqueur enough to bring it, but its limpid fragrance went perfectly with the early summer weather. Apparently it had been made by the West Wind Brigade's Brewer.

Calasin of Shopping District 8 paid a call to discuss something with Shiroe.

The "something" was the idea of hiring People of the Earth to handle clerical work for the Round Table Council—mostly light work, such as delivering documents and taking notes.

True, it would be hard to bind Adventurer players to work as light as that, and it would probably be quite expensive. They'd determined that, if possible, this way could work.

Calasin went home with a smile, saying that he'd start checking with the People of the Earth he happened to know right away.

Among the combat guilds, Isaac of the Knights of the Black Sword had stuck around for a surprisingly long time. Stopping by with a few of his Summoner subordinates, he began making arbitrary demands. "Hey, Machiavelli-with-glasses. Your place is huge and handy; let us do combat training here."

Before Naotsugu even had time to complain, the Summoners

summoned Undine of the Pure Currents and rinsed the cavernous first and second floors clean with a massive bead of water. Since there was no plumbing in this other world, this was incredibly helpful.

Isaac himself only chewed holes in the congratulatory fruit assortment Henrietta had brought by and left, but memorably, Captain Nyanta murmured, "The Knights of the Black Sword aren't such a bad lot." It was possible that Isaac had intended the visit to patch things up with Shiroe.

This was at least half of the reason that Shiroe had decided to purchase this abandoned building as their guild tower.

As one of the guilds participating in the Round Table Council, they were bound to have quite a few visitors. Shiroe's friend list had acquired more names over the past few days. They might not be friends he'd played closely with, but he had more opportunities to contact them now, and if he didn't register them, they couldn't telechat.

They'd probably have visitors in the future, and some of those visitors might have business that would need to be discussed for a long time. There was no telling whether a great uproar like the establishment of the Round Table Council would occur again, but if something of the sort did happen, they might end up needing a kitchen, a workroom, or a storehouse.

Due to these considerations, they'd chosen this building. It was on the outskirts of town, but it had more than enough space.

"Plus, it's like they say: Better too big than too small."

"That's what she said, right, Naotsugu? You would think like that."

"Shiro! Dude. Hey. Akatsuki keeps calling me an idiot because you say stuff like that. My-stock's-in-the-toilet city."

Naotsugu was one of Shiroe's oldest friends, and the one he found it easiest to relax with. Having completely useless conversations like this was incredibly restful.

"Here, now. Shiroechi and Naotsugucchi. If mew don't hurry and clean up, mew won't get dinner."

"Is it curry? Are we having curry?! I love curry!"

"...Dang it, Naotsugu. Yes. We're having curry today."

"What, for *real*?! Whoo-hoo!"

And thus, Nyanta and Akatsuki joined them.

In his long history with *Elder Tales*, even Shiroe had joined a guild before. Now, though, he knew he hadn't been part of that guild in the truest sense of the word; he'd only been a guest.

It wasn't the structure known as a guild; it was companions and a place to belong.

It meant holding these things important and protecting them.

That was something he ought to have learned from the Debauchery Tea Party: The will of the companions who gathered there was much more important than whether it was a true "guild" or not.

When the town began to turn red, it always gave Shiroe a special feeling. Back when *Elder Tales* was a game, sunset had been nothing more than an on-screen effect, but in this other world, it was different.

With sweet, sad cries, blackbirds flew low on their way home to the forest.

Adventurers returning from the hunt filtered into the plaza, having a look at the stalls that lined the central avenue as they passed. Groups that had bagged lots of prey discussed their plans for the next outing in high spirits, and those that hadn't had much luck swore to vindicate themselves next time. The vine-tangled ruins glowed red madder, and the shadows of the warriors and the town's artisans grew longer and longer, regardless of whether they were Adventurers or People of the Earth.

In the space of a week, the sunset had acquired a fragrance.

Numerous stalls sold evening meals, sought out by weary Adventurers and production-class artisans alike who'd finished the day's work. Even the taverns run by People of the Earth now had the smell of sweet-tasting alcohol and simple food wafting from their doors.

The sky gradually darkened. Copper slowly changed to smoky rose, then deep blue, then indigo. In the midst of a sunset that felt slower than it had in the old world, the townspeople wound up their day and made preparations for tomorrow.

"There's the evening star, my liege."

"Forget that, I'm hungry. I'm so hungry I can't move. Starvation city."

Akatsuki and Naotsugu, who seemed to have finished carrying their cargo, were cooling themselves by the window.

In the sunset, too early yet for lamps to be lit, Shiroe's two friends turned back to him.

Their peaceful, inquisitive expressions convinced Shiroe that this was indeed his place.

Inside him, the Debauchery Tea Party was growing distant. It had taken a very long time. Shiroe thought, with regret, that he might unwittingly have hurt many people and places by comparing them to his old home.

He hadn't even understood the easy things. He'd taken the long way around. As Shiroe castigated himself for having nothing but faults, the other two looked at him blankly. "What's the matter, my liege?" "You're hungry, too, huh? Empty stomachs are no joke."

"Hm? Where's the captain? Isn't he back yet?" Pulling himself together, Shiroe realized that Nyanta wasn't there. He'd gone out to buy some more spices.

"Yeah, now that you mention it, the captain's late. He'd better not be shopping and snacking. If he is, I'll have to mete out his punishment."

"That wasn't terribly clever."

Even as he listened to their banter, Shiroe began to feel a bit concerned. Just then, from the floor below, an easygoing voice called, "Shiroechi~. Naotsugucchi~. Akatsuki~."

Nyanta seemed to have returned.

As they went downstairs, talking among themselves (did he need help carrying things? No, nothing would be that heavy in this other world), on the bare moonlit floor, they saw a figure so slim it might have been made of wire. It was Nyanta.

"What's up, Captain? I'm starving. Let's get that curry eaten, stat."

"Yes, venerable sage. I'm hungry as well."

Sounding childlike, Naotsugu and Akatsuki leaned out partway down the stairs. Nyanta laughed—"Mya-ha-ha-ha"—and pushed forward two shapes that had been clinging to his back.

"......Uu."

"Um, ummm..."

"If it isn't Touya and Minori!"

It was the Kannagi girl, who was blushing so fiercely that it showed even in the dark, and her Samurai twin brother. Over the past week, the newbies' hair had been trimmed and their equipment tidied. Nyanta urged them on.

"I found them on my way back from buying spices. They were circling this building, round and round and round. If it were me, I would've turned into butter candy."

"What's the matter, you two?" Shiroe asked. "Wasn't the Crescent Moon League moving today, too?"

The Crescent Moon League had been scheduled to move into a guildhall two ranks higher that day. Once they'd finished moving, there'd probably be another banquet. Marielle loved it when things were lively, and he couldn't imagine that she'd send two of her precious newbies out into the night all by themselves.

"No, uh, mister. Listen, we…"

"Hm?"

From where he stood on the first floor, Touya looked up at Shiroe, standing halfway up the stairs, and spoke in a young, ringing voice.

"—We're here to join your guild, mister."

"Huh…?"

"We came because we hoped you would teach us, Shiroe. …We've imposed on the Crescent Moon League for the past week, but we haven't joined it. …We *didn't* join. Touya and I are the only players who left Hamelin who haven't joined a guild yet." Minori conscientiously supplemented her brother's frank, straightforward words.

"We were able to do our best because of all the stuff you taught us, mister. If you've started a guild, we want to join it. Maybe I'm weak, but I'm gonna get stronger."

"I may just be in the way as well, but… I've decided not to use that as an excuse anymore. Please let us stay with you."

"Ah…… Um."

He might turn them down.

What would they do if he did?

The young twins spoke as eloquently as they possibly could. They were so stiff that their tension was obvious at a glance.

He'd heard vague rumors of the sort of treatment they'd been subjected to in Hamelin. For players who were new to *Elder Tales* and had no acquaintances or people to rely on, the experience must have been incredibly painful.

At the Crescent Moon League, they would have had lots of friends who'd been in the same situation and whose skills were at about the same level. He was positive that they wouldn't have been treated badly. What must they have felt when they turned down the chance to join the Crescent Moon League and came to Shiroe, knowing that, if he refused them, they'd have nowhere left to go? Shiroe could only guess, but he could sense the desperation in their resolution.

They'd played together for one week, the last week that *Elder Tales* was a game. Shiroe didn't know what he'd said to them that could have attracted them to him in that short time.

He'd never been a role model for anyone in that way before, and so their wish left him speechless, unable to respond properly.

As he watched Shiroe, Nyanta's narrow eyes narrowed further in an excess of kindness. He spoke to him, calmly.

"Shiroechi. Mew mustn't just stare like that. Mew're the GM."

GM.

Guild master.

The leader of a guild.

He was right, Shiroe realized. He was so used to his companions that they could practically read one another's minds, and so even after he'd created a guild, he hadn't been all that conscious of being a leader.

...Or of being a role model for someone.

Even though he'd come this far following role models of his own, he'd never imagined that he'd become someone like that.

Shiroe turned to look back at his two hungry companions, who'd poked their heads out over the edge of the stairs. Naotsugu gave a sly grin and said, "Well, duh," flashing him a thumbs-up sign. Akatsuki nodded, her expression just a little softer than usual.

"All right. Log Horizon welcomes you, Touya and Minori. As new recruits, your first mission is to come eat curry rice with the top brass. ...Are you ready?"

"Yes, sir!" "Mister!"

Two young voices chimed in, and now they were six.

*   *   *

In the world that had once been *Elder Tales*, a new guild was formed.

Its name was Log Horizon.

And so this small band of companions established itself in a ruin, pierced by an ancient tree, on the outskirts of Akiba.

Log Horizon 2—The Knights of Camelot—The End

[HONESTY]
AINS

[KNIGHTS OF THE BLACK SWORD]
ISAAC

[SILVER SWORD]
WILLIAM MASSACHUSETTS

[WEST WIND BRIGADE]
SOUJIROU SETA

HEROIC

[GRANDALE]
WOODSTOCK W.

[LOG HORIZON]
SHIROE

[SHOPPING DISTRICT 8]
CALASIN

[RODERICK TRADING COMPANY]
RODERICK

[D.D.D.]
CRUSTY

⟨MEMBERS OF THE FIRST ROUND TABLE COUNCIL⟩

HERO TALES

WITH AKIBA'S DESTINY ON THE LINE, TWELVE GUILDS ANSWERED SHIROE'S CALL. AN IN-DEPTH EXAMINATION OF THE LEADERS OF THE GUILDS THAT REPRESENT AKIBA!!

[MARINE ORGANIZATION]
MICHITAKA

EPISODE

[CRESCENT MOON LEAGUE]
MARIELLE

[RADIO MARKET]
AKANEYA ICHIMONJINOSUKE

SEATING
ORDER

GUILD

HONESTY

CLASS

KANNAGI

SUB CLASS

SCHOLAR

[
The sharing of knowledge
is this world's living will.
]

The guild master of Honesty,
which proactively promotes the
accumulation and disclosure of
raid information. He has mapped
out and posted strategies for the
Festival of the New Emperor's
Return and the Nine Great Gaols
of Helos and has made other great
contributions to the revitalization of
the entire server. On the other hand,
his doctrine of sharing information
often makes him clash with the top
guilds.

[MITHRIL EYES]
WILLIAM MASSACHUSETTS

SEATING
ORDER

GUILD

SILVER
SWORD

CLASS

ASSASSIN

SUB CLASS

HUNTER

[
Who cares about
the council?
I'll do what I want!
]

The guild master of Silver Sword,
which (back when most Japanese
guilds tended to play on the
domestic Yamato server) proactively
conducted the first expedition to
Korea and acquired lots of unknown
items. Although planning and
strategy are emphasized in raids, he
was famous for asserting that one
couldn't even gather information
unless they fought, as well as for
continuing to take an aggressive
stance post-Catastrophe.

[BLACK SWORD]
ISAAC

[
Guys with no bloodlust
are boring! Fight like
you're gonna kill me!
]

The leader of an elite combat guild
whose policy is to admit only players
who've maxed out the level counter.
This is the guild that's closest to an
outsider's image of "a group of
game junkies." Isaac himself is highly
respected. He carries the magic
Black Sword of Pain, and many
consider him to be the toughest
Guardian on the server.

SEATING
ORDER

GUILD

KNIGHTS OF
THE BLACK
SWORD

CLASS

GUARDIAN

SUB CLASS

GLADIATOR

[BERSERKER]
CRUSTY

[
Live until you die: That's
the same in every world.
]

In addition to leading D.D.D. (the
top combat guild on the Yamato
server in terms of difficulties
overcome, number of members,
and total power), he always
dominates large-scale raids on the
front line. A distinguished raid player
who made it through the Tower of
the Oracle, a worldwide region raid
said to be impossible for Japanese
players.

SEATING
ORDER

GUILD

D.D.D.

CLASS

GUARDIAN

SUB CLASS

BERSERKER

[YOUNG GENT]
CALASIN

[FAIRY DOCTOR]
RODERICK

[Sell, sell, sell until the
storehouses are empty!]

The guild master of Shopping
District 8, an emerging force and
the youngest of the three major
production guilds. Because *Elder
Tales* was a paid game, the average
age of users is fairly high; however,
Shopping District 8 has a relatively
young membership, and there's a
casual energy about it. Ever since
Calasin's appearance, the liquidity of
item circulation among Adventurers
has risen and prices have stabilized.

SEATING
ORDER

GUILD

SHOPPING
DISTRICT 8

CLASS

SUMMONER

SUB CLASS

TRADER

[That's an intriguing
discovery. Let's
experiment right away.]

Guild master of the Roderick
Trading Company, which holds
many fantasy-class recipes
obtainable in That Which Saves
Defiled Souls, the Swan of Tuonela,
and others. The Roderick Trading
Company's objective is to produce
and sell ultra-difficult production
items. Particularly in the field of
consumables, such as potions and
magic gems, it's unrivaled by other
guilds.

SEATING
ORDER

GUILD

RODERICK
TRADING
COMPANY

CLASS

SUMMONER

SUB CLASS

APOTHECARY

EPISODE

[MASTER SWORDSMAN] SOUJIROU SETA

SEATING ORDER

GUILD

WEST WIND BRIGADE

CLASS

SAMURAI

SUB CLASS

MASTER SWORDS-MAN

[Of course I'd cut down an enemy. Wouldn't anyone?]

Guild master of the West Wind Brigade and former Debauchery Tea Party member. Although there are many guilds that give raids as their targets and early arrivals have a great advantage in the field, his guild has been responsible for military achievements that are unusual for a new group, and it continues to extend its influence. Soujirou himself is notoriously harem prone, and his "it guy" status has made him the target of a lot of jealousy since *Elder Tales* was a game.

[IRON-ARM] MICHITAKA

SEATING ORDER

GUILD

MARINE ORGANIZA-TION

CLASS

MONK

SUB CLASS

BLACKSMITH

[I keep pulling all the short straws. What's the deal?]

The Marine Organization, a giant production guild, is divided into several departments, and the department supervisors are known as "managers." Michitaka is the "general manager" who supervises them. Since many people are involved in the game, there's quite a bit of interpersonal trouble, and he's famous for running the largest guild on the Yamato server as a huge Blacksmith bursting with charisma in spite of it all.

HEROIC

SHIROE [MACHIAVELLI-WITH-GLASSES]

[
If you're going to give
up that easily, we have
no hope.
]

The skilled counselor who
supported the steady advance
of the legendary play group, the
Debauchery Tea Party. In the real
world, he's a university student
who's studying engineering, and he
analyzed game play records from
logs and videos, mapped dungeon
spaces using 3-D CAD, and came
up with battle maneuvers and other
strategies. He's a mild, subdued
young man, but when he makes up
his mind to do something, he acts
decisively and cuts down anything in
his path.

SEATING
ORDER

GUILD

LOG
HORIZON

CLASS

ENCHANTER

SUB CLASS

SCRIBE

MARIELLE [AKIBA'S SUNFLOWER]

[
You've got that
right. After all, it's our
darlin' Akiba!
]

Her open-minded, tolerant
personality and her kindness to men
and women alike have made her
very popular in Akiba. She hasn't
made any great achievements on
raids or in production, at least in the
gaming sense, but she has a wide
network of acquaintances, so she
knows all sorts of information. Her
generous bust is one of her charms.
She and her accountant, the glasses-
wearing beauty Henrietta, have
been friends since their student
days.

SEATING
ORDER

GUILD

CRESCENT
MOON
LEAGUE

CLASS

CLERIC

SUB CLASS

WOOD-
WORKER

[CANNONBALL] WOODSTOCK W.

SEATING ORDER

GUILD

GRANDALE

CLASS

ASSASSIN

SUB CLASS

ANIMAL TRAINER

[THE RETIREE] AKANEYA ICHIMONJINOSUKE

SEATING ORDER

GUILD

RADIO MARKET

CLASS

SORCERER

SUB CLASS

MECHANIST

> Accelerate like you're falling from the sky, and you're always at your best.

A former member of the Knights of the Black Sword. Their elitism irked him, and he formed his own guild. It supplies low-to-midlevel consumables, and in short-term markets, it makes higher profits than the three big production guilds. He's well known both inside and outside the game. In addition to making an official website for his guild and widely recruiting members, he conducts etiquette tutorials for newbies.

> This's a fine article. Shine, durability, workmanship—all exceptional.

A veteran player whose history in *Elder Tales* is as long as—or longer than—Shiroe's. The history of his guild, RADIO Market, is also long. He's never liked factions, and his frank administrative stance has earned the guild solid support as a refuge for solo players. The guild has many eccentric high-level players, including Akaneya, and it's known as a den of oddballs.

AFTERWORD

Hello! It's been about a month. This is Mamare Touno.

Thank you very much for picking up *Log Horizon 2: The Knights of Camelot*. When this book ran online, it was part of *The Beginning of Another World, Parts 1 and 2*, but that got split up and restructured, and now it's the second volume. In this book, the curtain finally rises on the adventures of Shiroe and the other Log Horizon members. Look forward to their future activity!

…And with that introduction, here's more about Sister Touno.

Thanks to all of you, *Log Horizon* made it into print, so I thought I'd take Sister Touno out to eat. To celebrate, you know.

That said, my frail little sister isn't physically up to long excursions, so we stuck close to home.

In this case, we didn't even have to think about it: We went to the *monja* place.

We live in Shitamachi, so *monja* (savory pancakes) are one of the standards.

Sister Touno didn't seem to have grasped the situation all that well, and the expression on her face said, "?, ?" It was like she was so much of a monkey that she didn't even understand the words *my treat*. Is my little sister dumb, or is it just that her big brother hasn't done many big brotherly things? I could dig my own grave real easily here, so I'll leave that aside.

As you've guessed, I haven't actually come out to my family about the books being published yet. It's not that I'm trying to keep it a secret or anything. It's just that, when I came clean about it the month before last, I got called a liar and ignored, and I lost the opportunity to explain.

This going out for *monja* doubled as a ploy to create another opportunity to explain, but the second we sat down, Sister Touno started threatening me.

Oh, Sister Touno. Do you distrust your big brother so much? I told her to order anything she wanted, and I guess it was a really bad move. She said some pretty mean things: "What are you plotting, stupid brother?"

I talked her down somehow, and we ate *monja* together.

Spicy cod roe and cheese *monja*, with mochi topping.

It isn't just Sister Touno: The whole Touno family tends to take a liking to something and only eat that one thing. The late Mother Touno would eat *soumen* noodles all summer long, and Touno himself went nuts over the Tohato company's "All Apricot" cookies and bought them by the case.

For Sister Touno, that something is *shibazuke* (eggplant or cucumber pickled with red *shiso* leaves) and cheese fish cakes. As you can see, the Touno family's eating habits are cheap, the Shitamachi way.

So the two of us ate our way through three spicy cod roe and cheese *monja* with mochi topping in a row. We had slightly flat soda, too.

Spicy cod roe and cheese *monja* with mochi topping is the most delicious *monja* in the world.

I tried to talk about the publishing thing several times, but every time I started to explain, Sister Touno would invade the *monja* border, so I didn't have time. Scrambling the *monja* and trying to hog it is a violation of the Shitamachi code of conduct.

Even though she's sickly, my little sister is excessively aggressive, and she really won't listen when people talk. She's as insolent as a Himalayan pika.

It wasn't my fault that when Sister Touno was in elementary school, she thought the characters for Oita Prefecture were read as "Daibu Prefecture" and that she got the English words *trumpet* and *trampoline* mixed up. I tried to correct her and she just wouldn't listen, all right?

"That was yummy and I'm full!" That satisfied smile of hers hasn't changed all that much since elementary school, so it's a sure bet the contents of her noggin haven't changed, either. ...Not that Touno—who said, "I'm stuffed! Mentaiko's mentastic!"—is much different.

...And so I'm still not "out."

All right, then: Touno family circumstances aside, *Log Horizon* is being brought to you at ferocious speed. In this volume, the twins Touya and Minori make their entrance, and Shiroe's world gets even noisier. These two are very hard workers, and they could become the engine for Shiroe's group.

The items listed on the character status screens at the beginning of each chapter in this volume were collected on Twitter in March 2011. I used items from IGM_masamune, RyosukeKadoh, ebius1, gontan_, hpsuke, kaze_syuki, makiwasabi, roki_a, sawame_ja, tepan00, black-usagi, kane_yon, and wataru_mg. Thank you very much!!

I can't list all your names here, but I'm grateful to everyone who made a submission. It was an embarrassment of riches, from really cool items to items that made me snicker. This wealth of items gives me ideas about this world's various knowledge and legends.

The good people of the editorial department came up with projects as well, including the Akiba map in this volume. For detailed, brand-new news, check out http://mamare.net. You'll find all sorts of other non–*Log Horizon* Mamare Touno information there, too.

Finally, I'd like to thank Shoji Masuda, who produced this book as well; Kazuhiro Hara, who drew even more extravagant illustrations for this volume than for the first one; Tsubakiya Design, who handled the design work; little F_ta of the editorial department! And Oha, who even took care of touching up the text! Thank you very much! Now all that's left is for you to savor this book. Bon appétit!

Mamare "I love monja*" Touno*

I WAS SURE THEY'D ORDER AN ILLUSTRATION FOR THIS SCENE, AND I WAS COMPLETELY WRONG.

IT'D BE A SHAME TO WASTE THE SKETCH, SO HERE IT IS.

HARA

▶LOG HORIZON, VOLUME 2
MAMARE TOUNO,
ILLUSTRATION BY KAZUHIRO HARA

▶TRANSLATION BY TAYLOR ENGEL

▶LOG HORIZON, VOLUME 2:
THE KNIGHTS OF CAMELOT
▶©2011 TOUNO MAMARE
ALL RIGHTS RESERVED.
▶FIRST PUBLISHED IN JAPAN IN 2011 BY
KADOKAWA CORPORATION ENTERBRAIN.
ENGLISH TRANSLATION RIGHTS ARRANGED
WITH KADOKAWA CORPORATION ENTERBRAIN,
THROUGH TUTTLE-MORI AGENCY, INC., TOKYO.

▶ENGLISH TRANSLATION © 2015 HACHETTE
BOOK GROUP, INC.

▶YEN ON
HACHETTE BOOK GROUP
1290 AVENUE OF THE AMERICAS
NEW YORK, NY 10104
WWW.HACHETTEBOOKGROUP.COM
WWW.YENPRESS.COM

▶YEN ON IS AN IMPRINT OF
HACHETTE BOOK GROUP, INC.

▶THE YEN ON NAME AND LOGO ARE
TRADEMARKS OF
HACHETTE BOOK GROUP, INC.

▶FIRST YEN ON EDITION: JULY 2015

▶ISBN: 978-0-316-26381-8

10 9 8 7 6 5 4 3 2 1

▶RRD-C

▶PRINTED IN THE UNITED STATES OF AMERICA

▶AUTHOR: **MAMARE TOUNO**

▶SUPERVISION: **SHOJI MASUDA**

▶ILLUSTRATION: **KAZUHIRO HARA**

▶AUTHOR: MAMARE TOUNO

A STRANGE LIFE-FORM THAT INHABITS THE TOKYO BOKUTOU SHITAMACHI AREA. IT'S BEEN TOSSING HALF-BAKED TEXT INTO A CORNER OF THE INTERNET SINCE THE YEAR 2000 OR SO. IT'S A FULLY AUTOMATIC, TEXT-LOVING MACRO THAT EATS AND DISCHARGES TEXT. IT DEBUTED AT THE END OF 2010 WITH *MAOYUU: MAOU YUUSHA* (*MAOYUU: DEMON KING AND HERO*). *LOG HORIZON* IS A RESTRUCTURED VERSION OF A NOVEL THAT RAN ON THE WEBSITE *SHOUSETSUKA NI NAROU* (*SO YOU WANT TO BE A NOVELIST*).

WEBSITE: HTTP://WWW.MAMARE.NET

▶SUPERVISION: SHOJI MASUDA

AS A GAME DESIGNER, HE'S WORKED ON *RINDA KYUUBU* (*RINDA CUBE*) AND *ORE NO SHIKABANE WO KOETE YUKE* (*STEP OVER MY DEAD BODY*), AMONG OTHERS. ALSO ACTIVE AS A NOVELIST, HE'S RELEASED THE *ONIGIRI NUEKO* (*ONI KILLER NUEKO*) SERIES, THE *HARUKA* SERIES, *JOHN & MARY: FUTARI HA SHOUKIN KASEGI* (*JOHN & MARY: BOUNTY HUNTERS*), *KIZUDARAKE NO BIINA* (*BEENA, COVERED IN WOUNDS*), AND MORE. HIS LATEST EFFORT IS HIS FIRST CHILDREN'S BOOK, *TOUMEI NO NEKO TO TOSHI UE NO IMOUTO* (*THE TRANSPARENT CAT AND THE OLDER LITTLE SISTER*). HE HAS ALSO WRITTEN *GEEMU DEZAIN NOU MASUDA SHINJI NO HASSOU TO WAZA* (*GAME DESIGN BRAIN: SHINJI MASUDA'S IDEAS AND TECHNIQUES*).

TWITTER ACCOUNT: SHOJIMASUDA

▶ILLUSTRATION: KAZUHIRO HARA

AN ILLUSTRATOR WHO LIVES IN ZUSHI. ORIGINALLY A HOME GAME DEVELOPER. IN ADDITION TO ILLUSTRATING BOOKS, HE'S ALSO ACTIVE IN MANGA AND DESIGN. LATELY, HE'S BEEN HAVING FUN FLYING A BIOKITE WHEN HE GOES ON WALKS.

WEBSITE: HTTP://WWW.NINEFIVE95.COM/IG/

Fragrant green winds blow across this new, yet somehow old land. The imaginary world of Theldesia is home to dragons and giants, monsters and demihumans. With a burden weighing upon your soul, go forth, O winged one <Adventurer>! This land spreads out before you like a blank page, make your mark in it!

LOG HORIZON

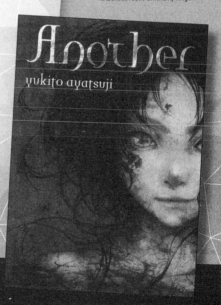